Dear Reader,

Welcome to another fun-filled month of Duets.

Duets #27

Award-winning author Kristin Gabriel is back with *Bachelor By Design,* book 2 in the delightful CAFÉ ROMEO trilogy, about a coffee shop that doubles as a dating service. *What better place to find both lattes and love!* And popular Superromance author Kay David joins the Duets lineup with the sizzling *Too Hot for Comfort.* Something is definitely cookin' in Comfort, Texas, between Sally and Jake—and it isn't steak!

Duets #28

Talented Jill Shalvis delivers her version of MAKEOVER MADNESS. *New and...Improved?* questions whether life is any better for the heroine when she goes from geek to goddess—and has to fight off men day and night! New author Jennifer LaBrecque serves up a delicious hero in *Andrew in Excess.* Andrew Winthrop is gorgeous, filthy rich—and in need of a temporary wife. Kat Devereaux knows just the woman—herself! But can these two make it down the aisle?

Be sure to pick up both Duets volumes this month!

Birgit Davis-Todd
Senior Editor, Harlequin Duets

Harlequin Books
225 Duncan Mill Rd.
Don Mills, Ontario
M3B 3K9 Canada

"Come on, let's make a run for it."

They raced the short distance from the picnic table to the red Ford Taurus, Trace keeping his body between Chloe and the direction the shots had come from. She opened the driver's door and dived inside the car, lying flat across the seat. Trace followed right behind her, closing the car door, then landing on top of her.

"I can't breathe," Chloe gurgled, her face pressed against the seat cushion.

Trace levered himself up on his elbows, giving her enough room to turn onto her back. He lifted his head far enough to peer out the windshield, searching the dark shadows for some sign of the shooter.

"Get down," she whispered harshly, grabbing his shoulders and pulling him toward her.

He sank onto her soft, voluptuous body and his breathing hitched. They fit together perfectly. The adrenaline fueling his blood turned into something more. His heart raced and his body reacted with a will of its own.

She stared up into his face. "I guess you'd better kiss me, Trace."

For more, turn to page 9

Too Hot for Comfort

Jake wished he had more in his hand than a plastic tackle box.

"Hey there," he said with as much dignity as he could muster. "I wasn't expecting a party or I wouldn't have dressed this casually."

Bob ambled over to the dock and Jake muttered, "Think you could help me out here, pal? Get me a towel or something?"

Ignoring Jake's question, Bob glanced down. "You always fish in the buff? What 'bout them skeeters?"

Just then Jake noticed Sally Beaumont making her way over to them. She was trying not to grin, but then she started to giggle. "Guess somebody forgot to tell you about your party, huh?"

"Hell, no," he said. "This is how we dress for bar-b-cues in Houston."

Her mischievous eyes met his. "What happens if you drop sauce somewhere you shouldn't?"

"Well, that depends," he drawled, "on where it lands and how good a friend you are with the one sitting next to you."

For more, turn to page 197

HARLEQUIN DUETS

ISBN 0-373-44093-6

BACHELOR BY DESIGN
Copyright © 2000 by Kristin Eckhardt

TOO HOT FOR COMFORT
Copyright © 2000 by Carla Luan

This edition published by arrangement with Harlequin Books S.A.

® and TM are trademarks of the publisher. Trademarks indicated with ® are registered in the United States Patent and Trademark Office, the Canadian Trade Marks Office and in other countries.

Visit us at www.eHarlequin.com

Printed in U.S.A.

KRISTIN GABRIEL

Bachelor By Design

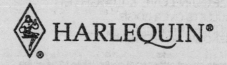

HARLEQUIN®

TORONTO • NEW YORK • LONDON
AMSTERDAM • PARIS • SYDNEY • HAMBURG
STOCKHOLM • ATHENS • TOKYO • MILAN • MADRID
PRAGUE • WARSAW • BUDAPEST • AUCKLAND

Dear Reader,

Welcome back to CAFÉ ROMEO. Before I go any further, I have to let you in on a secret. Out of all the Callahan brothers, Trace is my favorite. I can't explain it, and I'm not even sure I'd know how to handle a man like Trace in real life. I know I'd sure have fun trying. But let's face it—that's the beauty of fiction. You can be anyone you want—and you can be with anyone you want. So, sit back and enjoy the fantasy. And if you figure out a way to deal with a hunk like Trace, let me know.

Happy reading,

Kristin Gabriel

P.S. Be sure to watch for Beauty and the Bachelor, the final book in the CAFÉ ROMEO miniseries, available next month. Now that his two brothers have bitten the matrimonial dust, so to speak, poor Noah Callahan is panicking. And he's got good reason....

Books by Kristin Gabriel

HARLEQUIN DUETS
7—ANNIE, GET YOUR GROOM
25—THE BACHELOR TRAP

HARLEQUIN LOVE & LAUGHTER
40—BULLETS OVER BOISE
56—MONDAY MAN
62—SEND ME NO FLOWERS

For my daughter Jenny,
Who makes me smile at least once a day.

1

CHLOE D'ONOFRIO just didn't feel at home in prison, despite the fact that several members of her extended family resided there. Still, she faithfully made the rounds each visiting day, bearing gifts and D'Onofrio family gossip.

First she saw Aunt Wanda, serving two to five years for petty larceny. Then Cousin Kit, serving ten months for floating bad checks. Her other cousin, Nora, was in again for violating her probation.

And then there was her mother.

"Did you know I'm up for parole soon?" Eileen D'Onofrio asked, flicking a piece of lint off the sleeve of her bright orange jumpsuit.

"In twenty-one days. That's what I wanted to talk to you about." Chloe cleared her throat, then looked at her mother through the Plexiglas partition. She'd rehearsed this speech on the two-hour trip from St. Louis, determined to convince Eileen to go straight once and for all. "You'll have a much better chance of making parole if you've got both a job and a place to stay when you get out."

"I'm really overqualified for most jobs," Eileen mused. "And I refuse to work in another laundry."

She frowned down at her chapped hands. "Just look at what that harsh detergent has done to my nails."

Chloe leaned forward in her chair. "Mother, you can't be picky this time. And you absolutely cannot work for Uncle Leo again."

"But he let me set my own hours."

"You were a courier for his money-laundering operation!"

"He had a wonderful dental plan."

"You're going legit this time, Mom." Chloe set her jaw. "I mean it. Ramon needs you on the outside, and so do I."

Eileen frowned. "What's the matter with Ramon?"

Chloe didn't know where to begin. It seemed her younger brother was always suffering some sort of crisis. "Well, he's still upset about his broken engagement. I knew it was a mistake for you to fix him up with your cellmate."

"I thought having a girlfriend might give him some self-confidence. He's so shy around women."

"His *girlfriend* was convicted of attempted murder!"

"But Nanette seems like such a nice girl. And so pretty. By the way, she's not my cellmate anymore. Her conviction got overturned last month on a technicality. I heard she moved to Florida, so she's out of his life."

"Good," Chloe said. "Because the last thing we need in this family is another felon. Now, I think you should move in with me when you get out of here and I'll help you find a good, *legitimate* job."

"You can't afford another mouth to feed, honey. Especially when you're struggling to start a new business."

"I already got my first big job," Chloe announced, trying her best to sound nonchalant about it. "So money won't be a problem."

"You did!" Eileen's face lit up. "Oh, Chloe, that's wonderful. When did this happen?"

"Just yesterday, actually. I picked up Ramon from work at Café Romeo and ran into the owner. She treated me to a cup of coffee and the next thing I know, she's offering me a job to redecorate the place."

"Imagine that. Isn't she some kind of psychic?"

Chloe smiled. "Her name is Madame Sophia, and I believe she's a former fortune-teller. At the café she reads coffee grounds and predicts romance for her customers."

Eileen nodded approvingly. "What a great scam. She must be raking in the dough."

"She's legit, Mom. At least she believes in what she does. And it must be working, because she's remodeling the place to make it bigger. That's why she needs a decorator."

"So did you ask Madame Sophia to read your coffee grounds?"

"Of course not. You know I don't believe in that kind of nonsense."

"My sensible Chloe. I suppose you don't believe in love, either."

"Actually, I do. But it's hard to meet men these days."

Eileen clucked her tongue. "You're on the wrong side of twenty-five, dear. It's time to stop being so picky."

"I'm not picky," Chloe countered. "As long as they pass the FBI background check."

Eileen laughed, but Chloe wasn't joking. Growing up among the D'Onofrio men had taught her exactly what she didn't want in a man. They were all handsome, charming, stubborn male chauvinists. And they all had criminal records. Except Ramon, whom she'd managed to keep out of trouble. So far, anyway.

To be fair, Chloe's deceased father hadn't had a criminal record, either. But only because the masterful jewel thief had never been caught.

"Maybe I'll give Café Romeo a try myself," Eileen said playfully. "After spending the last three years in here, I could use some romance in my life."

"That's a wonderful idea," Chloe exclaimed, willing to show enthusiasm for anything that would keep her mother out of trouble. And out of jail. "As soon as you're free we'll go shopping. We'll buy you a whole new wardrobe."

"I need a perm, too," Eileen said, fingering her faded brown hair. "And maybe a color touch-up."

"We'll shoot the works." Thanks to Madame Sophia, Chloe would have enough money to give her mother a fresh new start. The coffeehouse owner might be a little flaky, but her job offer couldn't have come at a better time. Madame Sophia hadn't even asked for any references. All she'd required of Chloe was to sign on the dotted line.

And, oddly enough, to drink one cup of Café Romeo's special blend of Jamaican almond coffee.

"DON'T SAY I didn't warn you."

Trace Callahan looked up from the sheet of plywood he was measuring to scowl at his little brother. Only Noah wasn't so little anymore. He'd just turned twenty-six, and at six-three, stood an inch taller than his two older brothers. "Warn me? You've been predicting catastrophes ever since I told you Aunt Sophie confiscated our coffee grounds. Don't you think you might be just a little paranoid?"

Noah Callahan snorted. "That's the same thing Jake said. And looked what happened to him."

"Jake's not dead, he's engaged."

"Is there a difference?"

Trace shook his head in disgust, then pulled a stubby pencil out of his shirt pocket. He began marking off measurements on the wood, refusing to let this ridiculous conversation slow his progress on the expansion of Café Romeo. A common wall separated the coffeehouse from the now-defunct pizza parlor next door. He'd gutted the pizza parlor and stripped the oppressive red-and-black flocked wallpaper off the walls.

After spending several weeks remodeling the interior, he felt the place was finally beginning to come together. Just yesterday he'd cut the wide archway in the common wall that connected it to Café Romeo. He'd tacked an oilcloth over the opening to contain the dust, but he could still smell the fragrant aroma of fresh-ground coffee and hear the low murmurs of Aunt Sophie's customers.

He stuck the pencil back in his shirt pocket, then glanced at his brother. Noah might have more brawn than Trace, but obviously not as much brain. He was also an inveterate playboy. "Look, Noah, you've got to get over this marriage phobia of yours. It isn't healthy."

"And I suppose your plan to have women audition for a chance to be your wife is what you call healthy?"

"Definitely. I'm planning to marry for keeps. As soon as I find the one who fits all my requirements."

Noah visibly shuddered. "Well, I'm going while the going is good."

"Going where?"

"Cleveland, Ohio. I arranged a job transfer there as soon as I found out Aunt Sophie had gotten her hands on our coffee grounds. I don't want to take any chances."

"Don't you think moving out of state is a little extreme?"

Noah folded his arms across his chest. "You tell me. Our big brother recently proposed to a woman he's known less than a month. This is the same man who had a bumper sticker on his car that read Marriage is for Morons. And Aunt Sophie made it happen." Noah leaned toward him and lowered his voice. "Be afraid, Trace. Be very afraid."

"I like Nina," Trace said in defense of his future sister-in-law. He bent down and picked up the four-foot level off the floor.

"I like her too. But that doesn't change the fact that one of Aunt Sophie's crazy romantic predictions actually came true. And I'm not sticking around to be victim number three."

"Number three? Who's victim number two?"

"Just take a look in the mirror, pal," Noah said as he headed for the archway. "You're bride bait, and Aunt Sophie's all set to reel one in for you. As soon as Jake and Nina tie the knot, I'm outta here."

Trace watched his brother disappear behind the oilcloth. Noah was actually running scared. And for what? Some illogical fear that Aunt Sophie could make him fall in love with a woman against his will?

Trace wasn't about to let that happen. He'd be getting married all right, but to a woman of his own choosing. A woman who fit the exact blueprint of the future he wanted to build. And he'd told his aunt that already, in no uncertain terms. She'd taken the news well. He frowned down at the level in his hand. Maybe a little too well. Maybe he should have another talk with her, just in case....

As if she were truly psychic, Sophie Callahan appeared at that moment, bustling through the makeshift oilcloth door with Café Romeo's most inefficient waiter in tow.

"Trace, the place looks absolutely wonderful."

Sophie wore a hot-pink caftan and matching turban. Several gold bangle bracelets adorned each arm, making her sound like a wind chime whenever she moved.

Trace looked around the barren room. All the old booths had been ripped out, as well as the red shag carpet, leaving the old, worn floorboards bare. Plaster hung in chunks from the ceiling. Wires dangled from the newly installed drywall.

"There's still a lot of work left to do. Especially if you want to open this new section in three weeks. I could hire some extra help...."

"That won't be necessary," Sophie interjected. "I've got the perfect man for the job."

"Who?"

"Me." Ramon D'Onofrio stepped forward, his shoulder-length brown hair pulled back into a neat ponytail. He stuck his chin out and folded his arms across his narrow chest.

Trace swallowed a groan. Not Ramon. *Anyone* but Ramon.

"Don't you already have a job?"

Ramon turned to Sophie. "I told you he hated me. Didn't I tell you? I spill one cup of coffee on him and he holds a grudge forever."

"I'm sure that's not true," Sophie said. "Is it, Trace?"

Actually, it was damn close to the truth. That coffee Ramon had dumped in his lap had come perilously close to doing permanent damage. Ramon was obviously as dangerous as the rest of the infamous D'Onofrio family. Trace shuddered to think of the havoc Ramon could wreak with a nail gun. "Look, it's nothing personal. I just prefer to work with people who actually have some experience."

"I made a birdhouse in seventh-grade shop class," Ramon said, widening his puppy brown eyes. "And I'm always doing little repairs around the house."

"Hammer something for him," Sophie said, handing Ramon the sledgehammer on the floor.

Trace took a cautious step back. "That's really not…"

Too late. Ramon took a swing at one of the braces Trace had just installed to reinforce the unstable west wall. Wood splintered as the brace split in two at the impact. The wall creaked ominously and pieces of plaster rained onto the floor.

"There's more where that came from," Ramon said proudly.

Trace didn't doubt it for a moment. "I really can't afford you."

"No problem," Aunt Sophie chimed, picking a chunk of plaster out of her titian hair. "I'll pay Ramon's wages. He needs a sabbatical from waiting tables, but I don't want to lose him."

"I just can't take the stress anymore," Ramon explained, his voice quivering. "The menu is so complicated and some of the customers can be so rude. You dribble a little coffee on them and they start screaming about lawsuits and third-degree burns."

Sophie wrapped one arm around the waiter's narrow shoulders. "I thought working with his hands would be soothing."

Maybe for Ramon, but not for Trace. "How about a vacation instead? You could lie around on a beach somewhere and soak up the sun."

"Sand gives me a rash." Ramon swallowed hard, his Adam's apple bobbing in his scrawny neck. "For once in my life, I'd just like to be good at something. Just give me a chance."

Aunt Sophie leaned toward her nephew and lowered her voice. "Please, Trace. For me."

Damn. Now she had him. He'd give his right arm for Sophie if she wanted it. All the Callahan boys owed her for giving up her own career in the carnival to take care of them after their mother had abandoned them.

But Trace owed her even more.

That's why he'd agreed to remodel the addition to Café Romeo at cost. Even though his services as a freelance contractor normally brought in three times as much money.

And why he would agree to take on Ramon as an apprentice. Which might actually cost him his right arm. Not to mention a leg and numerous fingers.

"Anything for you, Aunt Sophie," Trace said, leaning over to kiss her cheek.

Her green eyes widened. "Anything?"

"Almost anything," he amended, before he found himself saddled with a blind date on top of everything else.

"But, Trace, I've found the perfect girl for you...."

He held up one hand. "Forget it. We've already talked about this. Besides, I already have a date tonight with Kimberly."

Aunt Sophie wrinkled her nose. "I've never liked Kimberly. She's too..."

"Sweet? Nice? Giving?"

"Exactly. She'll kill you with kindness. Or boredom. Or both. You need a woman who will challenge you. Who will add some excitement and unpredictability in your life."

"That's exactly what I don't need," Trace countered. He had his future drawn out as neatly as a set of blueprints. And he knew the exact specifications he required in a wife. He'd even made a checklist to use for rating potential candidates. He wouldn't be caught choosing the wrong woman like his father had, then suffering for it later.

"Don't be so stubborn," Aunt Sophie admonished. "I just happened to do a reading of Kimberly's coffee grounds, and believe me, that woman is completely wrong for you. Now if you'd just let me match you up with—"

Trace placed his hand over her mouth and slowly shook her head. "Quit while you're ahead, Aunt Sophie. Jake and Nina are happy and in love, and you're the one who brought them together. Why not just concentrate on their wedding? It's only a few weeks away."

Aunt Sophie removed his hand, her eyes glittering with excitement. "We could make it a double wedding! Jake and Nina, and you and..."

"Kimberly," Trace interjected. "Or Heidi, or Evonne. Those are the top three in the running to become Mrs. Trace Callahan. But there's no way I'll be ready to tie the knot in six weeks. I don't want to rush into anything."

Aunt Sophie arched one orange-tinted eyebrow. "Spoken like a man who hasn't met the right woman yet."

Trace couldn't argue with her. Not because he agreed, but because Ramon had started up the power saw and the noise made it impossible to think, much less speak. He turned to catch sight of the saw flailing wildly in Ramon's hands. "Put that thing down before you hurt someone!"

Too late.

LATER THAT EVENING, Trace sat at his dining-room table knowing he had a decision to make. Kimberly sat opposite him, poised and perfect. Her perfection had actually begun to irritate him a little, but that could just be a side effect of his pain medication.

"How was your dessert?" Kimberly asked, after taking a sip of her wine. She was dressed in a pearl-gray silk suit and a pristine white blouse buttoned up to the neck. Her makeup was just right, not too heavy and not too light. Her long blond hair fell like a silk curtain over her shoulders.

"Fine," he replied, putting down his spoon.

"Blancmange is my favorite." She flashed him a wide smile.

Blancmange. A fancy name for vanilla pudding. That was the problem. Everything with Kimberly was just so...vanilla. Trace sat back in his chair, more irritated with himself than her. She fit all his specifications, so what exactly was his problem?

He mentally ticked off his checklist for the perfect wife. She should be attractive, but not too pretty. Adept in the kitchen, as well as a neat housekeeper. A good conversationalist, but not argumentative.

Kimberly was all of these things, yet he'd almost fallen asleep over the soup course. Maybe he was just tired. It had been a rather trying day. He flexed his right foot, which was propped up on a chair, and winced slightly at the movement.

"Does it hurt?" she asked, staring down at the bulky gauze bandage on his big toe.

"The numbness is starting to wear off," Trace replied, trying to ignore the throbbing ache in his big toe.

She shook her head as she set her spoon down and pushed her empty bowl away. "I never realized how dangerous your occupation was before. You're lucky you only needed four stitches."

"Five," he corrected, shifting his foot slightly. "And I would have needed a lot more than that if I hadn't been wearing my leather work boots."

She smiled at him. Her Carol Brady smile that was beginning to set his teeth on edge. Funny how it had never bothered him before. But then, he hadn't considered the possibility of looking at the smile every day across the breakfast table for the next fifty years.

Until now.

"You really should be more careful." She meticulously brushed a few crumbs off the white linen tablecloth and into her hand. "At least your aunt was there to call the ambulance."

"The ambulance wasn't for me, it was for Ramon. He had a panic attack after he dropped the saw on my foot and started hyperventilating."

"Oh, dear," she murmured. But Trace got the feeling she wasn't really listening. Her total attention was now focused on scraping the dried pink wax drips off the crystal candleholder.

So maybe she wasn't all that exciting. He wasn't looking for that in a wife. He wasn't necessarily looking for love, either, he reminded himself. Affection, compatibility, and hopefully passion, but not love. At least not the heart-pounding, soul-searing love that had turned his older brother inside out.

Trace wanted order in his life. Stability. A family. He wanted...vanilla. Which meant he must want Kimberly. He'd probably get used to her smile. And the way her nose twitched when she chewed. All married couples had to make some adjustments, didn't they? It was possible she might even find one or two things about him that irritated her.

The wall clock chimed eight times. *Just get it*

over with, Trace told himself, tired of these annoying second thoughts. "Kimberly," he began.

She looked up from the candleholder. "Yes, Trace?"

The words stuck in his throat. He cleared it, then took a deep breath. "I'd like to talk about our future."

She leaned forward, daintily folding her hands together on the table. "Oh, I'm so glad. I've been wanting to talk about it for a while now, but I didn't know how to bring it up."

Some of Trace's anxiety lessened. That was another thing he liked about Kimberly. She wasn't pushy or demanding. She always waited for him to take the initiative.

"You go first," he said graciously, wanting time to compose a proper marriage proposal.

She gave him an affectionate smile. "I never knew how I wanted to spend my life until I met you. Then we started dating three months ago, and everything became clear." She sighed wistfully. "The first time we kissed I knew for sure."

Trace wished he could say the same. Unfortunately, their first kiss had created more doubts in him than desire. "You did?"

She nodded. "That's when I knew I wanted to spend the rest of my life in a convent."

He blinked. "What?"

"I'm going to become a nun," she said, her voice quivering with happiness.

"A nun?" he choked out.

She dabbed at her watery eyes with a paper napkin. "I've already applied to begin my novitiate at St. Mary's. I just wanted one last chance to say goodbye, Trace, and to thank you."

Thank him? He frowned at his sore toe as her words echoed in his head. He'd kissed her and she'd decided to become a nun. Not exactly a glowing endorsement for his sexual prowess. "A nun," he murmured, still rocked by her announcement.

"Are you surprised?"

"You could say that." He looked up at her. "How long have you been thinking about becoming a...nun?"

"Since I was a little girl." She steepled her fingers together and leaned toward him, looking more animated than he'd ever seen her. "But I didn't want to rush into anything, so I decided to have one last fling just to be sure."

A fling. He'd been ready to propose to this woman, and she'd considered him a fling! He shook his head, wondering where he'd gone wrong. In all the time he'd spent sizing up Kimberly as wife material, it had never occurred to him that *she* might not be interested. He stifled a snort. Not interested? She was about to take a vow of chastity!

"So sorry to eat and run."

He looked up, surprised to see Kimberly standing up and donning her jacket. "You're leaving?"

"We nuns don't like to keep late hours." She headed toward the front door, then paused to blow him a kiss over her shoulder. "I had a wonderful time tonight, Trace. Thank you for dinner."

"Thank you for cooking it," he said blankly. Then he pushed out his chair.

"No, don't get up," she said, holding one hand in the air. "I can see myself out. Besides, you and your toe need to rest."

He slumped back down in his chair as she waved goodbye and sailed out the door. A few moments later he heard the roar of a car engine and the squeal of tires. Sister Kimberly had a lead foot. He vaguely wondered if nuns got speeding tickets.

Then his gaze fell on the soiled plates neatly stacked at one end of the table. Too late he realized that Kimberly wasn't so perfect, after all. She'd left without doing the dishes.

He leaned his head back and closed his eyes. He couldn't do dishes with a sore toe. Maybe he should just throw them away. He'd never really liked that daisy pattern, anyway. Too girly. He'd picked them up cheap at a local thrift store when money had been tight. Now he could afford more masculine dishes. Maybe something with cars on it.

While he pondered if he should buy glasses to match, the doorbell rang.

"It's open," he called, lifting his head and opening his eyes, but not bothering to get up. No reason to aggravate his toe any more than necessary. Maybe it was Kimberly, back to tell him it was all a big joke.

But he didn't laugh when the sultry brunette walked into the room. She wore a short red silk suit that outlined a luscious hourglass figure. The kind of body a man could sink his hands into. With a conscious effort, he lifted his gaze from her full, round breasts to look at her face. He noticed her big brown eyes first, fringed with thick, dark lashes, then her pert nose and full, red lips.

This woman was no nun.

So who was she? And what was she doing in his condo? He swallowed as a curious mixture of apprehension and lust rose up inside of him. But before he could ask her anything, she placed both hands on the table and leaned toward him, unwittingly displaying her generous cleavage. Then she spoke.

"You're just the man I've been looking for."

2

CHLOE SILENTLY COUNTED to ten while Trace Callahan stared at her chest. Cursed with genes that made all the D'Onofrio women well-endowed, she was used to men paying avid attention to her physical assets and ignoring the fact that she was a savvy, intelligent woman. But this one seemed worse than usual.

She impatiently cleared her throat to get his attention. It worked. He looked up at her, his eyes slightly glazed. For the first time she noticed their unusual color—a deep, dark blue like polished sapphires. If she put any stock in physical appearance, she'd have to admit Trace Callahan was handsome. All right, just plain gorgeous with that square jaw, aquiline nose, and close-cropped dark hair. She couldn't help but notice how well the rest of him looked either, his biceps and broad shoulders clearly defined though his pine-green polo shirt.

"You're staring," Trace announced.

Chloe swallowed, her throat dry. "Me? You were the one who was staring."

"I always stare at beautiful women. Especially when they suddenly appear in my dining room." Then his eyes narrowed with suspicion. "Why exactly were you looking for me?"

She looked pointedly at the empty chair in front of her. "Aren't you going to ask me to sit down?"

"I'd rather you answered my question first. Or maybe I can answer it for you. Madame Sophia sent you here, didn't she?"

"She gave me your address, but..."

"I knew it," he interjected, shaking his head in disgust. "I knew it was too good to be true."

Chloe pulled out the chair and sat down next to him. "It?"

"I mean you," he muttered, then heaved a long sigh. "Look, we both know why you're here. Let's just skip the preliminaries and get right down to it." He leaned forward, closing the distance between them. "Kiss me."

Her mouth fell open. She quickly closed it again before he took it as a sign of encouragement. "Are you crazy?"

"No, just efficient. Once you kiss me, we'll both know if there's any future for our relationship. Although I should warn you that the last woman who kissed me decided never to let another man touch her lips."

Trace Callahan was not only a lunatic, but an incredible egomaniac. She smiled sweetly at him. "Thanks, but no thanks. I make it a habit not to kiss a man within the first five minutes of meeting him. Just one of my little idiosyncrasies."

"Suit yourself." He leaned back in his chair and folded his hands behind his head. "So tell me, Miss..."

"Please call me Chloe."

"Chloe. Do you make it a habit of going door-to-door looking for romance?"

She blinked. "I think you're confused again, Mr. Callahan...."

"Call me Trace." He smiled at her, but there was nothing sweet about it. His expression reminded her of a lion contemplating its next meal. "I probably am confused. In fact, you're probably just a delightful figment of my imagination. The medication is making me a little woozy."

"Medication?" she asked, wondering why she was surprised. There had to be some logical explanation for his odd behavior.

He winced as he lifted his bare foot up in the air. That's when she noticed he had it propped up on a padded chair on the opposite side of the table. His big toe was swathed in white gauze so thick it looked like a lightbulb. Before she could stop herself, she emitted a snort of laughter.

His jaw tightened. "Is something funny?"

"I'm sorry," she said, dissolving into uncontrollable, not to mention undignified, giggles. She took a deep breath and struggled to contain her amusement. "Did you hurt yourself?"

He drew himself up in his chair, obviously offended by her reaction. "My toe was almost amputated by a power saw today. The injury required several stitches."

Chloe stared at his long, lean foot in disbelief. "You mean that was the *horrendous* accident Ramon was so upset about? You cut your toe?"

He narrowed his eyes. "You know Ramon?"

She didn't like his tone. "Better than anyone. He happens to be my brother."

Trace closed his eyes. "That explains it."

"Explains what?"

"You're a D'Onofrio. That explains why I've felt uneasy ever since you walked through the door. Wherever D'Onofrios go, disaster follows."

She rolled her eyes. "Don't you think that's a bit of an exaggeration? Not all D'Onofrios are troublemakers." *Most of them,* she admitted to herself, *but not all.*

"Tell that to my toe."

"Let me see it," she said, standing up and walking over to the chair that held his injured foot. She reached out one hand to unwrap the gauze.

"Don't touch it!"

"I just want to take a look," she replied, ignoring his protest.

He grabbed her wrist.

"Are you a doctor?"

"No, I'm an interior designer. And in my professional opinion, white gauze doesn't go at all with this seat cushion. Didn't the pharmacy have anything in lavender?"

"Very funny."

"They say laughter is the best medicine."

"I prefer Novocain. Unfortunately, it's wearing off, so I'm not the best company right now. Maybe you could come back tomorrow. Or even better, next *year.*"

Some men just couldn't take a joke. "I'm afraid what I have to say can't wait until next year. It's about Ramon. He's very upset."

"He's upset? I'm the one who's been mutilated."

"Oh, come on. It's just a little nick." She gazed down at his foot. "I'll bet if you took off all that gauze, it would hardly even be noticeable."

A muscle ticked in his jaw. "Fine. Take it off and see for yourself."

Surprised by his acquiescence, she leaned over the chair and carefully began unwinding the gauze. All three yards of it. While she worked, she couldn't help but study Trace's foot. There was something almost intimate about seeing the bare foot of a total stranger up close. His was long and lean, with a high arch. The nails were clean and cut short straight across. The top of his foot was sprinkled with short, golden-blond hairs.

"Well, what do you think?"

Chloe thought she was much too interested in this man's foot. She forced her gaze to the toe in question. A neat row of tiny black stitches arched across the very tip. "I think you'll make a full recovery. Of course, that's just a layperson's opinion." She bit back a smile. "Have you thought about consulting a specialist?"

Trace carefully set his foot on the floor, his face set in a scowl. "No, but I do have a call into my attorney. Assault with a deadly weapon happens to be a felony."

She straightened, her amusement fading. "You can't be serious."

"Obviously, you're the one who can't be serious, since you consider this all one big joke."

"It's no joke," she agreed. "In fact, I don't find

it the least bit funny that you fired Ramon over something this—'' she pointed to his toe ''—inconsequential.''

''I happen to like my toe,'' he said through clenched teeth. ''And I'd like to keep it. Which means Ramon has to go.''

Chloe swallowed hard and willed the infamous D'Onofrio temper to stay under control.

''Just give him one more chance.''

''Why?''

Because she was terrified her brother would do something crazy if he lost this opportunity. He'd been despondent ever since his fiancée broke up with him—frustrated with his job as a waiter and life in general. He wanted a challenge. Excitement. Riches. Lately, he'd even talked about following in their father's footsteps. Ramon might not be the best waiter, or even a mediocre carpenter, but she knew for certain he'd make one hell of a lousy jewel thief. Which meant if she didn't do something fast, another D'Onofrio would end up behind bars.

''Well,'' Trace asked, breaking into her reverie, ''why should I give your brother a second chance to dismember me?''

As she stared into his deep blue eyes, her stomach suddenly went all queasy on her. Trace Callahan was too self-absorbed, too stubborn, and much too handsome to understand how much this job meant to someone as sensitive and insecure as her brother. And she'd be damned if she was going to beg.

''Why?'' She tipped up her chin. ''Because I can make it worth your while.''

He leaned back in his chair and gave her a slow, insolent once-over. "What exactly are you offering, Miss D'Onofrio?"

"Myself."

TRACE TIPPED so far back in his chair, he almost toppled over. He grabbed the edge of the table and pulled himself upright. This couldn't be happening. One moment Kimberly announces she's joining a convent, and the next moment a voluptuous, desirable woman sails into his condo and offers herself to him.

He must be dreaming. Or hallucinating. Perhaps the trauma of his accident was finally getting to him. Although, if a minor injury induced this kind of fantasy, he was almost willing to give Ramon free access to all his power tools just to see what else might develop.

Almost.

Of course, this was no dream. Chloe D'Onofrio was sitting right in front of him. In the delectable flesh. His common sense told him he could never consent to such an agreement. His body, on the other hand, was entirely ready, willing and able.

He cleared his throat. "That's an...intriguing proposition."

She sat down in the empty chair. "I call it good business. Tit for tat."

He closed his eyes, wishing she hadn't used that particular phrase. When he opened them again, she was still there, sitting with one long, slender leg crossed over the other, her short skirt barely reaching mid-thigh. He'd never seen legs like hers before. They were true works of art. And he was a devoted connoisseur. He tore his gaze from her legs. "Are you sure you're an interior designer?"

"Positive. And a damn good one, too. That's the reason Madame Sophia hired me to redecorate Café Romeo." She hesitated, then one corner of her mouth tipped up in a slow smile. "Or at least, one of the reasons."

"Aunt Sophie hired you?" he asked, reeling with this latest revelation. He'd been after his aunt for weeks to hire an interior designer so he could consult with him on some of the remodeling plans for the café. Only the *him* turned out to be a *her*. And even worse, a D'Onofrio.

She nodded and opened that sensual mouth, but he interrupted her before she had a chance to elaborate.

"Wait a minute," he said, as the rest of her words finally sank in. "What do you mean, *one* of the reasons? What other possible reason could there be?"

She arched one delicate brow. "You don't know?"

A heavy, sinking sensation filled him, but he didn't even want to consider that possibility. So he lied through his teeth. "No, I don't have the faintest idea."

She leaned toward him, her pink tongue darting out to moisten her lips. "No idea at all?"

He shook his head, his throat dry. If he didn't know better, he'd think she was purposely tormenting him. But Chloe could have no idea of the effect she was having on him. Trace had always prided himself on maintaining the upper hand in all his relationships—especially the romantic ones. Perhaps Kimberly had resigned herself to life in a convent because he'd been *too* good at hiding his feelings.

She settled back in her chair. "You're aware that your aunt reads coffee grounds?"

He sighed. "Unfortunately, yes."

"What you don't know is that she read my coffee grounds—and yours." Her brown eyes flicked over him. "For some inexplicable reason, she thinks we'd be a perfect match."

He groaned low in his throat as she confirmed his worst fears. "Impossible."

"I quite agree." She tucked an errant chestnut curl behind her ear. "Madame Sophia didn't want to tell me about it at first, because she believes romance should take its natural course. But then..." Her voice trailed off.

He looked at her. "But then...what?"

"But then she saw how upset I was after I'd heard you'd fired Ramon. I believe I might have even called you a few unsavory names in the heat of the moment."

"Such as?"

She blinked innocently at him. "I'm sure I don't remember."

He was sure she did, but he let her continue her story.

"Of course, that made Madame Sophia worry that I'd be prejudiced against you before we even met," Chloe explained. "So she told me about the reading and how we're destined to be together, and that fighting against destiny only makes the journey harder.''

He set his jaw. "I'm not planning on going anywhere."

"Your aunt seems like a very determined woman."

Determined was an understatement. She might not literally be able to move mountains, but she'd definitely caused a few avalanches in her time. If she was set on bringing Trace and this D'Onofrio woman together... He suppressed a shiver. He didn't even want to think about the consequences.

Of course that same wily determination had saved his butt more than a few times. And one time in particular. If it wasn't for Sophie, Trace might not even be here right now, ready to turn down Chloe D'Onofrio's incredibly tempting offer.

She seemed nice enough, for a D'Onofrio. But it was appallingly obvious that she was completely wrong for him. He frowned up at her, mentally listing all her flaws. A sassy mouth. A killer body. A classically beautiful face. A quick temper, judging by the sparks he'd seen in her big brown eyes. And worst of all, a brother named Ramon.

He sat back in his chair with a sigh. No, Chloe wouldn't even make it as a runner-up on his list for the perfect wife.

"Well, what do you say?" she asked. "Do we have a deal?"

Despite her obvious flaws, he found it harder to turn her down than he'd expected. "I'm flattered, Miss D'Onofrio...."

"Call me Chloe," she reminded him.

"Chloe," he echoed, mentally adding another flaw to the already long list. She had an annoying tendency to interrupt him when he was speaking. "I'm flattered, Chloe, by your very generous offer. I admire your loyalty to your brother and the lengths you're willing to go to help him. But I'm afraid I can't…"

"I'd do anything for Ramon," she said, interrupting him once again. "Family is very important to me."

"Me, too," he muttered. Family loyalty rated very high on his list of wifely requirements. He'd seen firsthand how betrayal could tear a family apart. But one plus didn't make up for all the glaring minuses that still tipped the scales against her.

"How important?"

He blinked. "What?"

"Exactly how important is your family to you?"

"What does that have to do with your offer to sleep with me?"

She stared at him. Then the corners of her mouth quivered until she couldn't contain herself any longer and burst out laughing. "*Sleep* with you?"

He scowled, wondering what was so damn funny. "Yes. In exchange for hiring back your brother."

"This is too much," she said, her laughter finally subsiding. She took a deep breath to compose herself. "Just what kind of woman do you think I am?"

"I…I…"

"And what kind of man would even consider using a woman that way?"

This had gone far enough. "I think you misunderstood me. I had no—"

"You know," she interjected, "I've met some male chauvinists before, but I didn't realize men like you still existed."

"If you'd just let me get a word in edgewise," he said between clenched teeth, "you'd find out I had absolutely no intention of taking you up on your offer."

But instead of mollifying her, his words actually seemed to offend her. Sparks lit her eyes. "So not only did you believe I was willing to prostitute myself, you have the nerve to sit there and tell me you're not the least bit interested!"

"I never said that," Trace growled. "I'm *very* interested. I'm so interested I can barely sit up straight. In fact, if you'd like me to prove it to you, I'll be more than happy to oblige."

"That won't be necessary," she said primly. "Because I'm definitely *not* interested. Now, may we please return to the subject at hand?"

He was both disappointed and confused. "What subject?"

She settled back in her chair, visibly calmer now. As much as he hated to admit it, she was just as appealing to him in the heat of anger. Maybe even more so. A rosy blush stained her creamy cheeks. Her brown eyes sparkled. His own blood raced in anticipation of what she might say or do next.

"Family loyalty," she replied evenly. "Ramon is the only reason I showed up here tonight."

He stifled a groan. *Ramon.* Why did she have to remind him? Although, perhaps it was a good thing she had, considering the directions his thoughts had taken just a scant moment ago. She was a D'Onofrio. Which meant she was off-limits.

She tilted her head to one side as she studied him. "So are you interested in my proposition?"

He scowled. "Maybe you'd better explain exactly what you mean by *proposition.*"

"Fine. I'll talk slowly this time so you understand." She leaned forward. "If you'll hire my brother back, I'll pretend to like you."

"Be still my heart," he said dryly. "Thanks, but no thanks."

She arched a brow. "I thought you said family loyalty is important to you. Are you really willing to disappoint your aunt? She was almost in tears when she heard my tirade against you."

"Tirade? I thought you just called me a couple of names."

"Among other things." She cleared her throat. "The point is, she has her heart set on bringing the two of us together. Are you willing to break it?"

Chloe couldn't have hit her mark better if she'd drawn a bull's-eye on his chest. The last thing he wanted to do was disappoint his aunt. He owed her. Big-time. Still, he couldn't marry the wrong woman just to make his aunt happy. He shook his head. "I'm sorry, Chloe," he said with a long sigh. "It just wouldn't work out between us."

"Of course not." She rolled her eyes. "That goes without saying. But if we *pretend* to give it a go, your aunt will eventually see the writing in the coffee grounds. She'll realize we're completely wrong for each other."

"You can say that again."

"We're completely wrong for each other."

He frowned at her. "That was just a figure of speech."

"I know. I just wanted to repeat it, in case you once again fall under the delusion that I want to sleep with you."

Her words pricked him more than he wanted to admit. "Not a problem."

"So do we have a deal?"

His common sense told him to turn her down and turn her out of his condominium. But his love for his aunt overrode his better judgment. "Yes."

"Good. I'll tell Ramon that he can start work again first thing in the morning." She stood and held out her hand. "Shall we shake on it?"

Trace complied, surprised by the strength of her grip. "Give me a chance to call my insurance agent first. I want to up my workman's comp to the max. Not to mention my life insurance." Then he stood up to follow her, momentarily forgetting about his sore toe. "Wait a minute. What about us?"

She turned around. "Us?"

"We should probably go out on a date or two just to make this look real." He limped toward her. "I'm free Friday evening."

She shrugged. "All right. The sooner we can convince your aunt we're completely wrong for each other, the better. Shall we meet at Café Romeo?"

"I'll pick you up at your place," he said firmly. "This is supposed to be like a real date, remember?

We can go to dinner first, then stop at Café Romeo for a cappuccino later.''

"Fine." She pulled a business card out of her purse and handed it to him. "My home address and telephone number are on my card.'' Then she turned and headed toward the door. "Do you want me to make reservations? I know a great Mexican restaurant."

"I hate Mexican food," he said, limping after her.

"How about Japanese?"

He grimaced. "Please tell me you're not serious.''

She sighed. "All right, what would you like to eat?"

"How about plain old American?"

She laughed. "My favorite."

"Mine, too. Seems we have something in common, after all.''

"Scary, isn't it?" she quipped, then sailed out the door.

Trace watched her walk toward her car, a sporty red Ford Taurus that matched the color of her suit. The way that skirt molded to her swaying hips made his mouth go dry. Then realization sunk in. He had a date with Chloe D'Onofrio in three days.

Scary was definitely the word for it.

BY FRIDAY, Trace was more than scared, he was downright suspicious. The night before he'd lain in his bed, unable to sleep, and replayed Chloe's unexpected visit in his mind. The more he thought about it, the more he was convinced she had orchestrated every aspect of their encounter—right down to the alluring shade of lipstick she wore. How else could he explain the fact that he had a date with Chloe D'Onofrio only three short days after vowing to his aunt that he'd never fall into one of her matchmaking traps?

Then another thought hit him, chilling him to the very marrow. Maybe Sophie had planned it this way all along. Asking him to hire Ramon, the power-saw incident, Chloe's visit and their unusual deal.

"Don't you think you're just a little paranoid," Jake Callahan said, after Trace had explained his suspicions to his brother. They stood in the large, plush dressing room of Sir Galahad Formal Wear.

Trace adjusted the blue silk cummerbund around his waist. "You tell me. I'm trying on tuxedos with my confirmed-bachelor brother, who is getting married in six weeks, thanks to Aunt Sophie."

"I've thanked her more than once," Jake replied, knotting his bow tie. "Nina is the best thing that ever happened to me."

"It was a fluke." Trace shrugged into a black cutaway jacket. "You don't really believe Aunt Sophie can read romantic futures in a pile of soggy coffee grounds."

"If you don't believe it," Jake challenged, "why are you so worried about it? Apparently this Chloe is all wrong for you, which is hardly surprising if she's anything at all like her brother."

"She's nothing like Ramon." Trace slipped into a pair of black patent-leather dress shoes. "But she's still...dangerous. You should see her, Jake.

Or maybe not." He grinned. "If you saw Chloe D'Onofrio, you might just decide to remain a bachelor."

The dressing room curtain was suddenly swept open. Nina Walker, Jake's fiancée, stood on the other side. "All right, Trace, quit trying to sabotage this wedding." Her voice sounded stern but her green eyes sparkled with amusement. "Or I may just have to kill you."

"Nina," Jake whispered, "you're not supposed to be in here. This is the *men's* dressing room."

She grinned. "Sounds like the perfect place to be to me. Unfortunately, you're both decent." She turned to Trace. "So who's Chloe?"

"No one for you to worry about," Trace replied, looking fondly at his future sister-in-law. Nina didn't have any competition for his brother's affections. He'd never seen Jake so besotted with a woman.

She smiled up at him. "So I can let you live?"

"You'd better, since I'm the best man. Somebody has to catch Jake when he passes out from a panic attack during the wedding ceremony."

"Ignore him," Jake said, drawing her into his arms and giving her a tender kiss on the lips. "If I start to panic, it will only be because it's taking so damn long to make you my wife. Six weeks seems like forever."

Nina laughed. "I agree. So why is everyone else calling it a whirlwind courtship?" She wrapped her arms around his neck. "I'm ready to start the honeymoon."

Jake responded with another kiss, this one longer

than the last. Trace folded his arms across his chest, waiting for them to come up for air. They'd been like this ever since they'd announced their engagement two weeks ago.

As much as Trace hated to admit it, he envied his big brother. Soon Jake would have exactly what Trace wanted—an adoring woman as his wife. A family of his very own.

He tugged at his bow tie. Not only had the Kimberly fiasco set him back, but now this situation with Chloe would cause an even longer delay. He just wanted a woman who fit all his requirements, who shared all his likes and dislikes, who didn't make him completely crazy.

Was that so much to ask?

He glanced at his watch, then impatiently cleared his throat. "Sorry to interrupt, but you two aren't on your honeymoon yet."

Nina turned to him, her cheeks flushed a becoming pink. "So who's Chloe?"

"Ramon's sister," Jake informed her. "She also happens to be Café Romeo's new interior designer, as well as Trace's date for this evening."

"Date?" A wrinkle creased Nina's brow. "What about Kimberly?"

"Kimberly is out of the picture," Jake said, sparing the details. "Chloe is in. Madame Sophia matched them up."

Nina's eyes widened. "Oh, Trace. How wonderful! You've finally met your match."

"You can say that again," Jake said with a chuckle.

"Chloe D'Onofrio is *not* my perfect match. I'm

only doing this for Aunt Sophie. Once she sees how wrong we are for each other, maybe she'll stop trying to interfere in my love life.''

Nina looked thoughtful. ''You know, it *is* possible Sophie made a mistake.''

''Hey,'' Jake interjected as he wrapped his arm around her waist. ''I thought you were a believer.''

''I am,'' Nina insisted. ''But Sophie did confide to me that there was a mix-up with your coffee cups when she secretly confiscated your coffee grounds. She wasn't exactly certain which coffee cup belonged to which Callahan.''

''Wonderful,'' Trace said dryly. ''I knew it was all a big mistake.''

''So give Noah a call,'' Jake said.

Trace scowled at him. ''Why?''

''So he can get together with Chloe. She must be *his* perfect match.''

Nina pulled a quarter out of her purse. ''I'll call him right now on the pay phone around the corner. He's investigating a possible arson case this afternoon, but he could probably take your place on this date tonight.''

''No!'' His tone was more strident than he intended. Clearing his throat, he spoke more calmly. ''Noah could never handle a woman like Chloe.'' He squared his shoulders. ''I'll suffer through it.''

''All right,'' Nina agreed with a shrug. ''But you two don't give your little brother enough credit. I was here with him earlier today when he tried on his tux.'' She sighed. ''He looked so handsome. Three women came in off the street when they saw him through the window.''

"Speaking of handsome," Jake said, holding out his arms and executing a slow turn in his tuxedo. "What do you think?"

She tapped one finger on her chin as she took her time studying her fiancé. Then she turned her analytical eye to Trace. "Well, if you want to know the truth…"

"We can take it," Trace said.

Nina's mouth curved into a slow smile. "Then I'd say Chloe D'Onofrio and I are the two luckiest women on the planet."

3

CHLOE HAD NEVER had so much trouble preparing for a date. First, her curling iron went on the blink, leaving her bangs hanging down in her eyes. Too pressed for time to go out and buy another one, she had to settle for sweeping her hair off her forehead and securing it with a silver filigree hair clip. Then her topaz ring snagged on her only decent pair of panty hose, causing a run from knee to thigh. She halted any further damage with a dab of clear fingernail polish, then rummaged through her closet for something long enough to cover up the run. She finally settled on a colorful broom skirt and a matching red peasant blouse.

Then there was Ramon.

"I'm the head of the family now," he said, propping his skinny form against the door frame in the open doorway of the upstairs bathroom. "And I don't like the idea of you dating Trace Callahan. Call it off."

"I made you a pot roast with carrots and potatoes for supper." Chloe leaned close to the mirror as she carefully applied a touch of mascara to her long, dark lashes. "If you eat all your vegetables, you can have some mocha ice cream for dessert."

Ramon wrinkled his nose. "I don't like pot roast. Besides, I have plans tonight."

Chloe turned to look at her brother. His shoulder-length brown hair was slicked back into a neat ponytail. He wore a blue pinstripe shirt and crisply pressed denim blue jeans. He'd shaved recently too, judging by the small tuft of toilet paper stuck to his chin. "Plans? What kind of plans?"

He shrugged. "I'd rather not say." Then his brown eyes widened in dismay. "And you changed the subject again. We were talking about Callahan."

She turned back to the mirror, able to see his reflection in the glass. "What about him?"

"He's not your type, Chloe. I've heard he even has a list of requirements for the perfect wife."

"Don't worry, Ramon. I'm not interested in the job."

"I still forbid you to go out with him. I don't trust the man, and I certainly don't like him. He wouldn't let me handle any of his precious tools at work today." His mouth drew down in a pout. "Except the broom."

"You're an apprentice," Chloe reminded him. "You've got to start somewhere. Just give it some time."

Ramon shook his head. "I don't have that much time. I'm already twenty-two years old."

She laughed. "I'll buy you a walker for your next birthday."

"I'm serious, Chloe. Life is passing me by. And what do I have to show for it? Nothing. Zilch.

Nada." He took a deep breath. "It's time to make some changes."

The hairs prickled on the back of her neck. "What kind of changes?"

He scowled. "You did it again. You changed the subject. We were talking about you and Callahan."

She turned to face him, a tube of raspberry-red lipstick in her hand. "Right now we're talking about you. I want to know exactly what kind of changes you're planning to make."

"It's a secret."

She took a step toward him. "Ramon, don't do anything foolish."

"What's that supposed to mean?"

"We both know what it means. I know the past few years have been rough for you. Especially after Dad died." She didn't want to admit they'd been rough for her, too. The sudden death of Theo D'Onofrio eight years ago had left Chloe, a naive nineteen-year-old, in sole charge of her sullen fourteen-year-old brother. She'd tried her best to raise him right, with plenty of unsolicited advice from her incarcerated mother and assorted D'Onofrios.

"I miss him," Ramon admitted. "He was my hero."

Just the words she *didn't* want to hear. "I loved Dad, too. But he had his faults. He was too smart to waste his life cracking safes. He could have done so much more."

Ramon's eyes sparked with anger. "Theo D'Onofrio was the best jewel thief in the country.

The police never even came close to touching him."

"I know," she said softly. "But the stress of evading them all those years took its toll. He was only forty-seven when his heart gave out."

Ramon's shoulders drooped. "The same thing could have happened if he'd been a plumber or a banker. Besides, he *loved* his work."

Sometimes Chloe wondered if her father had loved his work more than he'd loved his family. They'd never been able to stay in one place long—making it necessary for Chloe and Ramon to change schools often. They'd had to lie, too, whenever anyone asked them what Theo D'Onofrio did for a living. *He's in the security business* was their standard reply. Only they refrained from mentioning that his specialty was *breaking* security.

Still, it hadn't been a bad life. The D'Onofrios were a close-knit family, and they'd always been able to depend on each other. Which was the reason Chloe wasn't about to let her brother down—whether he wanted her help or not.

"Times are different now," she said briskly, turning back to the mirror. "The police have much more sophisticated equipment to track stolen merchandise. So if you're thinking of taking up where Dad left off, think again."

The doorbell rang, forestalling Ramon's reply. But she could see by the mottled flush on his cheeks that she'd hit a nerve. "That must be Trace."

"I'll get it," Ramon said, moving down the hallway.

Chloe picked up a pair of gold hoop earrings off the marble vanity top and hooked one through her ear. "Tell him I'll be down in a minute."

"I will," Ramon called over his shoulder. "As well as a few other things."

She stuck out her tongue at his retreating back, then walked down the hallway into her bedroom. After slipping on a pair of red leather flats, she took a long look at herself in the full-length mirror that hung on her closet door. Not quite satisfied with her appearance, she pulled the elastic band of the peasant blouse off her shoulders. Then up again. Then down again.

Her gaze fastened on her hair. Pulled back, it looked awful. Unfortunately, it looked even more awful flopping in her eyes after she took off the clip. Picking up a bottle of hair spray off her dresser, she feathered her bangs back with her fingers, then sprayed them into place. Not perfect, but definitely an improvement.

Chloe took a deep breath, surprised by the fluttery sensation in the pit of her stomach. She hadn't been on a real date in months. Between getting her business off the ground and keeping a watchful eye on Ramon, she simply hadn't had any time left over for romance.

Only this wasn't a real date. And Trace Callahan had made it clear he wasn't interested in a romance. Especially with her.

Good thing, too.

Because despite her skepticism about Madame Sophia's talents, she couldn't deny the pull between

them. There was something about Trace that
brought out the flirt in her. Something that almost
made her forget she didn't even like the man.

TRACE BROKE OUT in a cold sweat as he stood waiting on the dilapidated porch of the rambling Vic-
torian house. He'd been restless all day, wavering
between apprehension and anticipation. The pros-
pect of a date with Chloe D'Onofrio intrigued him,
aroused him and terrified him all at the same time.
Now that the moment had finally arrived, he didn't
know whether he should ring the doorbell again or
run screaming in the opposite direction.

Noah's warning echoed in his mind. *Be afraid,
Trace. Be very afraid.* Then he shook off the words
as well as his sense of foreboding. Trace Callahan
had never let fear dictate to him before, and he
wasn't about to start now.

Besides, it was only one date. How bad could it
be?

The front door swung open and Ramon stood on
the other side, a scowl on his face and a six-inch
carving knife in his hand. "It's you."

"Put the knife down, Ramon."

Ramon held the knife up in the air, the blade
glinting in the glow of the porch light. "This little
thing? I was just using it to slice up a roast."

"Put it down, Ramon." After almost losing his
big toe, Trace wasn't about to take any chances.

Ramon tipped up his chin. "And if I don't?"

"Then I'll have to take it away from you, and
you won't like the way I do it."

Ramon hesitated a moment, then dropped the knife into the potted plant just inside the front door. The hilt quivered slightly as the blade pierced the soil. "All right, have it your way."

"Thank you." Trace waited for him to move away from the door. "May I come in now?"

Ramon stood with his hands on his narrow hips, blocking the doorway. "Could I stop you?"

"No," Trace said genially, pushing past him as he stepped across the threshold and into the living room. "Is Chloe ready to go?"

"Depends." Ramon turned to face him. "Exactly what are your intentions toward my sister?"

"I intend to buy her dinner."

"I'm not worried about dinner. I want to know what you have in mind for dessert."

"Something sweet and soothing, which pretty much rules out your sister." Then he smiled. "Don't worry about it, Ramon. I'm not interested in Chloe that way." Which wasn't exactly the truth, but he didn't like the way Ramon was eyeing that knife.

"I hope not." Ramon moved a step closer to him, the top of his head barely reaching Trace's chin. "Because otherwise you'll have to answer to me."

"Thanks for the warning," Trace said dryly.

"Remember it." Ramon gave him one last glare, then turned on his heel and strode out of the room.

Trace watched him leave, grudgingly impressed with Ramon's efforts to defend his sister. The man might be a fruitcake, but he was a loyal fruitcake.

Left on his own, Trace could finally feast his eyes on the exquisite and spacious living room. Evidence of fine craftsmanship was everywhere. Intricate crown moldings lined the high ceiling. The large picture window was a showpiece in itself, accented with rose, amber and green stained glass. Marble insets flanked the hand-carved windowsill.

Trace stared in wonder around the rest of the unique room. Chloe obviously wasn't his perfect match, but he was falling hard and fast for her house.

He had to give her credit, though. She'd decorated it just right. The simple, tasteful furnishings and decor enhanced rather than detracted from the nineteenth-century grandeur of the setting. He just hoped she could do half as well with Café Romeo.

Saving the best for last, he moved toward the open spiral staircase. He'd never seen a staircase like this one before, although he knew a handful had been built in St. Louis sometime around the turn of the century. It was in amazing condition for its age, the wood gleaming and polished to a high sheen. With a feeling of reverence, he reached out one hand and ran it down the carved balustrade. He didn't know enough about real estate to guess the value of the house, but the staircase itself had to be worth a fortune.

He wondered who had built it. One of his hobbies was studying the techniques of local craftsmen from the nineteenth century. They had built some of the finest houses in the city. He bent down to look at the underside of the staircase, hoping to find a find a date or even the initials of the man responsible for this masterpiece.

He saw something far different.

"What the hell..." he muttered, angling his head for a better view. Then he heard footsteps behind him. But before he could turn around, something solid and heavy struck his temple. He blinked in surprise as a blinding pain streaked through his head.

Then everything went black.

CHLOE GAVE HER BANGS one last spritz of hair spray for good measure, then headed for the stairs. A loud thud made her pause at the top of the staircase. "Ramon?"

No answer. It was quiet down there now. Too quiet. She hoped Ramon hadn't scared her date away. Or maybe Trace hadn't shown up at all. In the past twenty-four hours, she'd wondered more than once if Callahan would really go through with this fake date.

Her doubts turned to uneasiness when she reached the landing. The living room was empty, but the front door stood open. She walked toward it and looked outside. The wide porch stood empty too, although a strange black Chevy Blazer was parked by the front curb.

Chloe closed the door and turned back into the living room. That was when she saw the knife sticking out of the potted plant. It looked as if someone had tried to murder her philodendron.

"Ramon?" she called again, picking up the

knife, then walking toward the kitchen. "Where are you?"

She moved through the kitchen door and her gaze settled on the oak pedestal table in the center of the room. It was set for one. The pot roast sat congealing on the counter, two thick slices of meat lying on the platter beside it. She set the knife in the stainless steel sink, then looked out the kitchen window at the driveway. Her brother's beat-up '83 hatchback was still there.

"Ramon?" she called, louder now as she walked down the long hallway, checking all the other rooms on the main floor. Could he possibly have gone upstairs without her seeing him?

Chloe moved back into the living room and headed toward the spiral staircase, a vague uneasiness settling over her. She'd just set her right hand on the newel post when she saw the shoes. She blinked in surprise, then leaned over the right side of the banister. Sticking out from under the staircase were two feet, wearing brown leather loafers, their toes pointing up toward the ceiling. She leaned further and saw that the feet were connected to a pair of long legs clad in tan Dockers.

"Omigod!" She rounded the newel post, and her knees hit the hardwood floor right next to the shoes. Bending down far enough to peer underneath the staircase, she saw Trace Callahan crammed in the narrow space between the floor and the bottom of the staircase.

His face looked pasty-white in the shadows.

"Trace!"

She grabbed his ankle and shook it. "Trace, are you all right?"

He didn't react to either her voice or her jostling. He just lay there deathly still. Her heart pounded in her chest as panic consumed her. She stood up, grabbed both his ankles and pulled with all her might. His body moved about a foot. She pulled again, grunting aloud with her effort. He was so impossibly heavy. She'd never moved over two hundred pounds of dead weight before. *Dead.* The awful word reverberated in her head. He couldn't be dead.

Could he?

At last, she'd pulled his body clear of the staircase. She dived to her knees again and clasped him by the shoulders. "Trace, please wake up. Please!"

The skin at his temple was mottled a dusky blue, and a thin red streak of blood was running down his cheek. His face was still pale, his lips almost bloodless. She wasn't sure he was breathing.

"Trace!" She shouted his name, her throat straining with effort and fear. She called it again. Then a third time.

No response.

Frantic now, she cupped one hand under his neck, tilting his chin up. His mouth fell open, revealing a straight line of white teeth. She took a deep breath, then clamped her mouth over his. Exhaling slowly, she tried to fill his lungs with air. But somehow, it wasn't working right.

Then he moved. His lips anyway, gently molding themselves against her mouth. His tongue darted forward and her eyes opened wide as it slid sleekly inside.

His eyes were still closed and she heard a low rumble deep in his throat. Then his hands rose. They reached up to cradle her face, holding her gently in place. Pure sensation overcame her shock as his mouth pressed against hers. She moaned softly as his fingers trailed down her throat, his thumbs stroking her collarbone. Then his hands moved over her bare shoulders, drawing her even closer to him.

He groaned again. Only this time it sounded more like a groan of pain than pleasure.

Chloe broke the kiss and sat up, watching him grimace as he brought his hand to his temple. She swallowed hard. "Are you all right?"

"What the hell happened?" His voice sounded weak and raspy.

"I don't know. I came down here and found you unconscious under the stairs."

His gaze focused on her. "Where exactly is *here?*"

"My house." She leaned forward. "I'm Chloe, remember? Chloe D'Onofrio. We have a date."

"Chloe." He closed his eyes. "I dreamed you were kissing me."

It seemed like a dream to her, too. She'd never been kissed like that before. It wasn't just his technique. The man had been barely conscious, after all. It was the unusual spark that had arced between them—connected them.

He opened his eyes. "Or *was* it a dream?"

"No. But it wasn't exactly a kiss, either—at least it didn't start out that way." She licked her lips. "That's not important right now. How do you feel?"

"Like someone has been using my head for batting practice. What happened?"

"I think you were attacked by a Chihuahua."

He shook his head as if to clear it, then winced. "I think I'm hearing things. Did you say a Chihuahua?"

She stooped to pick up the small ceramic dog lying upended near the base of the stairs. One pointed ear had been chipped off, and the remaining fragment was stained with a small amount of blood. She held it up for him see. "It used to be Ramon's pet, since he's allergic to animal dander. Now we use it for a doorstop."

"It also makes a handy guard dog," he said, gingerly fingering his injury. "I just wish I'd seen it coming."

"What exactly were you doing under the staircase?"

"The staircase," he echoed, closing his eyes once more. "Nice. Nice staircase. I...looked under it."

She frowned. "Why?"

His brow crinkled as if he was trying to remember the reason. At last he said, "Names. I was looking for names."

Names? That didn't make any sense. Which shouldn't surprise her, since he was suffering from a head injury. "Speaking of names, do you happen to remember yours?"

He opened his eyes and scowled up at her. "Of course."

"Tell me," she said, wanting to be certain.

"Trace Joseph Callahan. I'm twenty-seven years old and live on Ravenna Drive in St. Louis, Missouri." He arched a brow, then winced at the slight movement. "Am I right?"

"You looked older than twenty-seven."

"At the moment, I feel about eighty-seven." He struggled to sit up, his face blanching at the effort. "Make that ninety-seven."

She clasped his shoulder and helped pull him to a sitting position. He closed his eyes, then dropped his head between his knees.

She chewed her lower lip, wondering if she should call him an ambulance. "Are you all right?"

After a moment, he nodded. "Just a little dizzy."

"I still don't understand what happened."

He looked up at her. "Isn't it obvious?"

"No, not to me." She stood up and began to pace. "I find you unconscious under the stairs and I can't find my brother anywhere." She paused to look at him, twisting her fingers together. "Do you think Ramon is in trouble?"

"Definitely." He gripped the newel post, then rose unsteadily to his feet. "Attempted murder is a serious matter."

She blinked. "What are you saying?"

His brows drew together.

"Don't look at me like that. And don't pretend

to be shocked. Ramon answered the front door with a butcher knife in his hand. He made it perfectly clear that he doesn't want me anywhere near you. And, just yesterday, he assaulted me with a power saw.''

"That was an accident. And this is…preposterous. Ramon would never…could never hurt anyone.'' Her gaze flicked to his foot. "Not on purpose, anyway.''

"Chloe, I admire your loyalty, but this is pushing it a bit too far. The man is a menace. He belongs behind bars.''

Her blood turned to ice at his words. Ramon would never survive in jail. He could barely survive out of jail.

"I know he's your brother,'' Trace continued, his tone gentler now. "But I have to report him to the police. Otherwise, he's liable to kill someone with these crazy antics. And since I seem to be his favorite target, I'm afraid that someone will be me.''

"You don't understand,'' she breathed. "He's had a tough life. Our family is…different.''

A muscle twitched in his jaw.

"I do understand—better than you think. But Ramon has to take responsibility for his actions. And a lousy childhood or a dysfunctional family aren't excuses he can hide behind.''

His words transformed her fear to anger. "Look, this is ridiculous. I'm telling you, Ramon did *not* knock you unconscious. I give you my word.''

Trace folded his arms across his chest. "So who did?''

She shrugged, her mind racing to come up with a plausible suspect. "Well, there's my uncle Leo. Sometimes he drops by unexpectedly. Leo likes to hit first, ask questions later. Then there's Frankie."

"Frankie?"

"My cousin. He works as an enforcer for a loan shark. Sometimes he likes to practice on unsuspecting victims."

"Charming family. Ramon is starting to sound better all the time. Any other violent types?"

"Candy," she replied. "Another cousin. She's hated men ever since her high-school sweetheart squealed on her to the Feds."

Trace set his jaw. "You really expect me to buy all this?"

"It's the truth!" She tipped up her chin. "If you don't believe me, call my mother and ask her."

"Maybe I will. Especially if she can talk some sense into you. What's her number?"

"One-four-two-three-seven-six."

He arched a disbelieving brow. "That's her telephone number?"

"No, it's her prison number. You'll need it when you call the Women's Eastern Correctional Center at Vandalia."

Trace's jaw sagged. "Your mother is a..."

"Convict," Chloe said evenly. After her father's death, she'd promised herself not to lie about her family anymore. Honesty kept shame and embarrassment at bay. "The speed-dial number for the prison is taped on the back of the telephone receiver."

Trace stalked over to the telephone stand. "You've got *three* prisons listed here."

"Four, actually, if you count juvenile hall. Benson, Uncle Leo's stepson, hot-wired a car on his fifteenth birthday and went joyriding."

Trace kept staring at the speed-dial list. "Your mother is really in prison?"

Chloe heard both horror and pity in his voice. She didn't care for either. "Yes. But she'll be out in less than a month."

He turned to her. "Exactly how many D'Onofrios are behind bars?"

She glanced at the ceiling as she mentally calculated the number. "Six, if you count Benson. But he's not technically behind bars. Juvenile Hall is more of a rehabilitation facility."

"Six," he echoed, sagging onto the sofa.

"So you see," she said, joining him there, "I do have some experience with criminal behavior. Ramon just doesn't have it in him, no matter how much he might wish otherwise."

His eyes narrowed. "What does that mean?"

"Nothing," she bit out, wishing she'd bitten her tongue instead. Trace already thought badly enough of her brother without knowing he aspired to become a master jewel thief.

"Tell me."

"It's not important," she insisted, wishing he'd drop it, already.

He just stared at her, waiting. Was that empathy she saw in his blue eyes? Compassion?

"Fine," she said at last. "On one condition."

"You're hardly in any position to make conditions. You can either tell me right now or I pick up the telephone and call the police."

So much for compassion.

"Go ahead and call the police," she bluffed. "I'm not telling you anything."

But instead of reaching for the telephone, Trace leaned back against the sofa and closed his eyes, his face still unnaturally pale. For a moment she regretted arguing with him in his condition. She knew in her heart Ramon wouldn't purposely hurt anyone, but someone had definitely hurt Trace. And there was a high probability that someone was a D'Onofrio. Pangs of guilt and regret shot through her.

"Can I get you something," she asked, her tone softer now. "An aspirin, or maybe some ice for your head?"

"No, thank you."

"How about some pot roast? It will only take me a few minutes to reheat it in the microwave."

He cracked open one eye. "You cook?"

"Since I was twelve. Someone had to take over the meals after Mom went to prison the first time."

"Twelve." Trace sighed, both eyes open now. "I was seven when my Mom left. Only she never came back."

"I'm sorry," Chloe murmured, knowing firsthand the inadequacy of those words.

"Don't be. We had Aunt Sophie, and she couldn't have loved us more if we were her own sons.'' His mouth quirked up in a half smile. ''Even when we messed up.''

''Then you know why I still love my family. They're a little on the shady side, but they're all I've got.''

''A little?''

''All right,'' she conceded. ''A lot. Except Ramon. He's simply not a violent person.''

She waited for Trace to contradict her, but he didn't say anything. Maybe she'd convinced him. Maybe he'd already changed his mind about calling the police.

Chloe set her jaw. When she found the D'Onofrio who had attacked Trace, she'd string him, or her, up by his or her toes. On second thought, she'd do something even worse—she'd make the culprit eat her cooking. Trace had asked her if she could cook, not if she was a *good* cook. In her case, there was a big difference.

Only she couldn't do anything until she knew what Trace planned to do. Would he press charges against her brother? Or would he finally believe her assertion that Ramon was innocent?

''Chloe,'' he said at last, with the tone of a man who has come to a decision.

''Yes, Trace?'' She held her breath, awaiting his verdict.

''There's something else you should know.''

4

TRACE KNEW he shouldn't tell Chloe D'Onofrio anything but goodbye. Especially since he'd sincerely underestimated the damage she could do to his life. His pounding head was a powerful reminder of that. He needed to concentrate on his pain, rather than the apprehension he saw in her big brown eyes.

"Something else?" she said, nipping her lower lip between her teeth. "What is it?"

Leave. The word reverberated in his woozy brain. He could get up right now and leave her behind without a word. It was D'Onofrio family business, after all. No one had asked him to interfere. In fact, he could probably take that blow to the head as a hint to butt out.

So why wasn't he moving?

She reached out, the tips of her fingers lightly brushing his forearm. "Tell me, Trace. What else should I know?"

She should know that he never would have agreed to date her if he'd been aware of the extent of her felonious family background. She should know that he didn't interfere in other people's problems. He'd had enough problems in his own past to deal with. She should know that she wasn't responsible for the actions of her brother, or her family. That he didn't really blame her for any of this.

She should know...the truth.

"It's about the staircase," he began.

Her brow drew together. "What does the staircase have to do with Ramon?"

Instead of replying, he stood up, his knees wobbling just a little. Chloe was immediately standing by his side, lightly supporting him with her body. He closed his eyes for a moment just to enjoy the sensation.

He knew it wouldn't last long.

"Trace, I think you should lie down. You took a nasty blow, and you're not making a lot of sense right now."

"You'll understand soon enough," he said, walking slowly toward the staircase.

She walked beside him, still partially supporting him. "Understand what?"

He could hear the fear mingled with impatience in her voice. Hardly surprising. This woman had obviously endured a lifetime of unpleasant revelations. And he was about to add one more to the list.

"Lie down," he said, when they reached the staircase. He placed one hand on the thick newel post to steady himself.

"As I said before, I think you're the one who should lie down. But not on the floor."

"Just lie down," he insisted. "Then scoot underneath the staircase. Position yourself just as you found me."

With one last look of bewilderment, Chloe acceded to his wishes. She lay down on the hardwood floor and wiggled herself underneath the open staircase.

Trace waited, his body tensing. He didn't know what he expected to hear. A scream? A curse? A sob? Instead he heard the one thing he didn't expect—silence. Her reaction, or rather the lack of a reaction, made him wonder if he'd imagined it all in the first place.

"Well?" he asked, bending down slightly, but still unable to gauge her expression. "Do you see anything under there?"

She shot out from under the staircase and jumped to her feet. "I certainly do. The dust bunnies have been breeding like rabbits." Then she glanced at her watch. "Time to go! We don't want to miss our reservations."

Her false cheeriness confirmed for him that he hadn't imagined it. "It's still there, isn't it?"

"I didn't see anything out of the ordinary."

With a sigh of resignation, he lay down on the floor, grabbed the bottom edge of the staircase and pulled himself underneath it. His head screamed at him with every movement. But his eyes saw everything clearly. Taped to the underside of the stairway in a sealed Ziploc gallon bag were dozens of sparkling loose diamonds, all shapes and sizes. Even in the dark the jewels winked at him like stars in the sky.

The next moment Chloe slid in beside him, her

back on the floor, her head right next to his. She tilted her gaze toward him. "I can explain."

He couldn't wait to hear it. Would she tell him the truth or make up an elaborate lie? And would he be able to tell the difference? "Go ahead."

She hesitated. "All right, I can't explain. But that doesn't mean there's not a perfectly logical explanation."

"Such as?"

"Such as...these aren't what they look like."

"They look like flawless diamonds worth thousands of dollars."

"They could just be really good fakes. Sometimes you can hardly tell the difference."

Trace stared at the bag, considering her argument. He supposed they could be fake, but that brought up another question. "If that's true, then why did someone go to all the trouble to hide them?"

"Well...maybe someone is fencing them as the real thing. They do look authentic."

"There's one way to find out." As soon as he said the words he felt her stiffen beside him.

"I don't think that's a good idea."

He turned slightly to get a better view of her face. "You haven't even heard my idea yet."

She scowled. "I can make a wild guess. You want to take them to a jeweler so he can examine them and give us his expert opinion. Or did you have something else in mind?"

"No, that about sums it up. At least then we'd know what we're dealing with."

"We?" she echoed, her tone slightly sarcastic. "This isn't your problem, Callahan. This is my house. My staircase."

"Your diamonds?" When she didn't deny it, the hairs prickled on the back of his neck. He hadn't even considered Chloe might be involved in something shady. He suddenly wondered why he'd been blind to that possibility. Was it the way she looked? Talked? Kissed?

He closed his eyes for a moment, not wanting to think about that kiss. It confused him too much. Made perfectly clear issues suddenly cloudy.

"They're not my diamonds," she said firmly. "But this is a family problem. I'd rather you didn't become involved."

"It's too late. I became involved the moment your brother conked me over the head. And now we know why. He didn't want me to find the stash."

"That's pure speculation," she replied, although she didn't sound too convinced herself. "Why wouldn't he...I mean, whoever hit you, just take the diamonds and run?"

Trace shrugged. "Maybe he heard you coming and panicked. Or maybe he thought he'd killed me and panicked. Criminals aren't always logical. Or smart."

"Believe me, I know." She turned her face to him. "So now what?"

They were lying so close together that he could feel her soft breath on his cheek. "We call the police."

Chloe immediately wiggled out from beneath the staircase. Trace followed her, moving more slowly. She was pacing back and forth across the living room by the time he got to his feet. He watched her for a moment, then he walked toward the telephone.

"Wait," she cried, reaching out to stop him.

He turned to face her. "Chloe, I know you're upset. I know you don't want to face the facts about your brother. But shielding him won't help him. Ramon will just dig himself deeper and deeper into trouble." He took a step closer to her. "I'm furious with Ramon for knocking me out, but I could probably deal with him one-on-one and leave the police out of it."

He steeled himself against the way her brown eyes filled with hope. "But the diamonds are another matter. We're talking about a possible felony. We don't have any choice but to turn him in to the authorities."

"You're right."

He blinked, surprised at her easy capitulation. He turned toward the telephone once again.

Chloe whirled in front of him, effectively blocking his path to the phone. "But we don't have to turn him in yet. I still don't believe Ramon hit you, but…" Her voice trailed off and a spark of anger flashed in her eyes.

"You do believe he stole the diamonds?"

"Yes." She threw her hands up in the air. "Why couldn't he have started small? A gold bracelet here, a semiprecious stone there? Instead he steals enough diamonds to land him in prison for a life-time!''

"Wait a minute," he interjected, slightly confused. "Did Ramon tell you he planned to rob a jewelry store?"

"Not in so many words. But I could see the warning signs." She looked up at Trace. "Why didn't I try harder to stop him?"

"You can't blame yourself."

"Yes, I can," she countered. "I promised my mother I'd look after him the first time she went to prison. And I've tried to keep that promise ever since."

His gut clenched at her words. She'd only been twelve years old and already taken on the responsibilities of an adult. "Ramon is a man now, not a little boy. You're not responsible for his actions anymore."

"He's still a little boy inside. Sensitive and impulsive." She laid her hand on his chest. "Let me find him. Let me try to convince Ramon to turn himself in. They'll go easier on him then."

He shook his head. "The police could be on his trail right now. I'll bet they're definitely on the trail of the diamonds. If they find them here, you could be considered as an accomplice."

She tipped up her chin. "I can take care of myself."

Trace knew it wasn't a bluff. From the sound of it, she'd been taking care of herself since she was a child. But this was serious. Still...he couldn't quite resist the raw appeal in her eyes.

"Twenty-four hours," he clipped. "I'll give you twenty-four hours to find your brother. Then we go to the police."

She threw her arms around his neck. "Thank you! You won't regret it—I promise."

He didn't regret it. Not at this very moment, with Chloe warm and pliant in his arms. He lowered his head and captured her mouth with his, hearing her tiny gasp of surprise. Wrapping his arms around her waist, he pulled her closer, relishing the way her body molded so easily against his own. Seeking an answer to the question that had plagued him ever since she'd tried to give him mouth-to-mouth resuscitation. Now he knew for certain.

It hadn't been a fluke.

The same strange current arced between them— making him feel almost as if their souls were connecting as well as their lips and their bodies. It exhilarated him—and terrified him.

He broke the kiss, pressing his cheek momentarily against her hair while he regained control of his equilibrium and his breathing. "This is quite a date."

She laughed, sounding a little breathless herself. Then she stepped out of his arms. "Short but memorable."

He frowned. "Does that mean it's over?"

She nodded. "If I only have twenty-four hours to find Ramon, I need to begin looking right now."

"Do you even know where to start?"

She picked up her purse off the coffee table.

"Ducky's Bar on Benton Street. That's one of Ramon's favorite hangouts."

"Benton Street?" he echoed in disbelief. "You can't go down to that part of town alone at night. It's bad enough in daylight."

She slung the purse strap over her shoulder.

"I'll be all right."

"I'm going with you." He pulled his car keys out of his pocket and headed toward the door. "I'll drive."

She stood her ground. "I think I should handle this on my own."

"You're wrong."

Her eyes widened. "I'm wrong? Just like that?"

"It's nothing personal," he assured her. "Many women don't realize what's best for them. I've been to Ducky's a time or two and it's no place for a lady. I think it's best if I go along for protection."

She stared at him for a long moment. "Do you know what year this is?"

"Two thousand," he replied without any hesitation. "I already told you, I'm fine. A blow to the head can't stop Trace Callahan."

"Too bad," she muttered, as she watched him walk out the door.

DUCKY'S BAR sat nestled between Eve's Tattoo Emporium and Barney's Bail Bonds at the far end of Benton Street. Peeling yellow paint adorned the cinder-block wall on the outside of the bar. Black paint concealed the windows and the plate-glass door, giving the building an ominous appearance.

Humidity hung heavy in the air and swollen gray clouds stretched across the sky. Trace glanced at Chloe as they walked along the litter-strewn sidewalk. She looked grim, determined, and too damn sexy.

"Hold it," he said, stopping in front of the door. "I've changed my mind. You can't go in there."

She looked up at him. "Excuse me?"

"Go back and wait for me in the car. I'll check out the place and see if Ramon's made an appearance."

Annoyance flashed in her eyes. "I'm not waiting in the car. I can't believe you'd even suggest such a thing."

"And I can't believe you'd even consider going into a place like Ducky's Bar in that outfit."

She planted her hands on her hips. "You don't like the way I look?"

"You want my honest opinion?" He took a step closer to her. "I love the way you look. The problem is that every hoodlum in the bar is going to love it, too. I can't help you find Ramon if I'm too busy fighting off all your admirers."

"In the first place," she said, her voice low and tight, "I never asked you to fight anyone. You're barely able to walk, much less defend my honor. And in the second place, it may surprise you to learn that not every man looks at a woman as a sex object."

His jaw tightened. "This has nothing to do with sex and everything to do with that blouse you're wearing. Or should I say, barely wearing." He

frowned at the way the red peasant blouse exposed
her creamy white shoulders and generous cleavage.
"Don't you have a sweater or something you can
put on?"

"A sweater?" She rolled her eyes. "It's ninety
degrees in the shade."

Standing so close to Chloe made it seem more
like a hundred and ninety. He reached out and
pulled up the elastic neckline of her blouse, tugging
it up to her chin. "There. That's much better."

"I think you're overreacting," she muttered, tugging her blouse back down but keeping it on her
shoulders this time. "But I don't have time to argue. We're here to find Ramon, remember?"

"Just let me do all the talking." Trace moved
toward the door. "This Ducky woman may be the
owner, but I've heard she's a real wacko. She's
been married four times."

"That hardly makes her crazy," Chloe said
wryly. "Just unlucky in love."

"Her husbands were the unlucky ones. They're
all dead."

She stopped short.

"Just what are you implying?"

"I'm not implying anything. I'm just telling you
she's a rough old broad who needs careful han-
dling." He smiled. "But I'm sure I can soften her
up. Women find it hard to resist me."

"It must be your modesty."

"Must be." Then his smile faded as his gaze
flicked to her blouse. "Let's make this quick. And
try not to draw attention to yourself."

She didn't say anything as he held the door open for her. He followed her inside, taking a moment for his eyes to adjust to the haze of smoke in the air and the low lighting. An old Hank Williams tune wailed from the jukebox, accompanied by the shrill bells and whistles of the two pinball machines in the corner.

Trace had only taken three steps inside the bar when a burly bouncer blocked his path.

"I'd like to see some identification."

"What about her?" Trace asked, watching as Chloe walked past the bouncer unimpeded.

"What about her?"

"You didn't card her, so why single me out? You can't seriously believe I'm under twenty-one."

"Must be your baby face," the bouncer sneered. "You're one of them pretty boys that all look about twelve years old."

No one in their right mind would ever call the bouncer a pretty boy. He wore his dark hair in a military-style crew cut and had a long scar running along his forehead, just above his bushy eyebrows. His nose veered a little to the left.

Trace could see Chloe frowning at him from the bar. "I'm twenty-seven. So why don't you quit wasting my time."

"Why the hell do you keep stalling? Got something to hide? I want to see some ID and I want to see it now."

Trace could either argue with the cretin or join Chloe. "Fine," he muttered, reaching into his back pocket for his wallet. Only he came up empty. Both pockets were empty. *"Damn."*

"Got a problem, pretty boy?"

Trace definitely had a problem—and his name was Ramon. Not only had Chloe's little brother sicced his Chihuahua on him, he'd also stolen his wallet. Which meant Trace had no money, no credit cards, and no identification.

This just wasn't his day.

"Would you believe somebody stole my wallet?"

The bouncer snorted. "That's original. I've tossed out underage teenagers with more imagination."

Before Trace could reply, Chloe ambled over to them. "What's going on here?"

"Let me handle this," Trace said.

The bouncer's eyes narrowed. "Is that any way to talk to your girlfriend?"

"I'm not his girlfriend," she interjected.

The bouncer turned to her. "That's good to hear. Why don't you let me buy you a beer? Then we can have a little private conversation."

Trace stepped in front of Chloe. "Forget it. She's off-limits."

"Trace..." she began.

But this was one time Trace didn't intend to let her interrupt him. He took a step closer to the bouncer. "The woman belongs to me. If you have a problem with that we can handle it outside."

The bouncer smiled, the light reflecting off the gold crown on his front tooth. "Lead the way."

"Neither one of you are going anywhere!" Chloe exclaimed, stepping between them. Then she glowered up at the bouncer. "What exactly is your problem, Viper?"

"Viper?" Trace echoed, looking from Chloe to the bouncer.

"Meet my cousin," she said, nodding toward the bouncer. "Viper D'Onofrio. Viper, this is Trace Callahan."

Viper shook his head. "Another pretty boy. Why don't you go for a real man, like my lawyer? That's what I wanted to talk to you about. He told me he'd really like to date you."

"Your lawyer is a slimeball."

"Maybe so. But just think how useful it would be to have him in the family. Free legal advice twenty-four hours a day."

"If you think it's such a great idea, you date him," she retorted. "Besides, I'm not here to talk about my love life. I'm looking for Ramon."

"Your brother Ramon?"

Chloe arched a brow. "How many Ramons do you know?"

He shrugged, avoiding her direct gaze. "Even if I did see him, I'm no snitch."

"Then I'll have to ask Ducky. You told me she knows everything that goes on in this place." Chloe looked around the crowded bar. "So where is she?"

Viper hesitated, his suspicious gaze flicking over Trace. "What about this guy? He claims he doesn't have any ID. How do I know he's not a vice cop disguised as a jerk?''

"If I was a cop I'd arrest you for impersonating an ape. Now, as soon as we find Ramon we'll find my ID. He has my wallet.''

She closed her eyes with a groan. "Oh, Trace, he didn't.''

"He did. Unless the Chihuahua ate it.''

Viper flashed his gold tooth. "Sounds like Ramon is finally living up to the D'Onofrio name. Now my cousin Chloe here is another story. She's a downright embarrassment to the family. In fact, we used to call her Squeaky, 'cause she's so squeaky clean.''

Chloe glowered at him, which only seemed to amuse her cousin.

Viper gave a low chuckle. "And because she was always squeaking on all of us, a real tattletale—ow!'' he yelped, his words abruptly cut off as a tiny woman with short, iron-gray hair twisted his ear between her bony fingers.

"That's enough out of you, Virgil D'Onofrio. I've told you before to stop harassing my customers.''

"But, Ducky,'' he protested, as she pulled him by the ear toward the bar.

She reached over the counter and pulled out a bucket and sponge. "If you don't have anything better to do, you can mop those bathroom floors. I want them shining by the time you're through.''

Viper rubbed his red ear. "But, Ducky....''

She planted both hands on her narrow hips.

"And if I hear one more 'But, Ducky,' I'm going to use that sponge on your mouth—*after* you've scrubbed those floors."

Trace found himself suddenly approving of the buxom, chain-smoking, tough-talking dynamo. Even if she did look like a charter member of the Hell's Angels.

Viper paled and backed away, obviously smart enough to take her threat seriously. "Yes, Ducky."

"And don't just barge into the ladies' room without knocking like you did last time," she admonished as he disappeared behind the men's-room door.

The little iron-haired tyrant lit a cigarette, then turned back to Trace and Chloe. "Welcome to Ducky's."

Chloe smiled as she turned to her date. "Trace, I'd like you to meet my grandmother, Ducky D'Onofrio."

5

CHLOE BIT BACK a smile at the stunned expression on Trace's face. She probably should have told him sooner, but the man seemed to bring out the worst in her. Especially after he'd practically accused her grandmother of killing off her husbands. Ducky might not be totally legit, but she wasn't dangerous. Or, at least, not lethally dangerous.

Ducky enveloped her granddaughter in an affectionate hug. "It's been too long, Chloe. Now, let me take a good look at you." Ducky stepped back and held her at arm's length. "Not bad." She reached out to pull the peasant blouse off Chloe's shoulders. "There, that's much better."

This time Chloe's smile broke through when she saw a muscle flex in Trace's cheek. She had to give him credit, though—he exercised surprising restraint.

Ducky turned around and elbowed Trace in the ribs. "Bet you find it hard to believe I'm old enough to be a grandmother."

He placed a hand over his ribs. "Well, I…"

Ducky glanced at her granddaughter. "Is he always this slow or is he just overwhelmed by a double dose of D'Onofrio beauty?"

Chloe leaned over to kiss her wrinkled, rouged cheek. "You've been making men speechless for the last forty years, Ducky. What do you think?"

Ducky snorted. "I think it's a shame you never went into the con game, girl. You're one smooth talker."

"Then I should be able to talk you into two ice-cold beers—on the house."

Ducky cackled. "You've got 'em. Go on and sit at my special table. I'll be right there."

Trace watched her grandmother bustle off toward the bar, a dazed expression on his face. Coping with more than one D'Onofrio at a time tended to have that effect on people. Especially when one of those D'Onofrios was Ducky. Chloe loved her spry, unconventional grandmother, despite her flirtation with the wrong side of the law.

Ducky had been there after Chloe's mother went to prison, providing advice and comfort. Intensely loyal to everyone in the family, Ducky had taken a special interest in Chloe. She'd encouraged her granddaughter's dream to go to design school and even cosigned her college loan papers. Ducky might not be your typical grandmother, but Chloe loved her fiercely.

"She's really your grandmother?" Trace whispered as they seated themselves at the secluded table.

She nodded. "My father's mother. Only she doesn't allow her grandchildren to call her anything but Ducky."

He scowled at her. "You might have told me sooner."

She batted her eyelashes at him. "But, Trace, I thought you already knew everything."

Before he could reply, Ducky arrived at the table with three frosty bottles of beer in her hands. She held Trace's bottle just out of his reach. "I don't serve a drink to a man unless I know his name."

"I'm Trace Callahan," he replied.

Chloe leaned forward. "Ducky, we can't stay long."

Ducky sat down at the table. "You'll stay long enough for this Callahan to tell me what his intentions are toward you."

"My intentions are strictly honorable," Trace assured her.

"That's too bad," Ducky replied with a disappointed sigh. "A man with strictly honorable intentions isn't much fun. Have you even kissed her yet?"

"Ducky!" To Chloe's consternation, a hot blush crept up her neck. "This is only our first date. Besides, we're not here to talk about...kissing. We're here about Ramon."

"What's that boy done now?"

"He's in trouble," Chloe replied, glossing over the finer details. "I have to find him. Has he been here this evening?"

Ducky shook her head. "No, but he was here last night. Had some bimbo with him, too."

Chloe's eyes widened. "A girl?"

"More like an Amazon," Ducky said with a cackle. "Ramon definitely had his hands full."

"Who was she?" Chloe asked.

Ducky shrugged. "Beats me. I was busy in the back. I just got a glimpse of her."

"What about Cousin Viper," Trace asked, "didn't he ask to see her ID?"

"Nope." Ducky tipped up her beer bottle. "He was too busy checking out her other vital statistics. She was one of those flashy blondes who wear too much makeup and look more than a little shopworn. I was afraid Ramon might be in over his head."

Chloe slowly shook her head. "I didn't even know he was dating anyone."

"I'm not sure I'd call it a date," Ducky said. "She flirted all night with Virgil. But your brother looked too nervous to notice."

"Poor Ramon," Chloe murmured. "He hasn't had much luck with women. No wonder he's been acting a little odd lately."

"How can you tell?" Trace asked.

She ignored him. "Is there anything else I should know?"

Ducky set her beer bottle on the table. "I shouldn't have told you that much. It's time to let him go, Chloe. Ramon is a big boy now and he doesn't need you to look after him anymore."

Chloe blinked, surprised by the vehemence in her grandmother's voice. "But he's family."

"Of course he's family. But there's more to life than work and cleaning up Ramon's messes. Just look at you." Ducky's mouth drew down in a frown. "Out on a date with this mouthwatering man and you're wasting it by worrying about your little brother."

Her words pricked. How could Chloe enjoy a date with Trace or any other man if her brother was headed for trouble? How could she not lift a finger to stop it? "If you want to know the truth, Trace believes Ramon hit him in the head this evening when he came to pick me up."

"Impossible," Ducky said, without a flicker of her false eyelashes. "That isn't Ramon's style. He's not a violent person."

"He almost cut off my toe yesterday," Trace said dryly.

"And tonight he answered the door with a carving knife in his hand."

Ducky shook her head. "The sight of blood makes him hysterical. You must be mistaken, Mr. Callahan."

"I have stitches to prove it," Trace insisted. "But that's not all. We found a bag full of—"

"Potato chips," Chloe interjected, before Trace could spill the beans about the diamonds. "They were lying on the kitchen floor and Ramon had disappeared. I thought maybe something had happened to him." She was lousy liar, which was evident by the expressions on the faces of her audience. But it was too late to backpedal now. "You know how Ramon loves potato chips. He wouldn't leave a bag just lying around, especially on the floor. But maybe I am overreacting just a bit." She pushed her chair back and stood up. "Ready, Trace?"

He looked at the untouched beer in front of him. "Uh...sure."

"'Bye, Ducky." She leaned over and kissed her grandmother's cheek. "Be good."

"I'll be good if you'll be a little bit bad," Ducky replied. Then she turned to Trace, her brown eyes serious. "I want you to promise that you'll take good care of my granddaughter."

"Ducky..." Chloe muttered.

"Promise me," Ducky said, her voice more intense now and her bony fingers squeezing his forearm.

He winced. "I promise."

Ducky's shoulders relaxed. "Thank you." Then she turned to Chloe. "I like him. I think you should keep this one."

"Ducky, like I told you before, this is only our first date." *And our last.* She was surprised Trace Callahan had stuck around this long. It was highly doubtful he'd come back for more. "Besides, he thinks women should be seen and not heard."

"I never said that," Trace protested. "I simply said some women don't always know what's best for them."

Ducky laughed. "Neither do some men."

"WHAT WAS THAT all about?" Trace asked as he steered his car away from the curb. A soft rain had fallen while they were inside Ducky's Bar, making the pavement glisten under the streetlights.

Chloe sat silently in the passenger seat, staring at the purse on her lap. "What?"

"The potato-chip story. It was pretty stale."

"I know. But I didn't want Ducky to find out about the diamonds."

"Afraid she'd want them for herself?" he asked wryly.

"Yes."

Trace almost missed his corner. He maneuvered the turn, then glanced at her. "You're joking."

"Unfortunately, no." She didn't say anything for a long moment. "Look, the D'Onofrios aren't exactly like other families."

That was the understatement of the century. Trace had never met anyone like Chloe. He never wanted to meet anyone like her grandmother. Especially in a deserted alley. His forearm and ribs still hurt.

"You really think she'd take the diamonds from you?"

"To protect me," Chloe replied. "But then she'd probably sell them on the black market. Ducky's cleaned up her act over the years, but she still runs a poker game in the back room. It's in her blood. A bag of diamonds might prove irresistible to her."

"It's in her blood, but not in yours?"

"Must be some sort of genetic mutation."

"Lucky for you," he said, and meant it. He flipped on the windshield wipers as intermittent raindrops splattered against the front windshield. "Exactly how long has this crime gene been in your family?"

"I believe it started with my great-great-grandfather. He was a professional gambler who got shot in the back after he was accused of cheating. Over the years that story's been romanticized, making him some kind of rogue hero. Ramon was even named after him."

"So, *was* he a cheat?"

She shrugged. "Who knows? All that matters to me is making sure the current Ramon D'Onofrio isn't accused of anything."

Trace glanced over at her. "But we already know he stole the diamonds."

"He may be the prime suspect, but we still don't know for certain," she said, her fingers fidgeting with the gold clasp on her purse. "And even if he did steal them, there's no reason he can't put them back where they belong."

Trace pulled up in front of her house, cut the engine, then turned to look at her. "That wasn't part of our agreement."

But Chloe wasn't looking at him. Her gaze was fixed on the front door. The *open* front door. "Didn't I lock the door when we left?"

"I watched you lock it. Which means—"

"Which means," she interjected, her expression grim as she popped open the passenger door, "it's time to settle this once and for all."

Trace jumped out of the car and hastily followed right on her heels. He didn't want her confronting Ramon alone. If the guy was desperate, there was no telling what he might do—even to his own sister.

Chloe stopped abruptly in the open doorway, and Trace plowed into her. He grabbed her shoulders to keep her from falling, then almost fell over himself when he looked past her into the house.

It was a mess.

His fingers flexed on her smooth, bare shoulders as he surveyed the living room. Furniture lay up-ended on the floor, the upholstery ripped to shreds and the white stuffing pulled out and scattered over the floor. The twenty-seven-inch television set had been tipped on its side and the back panel removed, the picture tube and electrical components exposed.

Chloe leaned back against him for a moment, almost as if she couldn't support herself. He breathed in the subtle raspberry scent of her hair and his gaze fell on her slender neck, now so close to his lips. They tingled slightly as he imagined skimming light, caressing kisses over that creamy skin.

But the fantasy abruptly ended when Chloe straightened and strode into her living room. She turned in a slow circle as she took in the devastation.

He took a deep breath to collect himself, then followed her inside. "What the hell happened here?"

"Isn't it obvious?" she muttered before disappearing down the long hallway.

He followed her wordlessly as she surveyed the rest of the house, both upstairs and down. Each room had been searched, with no care given to the mess left behind. At least the unique windows, carved moldings, and priceless staircase hadn't been damaged.

Chloe saved Ramon's bedroom for last. Squaring her shoulders, she opened the door. Then she let out a gasp.

It was the worst room of all. The closet stood empty, the clothes flung haphazardly over the floor. The dresser had been upended, the wood panels on the back and bottom pried off. The mattress lay at a drunken angle on the bed, slashed open through the blue-striped sheet right down to the other side.

Chloe bent down to pick up a small, ragged clown doll off the floor. Time had faded its curly red hair and orange polka-dot suit, but the jagged tear from nose to navel was brand new.

"Dad gave this to Ramon when he was ten years old," she said, her voice void of emotion. "It used to be his when he was a little boy and Ramon wanted it so badly. He promised he'd never let anything happen to it."

Trace carefully took the clown from her hand and set it on the tilted mattress. Then he enfolded Chloe in his arms. He gently cupped the back of her head with his hand, burying her face in the crook of his shoulder. "Go ahead and cry."

Her head snapped up, her brown eyes blazing. "Cry? I'd rather kick something. Or rather, someone! How dare *anyone* destroy my house just because they couldn't get their greedy hands on the diamonds."

"How do you know they didn't?" Trace asked, realizing he hadn't yet checked underneath the stairs.

"Because I've had them with me all evening." She held up her purse. "Safe and sound."

His jaw sagged. Thousands of dollars' worth of diamonds had been in her purse, in his car, and in Ducky's Bar. And he hadn't known it. A hundred possible scenarios popped in his head, all of them bad. "Are you completely crazy?"

"I'd call it prudent." She glanced around the room. "Especially considering what happened here."

"What if the police had made a traffic stop and searched your purse?"

"For what? A pencil?"

"For any number of reasons," he said, now pacing back and forth across the floor. "Or what if we'd been in a car accident and some emergency-room nurse had found them? Or some guy had decided to mug you outside of Ducky's?"

"I had you for protection."

"You might have mentioned to me that you also brought a stash of hot diamonds along for the ride."

She stared up at him. "Why are you so upset about this? I'm the one who deserves to be upset. My house has just been ransacked."

"Thanks to your brother."

Her eyes widened. "You think Ramon did this?"

"Oh, please. Don't tell me you're still going to keep defending him. He just killed a clown."

"How many times do I have to tell you," she said, her voice weary now. "This is not Ramon's style."

Trace shoved the mattress back into position on

the bed, then sat down, pulling her down beside him. "I think it's time you faced facts, Chloe. Ramon is on some sort of crazy crime spree."

She turned to face him. "*Accidentally* nicking you with a power saw does not make him public enemy number one."

"It was more than a nick," he said, stung by her sarcasm. "But I don't even care about that anymore. He's become much more dangerous in the last few hours." Trace let his gaze wander around the room. The destruction had a malevolent air about it. "You're not staying here tonight."

She blinked at him. "Is that an order?"

"Yes. And it isn't up for debate. It's not safe here. Can you stay with Ducky?"

"Of course. But I have no intention of going anywhere."

"Chloe, be sensible."

She rolled her eyes. "I like you so much better when you don't open your mouth."

"That's funny," he replied, "I was just thinking the same thing about you." *Except when you kiss me.* He looked away from her mouth and stared hard at the floor. Why did this woman have to make everything so difficult? Why did she have to have a face like an angel and a body that made him burn? Why couldn't he just walk away?

"I know you prefer women to be seen and not heard, but I'm not built that way."

"Believe me," Trace muttered, "I'm not complaining about the way you're built."

Her cheeks flushed a becoming pink.

"Well, if you'd pay as much attention to my brain, maybe we could actually accomplish something."

"I happen to think you're a very intelligent woman," he said honestly. "Except where your brother is concerned. Even you have to admit you're more than a little biased."

"Maybe so. But, as I said before, I know Ramon better than anyone. He may have stolen those diamonds, but he didn't do this." Her hand swept around the room.

"Then who did? Some other D'Onofrio?"

She slowly shook her head. "Not unless it was Uncle Pete. He's not technically my uncle anymore, since Aunt Mary divorced him. None of the family has had anything to do with him since his arrest for pandering. Even the D'Onofrios know where to draw the line."

"So you think Uncle Pete is responsible?"

"I don't know what to think. It's even possible this mess has nothing to do with the diamonds. Maybe this is just a run-of-the-mill burglary."

"Maybe," he conceded. "Have you noticed anything missing?"

"Just my brother."

"So much for that theory."

"Do you have a better one?" She tipped up her chin. "Besides blaming Ramon?"

"It's still the most logical explanation," he insisted. "But have you considered he could have an accomplice? Or even more than one?"

"No." She frowned. "Actually, the thought

never even crossed my mind. Ramon doesn't have a lot of friends.''

"They wouldn't necessarily have to be friends. What about the bimbo Ducky mentioned?''

"I suppose it's possible,'' she conceded, her expression growing thoughtful.

"I'd say it's highly likely. Which means we definitely have to call the police.''

She turned to him. "But...''

"No buts,'' he said, steeling himself against her entreaties. "We've taken enough risks tonight already. I still can't believe you brought those diamonds along with us.''

"That again?'' One corner of her mouth twisted in exasperation. "Even if by some wild chance the police *did* discover them in our possession, all we'd have to do is explain the situation. They'd have no reason to suspect either one of us.''

"Unless *one* of us is a convicted felon.''

"I'm not!'' she said hotly.

"I am.''

CHLOE GAPED at him in disbelief. Then she closed her mouth and tried to pretend his admission hadn't just knocked the air out of her lungs. Why should it shock her so much? It wasn't as if she'd never met a convicted felon before. *Met one?* Over half the D'Onofrio family had done time.

But Trace Callahan?

"You don't believe me?'' he said, a half smile tugging at his mouth.

"Frankly…no," she said at last. "You're just not the type."

"Should I take that as a compliment?"

"Of course." She frowned at him, still confused by his confession. "So what happened? Were you framed?"

He shook his head. "Nope. Definitely guilty. Some friends and I hot-wired a car, then got involved in a high-speed chase. I was the driver."

"How old were you?"

"Eighteen. To make matters worse, I had an extensive juvenile record. Vandalism, petty theft, disturbing the peace—you name it, I probably did it."

Her gaze drifted to his mouth as he spoke. She'd kissed him tonight. Twice. Even worse, she'd *enjoyed* kissing him. "Why didn't you tell me sooner?"

"It's not exactly something I'm proud of, Chloe. I messed up. Big-time. But I'm not the same man anymore. I've turned my life around and I have Aunt Sophie to thank for it."

"What did she do?"

"She talked the judge into giving me the minimum sentence. She also told me in no uncertain terms that my mother wasn't ever coming back."

Chloe blinked. "That sounds a bit harsh."

He nodded, a muscle knotting his jaw. "True. But I needed to hear it."

"Why? That seems so cruel."

"My mother left when I was six, and my first brush with the law happened when I was nine. I threw a rock through a neighbor's window. Over the next ten years, my behavior grew progressively worse." He chuckled, the tension leaving his body. "Now I wonder how Aunt Sophie kept herself from throwing *me* through a window."

"You wanted attention," she surmised, remembering how Ramon had always caused the most trouble when their parents weren't there for him.

"That's right. Specifically, my mother's attention. I guess some part of me believed that she'd hear about my problems and come back and rescue me from myself."

"But she never did," Chloe said softly.

He shrugged it off. "I had Aunt Sophie. She treated me as if I were her own son. She loved me enough to tell me the hard truth—my mother was never coming back and I could either make something of my life or destroy it. But whichever I chose, she'd always be there for me."

Chloe's throat tightened at his words. At the image of a little boy who missed his mother so desperately. Anger surged through her at the selfish, callous Mrs. Callahan. "How could any mother abandon her children!"

"She wanted a different life," he said evenly. "Not to mention the fact that she and my father were far from a perfect match. So she ended up in Europe and eventually remarried. But Jake, Noah and I are the only children she ever had."

"She didn't deserve you," Chloe said fiercely. "Did she ever call or write or send birthday presents?"

"Nope," he replied. "It was a clean break. Her

sister, my Aunt June, kept in touch with us though, and told us about her. Told us she was happy."

Anger roiled inside Chloe until she wanted to punch something. Why did his story affect her so much? It was sad, but she didn't know this woman. She hardly even knew Trace.

Then it hit her.

Her mother had abandoned her, too. Only she hadn't gone to Europe, she'd gone to prison. Maybe she hadn't wanted to leave Chloe and Ramon, but that hadn't stopped her from taking risks. She'd gambled and lost—and all of them had suffered the consequences.

Without conscious thought, she reached out and clasped Trace's large hand, squeezing it gently. No wonder she'd felt that odd connection between them. They shared more than passion. They shared heartache and loss.

She gazed up into his eyes as her anger transformed itself into something else entirely. Her heart pounded in her chest and her breathing grew fast and shallow. She let her hand trail over his wrist and up his arm, so lightly she barely touched him. His body stilled and she heard his quick intake of breath as her fingers traced his shoulder and the strong column of his neck, slowly circling the top button of his collar.

"Chloe," he groaned, not making a move to stop her.

She didn't say anything, just kept touching him. His long, lean jaw, his cheek and the line of his brow. Her fingers drifted into his thick dark hair, brushing through it until she reached the crisp, tight curls at the nape of his neck.

He reached out to cup her cheek, taking his turn to touch and torment. His broad fingers outlined her cheekbone and the delicate shell of her ear. Then he lightly trailed the tips of his fingers down her neck, the sensation causing an odd warmth to spread throughout her body. His fingertips teased the edge of her peasant blouse, back and forth in agonizing slowness. His blue eyes darkened and his breathing grew ragged, but his fingers never stopped moving.

A hot blush suffused her chest and she closed her eyes, amazed that such a delicate touch could have such a devastating effect on her.

The jangle of the telephone on the floor beside her bed made them both jump. Trace's hand stilled just above her breasts. They stared at each other for a long moment, until the telephone rang again.

"I'd better answer it," she whispered. Struggling to compose herself, she reached for the phone, her skin still tingling where Trace had touched her. She took a deep breath. "Hello?"

Her eyes widened when she heard the voice on the other end of the line. Then she cupped the mouthpiece with her hand and looked at Trace. "It's Ramon."

6

TRACE WATCHED as Chloe paced back and forth, twisting the phone cord between her fingers. Judging from her stark silence, Ramon was obviously doing all the talking.

He ran one finger around the collar of his shirt, unsettled by what had almost happened here. Being attracted to Chloe D'Onofrio was one thing. Acting on that attraction was quite another.

"Listen, Ramon...." Her voice trailed off as she looked at Trace with frustration.

Trace was frustrated, too. This fake date wasn't turning out at all the way he'd planned. Even worse, there was nothing fake about his reaction to her. His fingers itched to touch her again. He wanted to hold her. Kiss her.

"You can't be serious," she said, her fingers tightening on the telephone receiver. "Ramon—"

Trace watched Chloe's lips press firmly together as her brother obviously cut her off again. Those delectable lips had attempted to breathe life into him earlier this evening.

And it had worked.

These last few hours with Chloe had been more lively, more exhilarating, more unpredictable than anything he could ever remember experiencing. She was like no woman he'd ever met before. And she was completely wrong for him.

She was a D'Onofrio, he reminded himself. *Strike one.* She was Ramon's sister. *Strike two.* She made him completely crazy. *Strike three.* He didn't want craziness in his life. He'd had enough of that growing up around Aunt Sophie.

Now he just wanted to get his life back under control.

"Ramon, please," she entreated into the receiver.

He moved toward Chloe. "Let me talk to him."

She shook her head and turned away from him. "All right, I'm listening...."

Time to take matters into his own hands.

He reached for the telephone receiver, pulling it gently but firmly out of her grasp. Then he held it up to his ear. "Ramon, this is Trace."

Chloe glared at him, but he ignored her. She was obviously too emotionally involved to handle this on her own.

"What the hell are you still doing there?" Ramon sputtered. "No, don't tell me. I don't want to know. Whatever it is, you'd better stop it right now. I mean it, Callahan, if you lay one finger on my sister—"

"It's time to stop playing games, Ramon. We know you're guilty and you know you're guilty. Now why don't you take it like a man and turn yourself over to the police? The longer you wait, the harder it's going to be on you."

Ramon replied with a loud click.

Trace stared at the receiver for a moment, then handed it to Chloe. "He hung up on me."

"Now, there's a shocker."

He blinked at her tone. "You're upset."

"No, I'm not upset." She slammed the receiver down on the telephone base. "I'm furious."

"Ramon does have that effect on people."

"Ramon?" She gaped at him in disbelief. "What about you?"

"Me?" For a moment, he wondered if she was hysterical. She certainly wasn't making much sense. "What did I do?"

"Well, for starters, you practically ripped the phone out of my hand. Then you probably scared Ramon out of his wits by bringing up the police and telling him he should turn himself in."

"I had to do something. From the sound of it, you certainly weren't getting anywhere with him."

"I was *listening*." She sat down on the side of the bed. "You should try it sometime, instead of barging in where you're not wanted."

"I listen," he replied, stung by her words. *Not wanted.* She'd wanted him a few moments ago, before Ramon had interfered. Or had she? Maybe Trace had just assumed the explosive reaction between them was mutual. Maybe this date had only become real for him. "Look, I'm sorry if I offended you. It's been a long, eventful evening. I'm sure we're both tired."

She stood up abruptly. "You're right. I think it's time for you to go."

"Don't you want me to wait until the police arrive?"

She blinked at him. "The police?"

He motioned at the chaos around them. "You have to report this."

"Says who?"

He took a deep, calming breath, refusing to let himself lose his temper. Again. "I'm not trying to tell you what to do. It's your house, your brother, your mess. But any reasonable person…"

"Would realize that Ramon won't come within a mile of home if there are police cruisers parked outside. Besides, it doesn't look like anything's been stolen. Whoever did this was on a search-and-destroy mission."

"Searching for the diamonds," he added. "Which means they could come back here at any time." He set his jaw. "You can't stay here alone."

She arched a brow. "Trace…"

"I mean," he interjected, mentally kicking himself, "I'd rather you didn't stay here alone. If you don't want to leave, then I'll sleep here."

"No," she said, a little too quickly. "That's not necessary. You've already done too much."

Not nearly as much as he wanted to do. Which worried him almost as much as the thought of her staying here alone. His willpower was strong, but not superhuman.

"I'll call Viper," she offered at last. "I'm sure he won't mind camping out on the sofa."

"Fine." Trace knew he should feel relieved instead of frustrated. He'd finally won an argument.

Instead, his concern deepened as he reluctantly followed Chloe out of the bedroom and down the spiral staircase to the front door.

She walked out onto the porch with him. "Good night, Trace. This is one date I'll never forget."

"Me either," he muttered, still uneasy about leaving her. "Lock all your doors and windows."

She gave him a mock salute. "Yes, sir."

He grinned in spite of himself. "All right. So maybe I do tend to come on a little strong. I'll try and work on it."

She smiled, the moonlight casting an ethereal glow on her face. "Don't try too hard. Some women like a man telling them what to do."

"But not you?"

A sultry breeze fluttered the broom skirt around her slender legs. "I guess I've been on my own too long to start taking orders now. Madame Sophia must have been wrong about us."

"Definitely." He took a step closer to her. "Will I see you tomorrow?"

She nodded, her eyes large and luminous as she looked up at him. "I'll be at Café Romeo after lunch. I need to measure the windows."

"I'll be there," he promised, resisting the urge to brush back the silky hair on her temple. It was even harder to resist kissing her good night. But he'd had all the temptation he could take for one evening. So he just stood there, watching her, the air crackling between them.

At last Chloe moved toward the door. "Good night, Trace."

"Good night." He headed down the wooden steps, then he turned abruptly. "Wait a minute."

She paused in the open doorway. "What?"

"You never told me about your phone conversation with Ramon. Did he tell you where he was?"

"No."

"Well, did he happen to say when he was coming back? Or where he got the diamonds? Or why he left me under the staircase?"

She took a step back into the house, the old screen door closing between them. "I didn't get a chance to ask him. He was sort of rambling."

He climbed back up a step and held the door open. "About what?"

"This and that. I'm so tired now I can't even think straight. I'll tell you all about it tomorrow." She reached for the door.

"Chloe, wait..."

But he was too late. The door swung closed and Chloe disappeared inside, locking it after her.

He swore softly under his breath, certain she was keeping something from him. Part of him wanted to bang on the door demanding answers. Unfortunately, that was the part of him she didn't like. He clenched his jaw, wondering what the hell he should do now. He could leave and hope she followed through on her intention to call Viper. Or he could park his car on the corner and watch over her himself.

His stomach growled as he made his way to the Blazer. With any luck he still had some licorice in his glove compartment.

It was going to be a very long night.

THE NEXT DAY, Trace couldn't stop looking at his watch. He brushed fine sawdust off the crystal and swore softly under his breath. Two o'clock. He'd been at the Café Romeo for hours. Where the hell was Chloe?

He considered himself a patient man. In his business, patience was a necessity. Hurrying through a project cost both time and money, resulting in wasted materials and shoddy workmanship. He brought that same studied patience to his personal life, too.

Like his perfect-wife project.

His search might be slow and pedantic, but with his method a happily-ever-after outcome was practically guaranteed. No whirlwind romances for Trace Callahan. No headlong rush into marriage without looking at the future from every conceivable angle.

But even a patient man can be pushed too far. Especially a man who has spent a sleepless night cuddled up to a steering wheel. His neck still ached from reclining in the driver's seat for several hours. At least he hadn't seen anyone trying to sneak into her house. Even better, Chloe hadn't seen him keeping watch.

She also hadn't called her cousin Viper, which only added to his irritation. Maybe she didn't plan to show up here today, either. He should have demanded answers from her while he had the chance. Instead, he'd let her practically push him out the door without explaining Ramon's phone call. The phone call that had come just in the nick of time.

He closed his eyes, remembering those heated

moments before the telephone had jolted them back to reality. Her skin like silk beneath his fingertips. The unsteady rise and fall of her chest. Her lips slightly parted, so lush, so inviting. He swallowed hard and opened his eyes. Good thing she had pushed him out the door, or they might still be on that bed.

He couldn't afford to take any more chances. It was bad enough that this mess with Chloe had delayed his auditions of Heidi and Evonne, the next two candidates on his list. Bad enough that he couldn't work up any enthusiasm about either one of them. Bad enough that he still hadn't called the police about those hot diamonds.

The memory of her voice teased his senses. *I'll be at Café Romeo after lunch.* He set down the plywood on the sawhorse with a bang. It was now two hours past lunch and Chloe was nowhere in sight.

If he was smart, he'd want her to stay that way. Only he couldn't seem to concentrate on anything else. He'd remeasured the chair railing three times already. Broke the blade on his jigsaw. And stubbed his sore toe against a four-by-four.

The oilcloth curtain separating the new addition from the existing Café Romeo suddenly swept open, blowing his blueprints off the table and onto the floor. Chloe walked in like a gust of fresh air, her brown eyes sparkling and a sexy flush on her cheeks. "Sorry I'm late," she said, slightly breathless. "I had lunch at Julio's. They have the best Mexican food in town."

"I hate Mexican food."

"Oh, that's right." She folded her sunglasses in her hand, but avoided his gaze. It was almost as if last night had never happened. "Anyway, there was a three-car pileup on Interstate 70, so I've been sitting in traffic. I hope I didn't keep you waiting."

"No problem," he said in a clipped voice, watching her pull a sketch pad out of her voluminous straw tote bag.

Chloe set down her bag, then looked around the restaurant. "Where's Madame Sophia?"

"Some clown asked her to go on a picnic."

"Clown?" she echoed, her mouth turned down in disapproval.

"The guy's a real Bozo," he said, somewhat surprised by the note of irritation in her voice.

"You're unbelievable," she exclaimed. "Other men may not be as tall as you. Or as handsome. They may not have sapphire eyes that make a woman's knees go weak. But that doesn't make every man except you a clown!"

He folded his arms across his chest. "I call 'em as I see 'em. But it so happened that Aunt Sophie's on a picnic with Bozo, a clown she used to work with in the carnival. He's got a big red nose, an orange wig, and a polka-dot clown suit."

"Oh." Chloe cleared her throat, obviously embarrassed by her blunder. But now her gaze met his squarely. "My mistake."

His mistake was looking into her brown eyes. They did strange things to his equilibrium. His own knees felt like they were made of Jell-O. He forced his gaze away, turning to pull out a chair for her at a nearby table. "We need to talk."

"We certainly do," she agreed, opening her sketchbook while he took the chair across from her. "Here are my preliminary sketches. As you can see, I've stayed with simple lines and muted tones, saving bright colors for accents and trim. Madame Sophia didn't give me a lot of direction, so if you see anything here that might be a problem, let me know so I can make the changes before I draw up the final plans."

"There is one thing you should know." Trace stared down at the sketchbook, vaguely noting the skillful artwork and tasteful color combinations.

"What?"

He looked up at her. "I don't want to talk about your sketches. I want to talk about your brother."

"That subject is off-limits. Now, what do you think about track lighting?

"Excuse me?"

"I realize track lighting is a little more expensive, but ambiance is important, especially for a coffeehouse as unique as Café Romeo." She paused, then frowned at his expression. "I take it you don't like track lighting?"

"I don't like you changing the subject. I want to know why your brother called last night. I want to hear the entire conversation, word for word."

She closed her sketchbook. "I'm a professional, Trace. I don't discuss personal matters during business hours."

"You're stalling again."

"Maybe I should come back when I can talk to Madame Sophia."

"You're not going anywhere until you tell me

what I want to know." He picked up a folded newspaper off the table and thrust it at her. "Did you see the article on the front page of today's paper? The headline is, Diamond Heist at Choice Jewelers. Suspect Still at Large."

"If we order the fabric before Thursday, I can get a great discount."

"If your brother turns himself in, he may be able to cop a plea. Where is he, Chloe?"

She stood, pulling a business card out of her bag. "Will you please have your aunt call me at her earliest convenience?"

Trace rose, rounding the table to stand in front of her. He'd reached the end of his patience. "Knock it off, Chloe. I deserve to know the truth."

The oilcloth drape swept open, heralding a new arrival, but neither one bothered to look. They were completely focused on each other.

Her eyes flashed. "The truth? The truth is that I don't take orders from anyone, Trace. Especially a man. So you can take your orders and your puffed-up ego and shove 'em in your...sock."

"There's no room in my sock, thanks to your brother. My toe is still swollen."

"Don't worry," she retorted, "it's still not as big as your head."

His gaze fell to her sassy mouth. Damn. The woman drove him crazy. Unfortunately, he could think of only one way to shut her up.

But before he could make a move, Chloe muttered under her breath, "Looks like we have an audience."

He glanced over his shoulder to see Nina and

Jake watching them, obviously fascinated. He turned back to Chloe. "It's my brother and his fiancée. They can wait until we settle this."

"It's settled," she insisted. "Ramon is my problem, not yours. I'll handle it. Just pretend it never happened. Even better, pretend we never even met."

"We're supposed to be dating," he reminded her. "Our love is written in the coffee grounds, remember?"

"Coffee grounds belong in the trash. So consider this our big breakup scene." She glanced toward Jake and Nina. "We'll even have witnesses."

He took a step closer to her, knowing most women found his height and size intimidating, but too frustrated to care. "What if I'm not ready to break up?"

"Get ready," she muttered, then she pushed past him and headed toward the door. "Adios, Trace. It's been fun, but no enchilada. You want ketchup and I'm more of the salsa type."

Salsa? More like a jalapeño pepper.

He'd never liked hot and spicy. Until now. "Wait…"

"Buenos nachos," she chimed, then slung her tote bag over her shoulder and breezed through the oilcloth partition.

Trace watched her leave, resisting the urge to race after her. Maybe this was for the best. He might be attracted to her, but there was certainly no future for them. And he could hardly barge back into her life when she'd just made it clear she wanted him out of it.

"Earth to Trace," Jake said, waving a hand in front of his brother's face.

Trace blinked, then realized Jake and Nina were now standing in front of him. "What?"

"Let me take a wild guess," Nina ventured, flashing a dimple. "That was Chloe."

"*Was* is the operative word," Trace said, picking his blueprints off the floor and laying them out on the table. "You just saw us break up."

Jake laughed.

"Oh, we saw plenty, little brother."

Trace scowled. "What's so funny?"

"Nothing." Nina elbowed her fiancé in the ribs. "You seem upset, Trace. Do you want to talk about it?"

"I'm not upset." Trace rolled up the blueprints. "Why should I be upset?"

Jake shrugged. "Maybe because she's a beautiful woman and you just let her walk out the door."

"Let her? How was I supposed to stop her? More to the point, *why* should I stop her? She's a D'Onofrio. I should be celebrating."

"You don't look too happy," Jake observed.

"I'm ecstatic," Trace snarled. "Besides, we only had one date. I'm lucky I survived it." He set down the rolled blueprints. "In fact, I'll buy you both a beer across the street at O'Malley's."

"Now?" Jake glanced at his watch.

"Right now," Trace insisted as he moved toward the door. "You can toast my bravery. I had a date with Chloe D'Onofrio and lived to tell about it."

CHLOE SAT in a dark corner booth at O'Malley's, staring gloomily into her coffee. It was strong and black and a little bitter. Nothing like Madame Sophia's special Jamaican-almond blend. Just the way no other man was quite like Trace Callahan.

She watched him through her lashes as he talked and joked with Jake and Nina at a table on the far side of the room. They hadn't seen her when they'd come into O'Malley's and she intended to keep it that way. She'd already walked away from Trace once. She wasn't sure she could do it again.

Dumping Trace was the only way to keep him safe. She certainly couldn't tell him about Ramon's phone call. Her nitwit brother actually wanted to split the diamonds with her, fifty-fifty. Actually believed she'd even consider the idea. Right now, all she was considering was locking her twenty-two-year-old brother in his room until he came to his senses.

She took a sip of her coffee, grimacing at the bitter taste. It matched the bitterness in her heart. Until last night, she'd hoped that Ramon was innocent. That somehow he hadn't been behind the theft of those diamonds. But his phone call had made his guilt perfectly clear. He knew about the diamonds. Knew they'd been taken from the hiding place under the stairway.

And now he wanted them back.

Too bad. She set down her coffee cup so hard it clinked against the saucer. She glanced up, then breathed a sigh of relief that no one at Trace's table had noticed. They were too caught up in their conversation. For a moment, she envied their easy camaraderie. The D'Onofrios were loyal and loving, but there had always been an underlying tension among them. Hardly surprising, when half of them were wanted by the law at any given time.

She'd just never imagined her brother would be one of them. Until last night. She'd played along with Ramon on the telephone, pretending to consider his offer to split the diamonds between them. That's when he'd suggested they meet tonight at ten o'clock sharp, by the Dairy Wizard, an abandoned ice-cream parlor out on Farmingham Road.

Chloe wasn't exactly sure what she'd do when she got there. Ramon had sounded different on the phone—almost desperate. She doubted he'd listen to reason. Which meant she had to come up with a plan.

She glanced at her watch. Not much time. After setting a small tip on the table, she eased out the back entrance, certain Trace hadn't spotted her. It was already past four o'clock. Somehow in the next few hours, she had to figure out a way to clear her brother, get rid of the diamonds, and forget about Trace Callahan.

Right now, all three sounded impossible.

7

BY SIX O'CLOCK that evening Trace had resigned himself to the fact that Chloe was out of his life. He celebrated by having a pizza delivered. It arrived half-baked.

By seven o'clock he'd begun to have second thoughts. He took two antacids and threw the remainder of the pizza in the trash. Then he sat on his sofa, staring at the stitches on his big toe.

By eight o'clock, he was climbing the walls. He had to see her. Talk to her. Convince her that she needed his help. His desire to see her again was more than just physical attraction. She obviously didn't realize the trouble she could be in for harboring a criminal. Protecting her brother was one thing, aiding and abetting quite another.

Shortly after nine o'clock he simply couldn't take it anymore. In an attempt to distract himself, he took a drive in his Blazer, cruising the suburban streets of St. Louis. It was a hot, balmy evening; the smell of rain was in the air. As he drove, he saw a group of young girls playing hopscotch on the sidewalk. An adolescent couple walked hand in hand in the park. An old man sat outside his tiny box of a house, lazily scratching his dog's head with the tip of his cane.

As hazy twilight descended on the tranquil neighborhood, Trace knew he had a choice to make. He could turn around and go home, or he could go after Chloe. Not that he wanted her in his life. She'd never be vanilla. But she needed his help. Especially since she was still obviously in denial about Ramon.

He pulled up to a stop sign, letting the car idle as he contemplated which way to turn. Left would take him home. Right would take him to Chloe. He reminded himself that she didn't want to see him again. That the last time he'd shown up at Chloe's door, he'd been threatened with a knife, then bashed on the head. Left would be safer. Smarter. Duller.

He turned right.

WHERE WAS A MAN when you really needed one?

Chloe tightened the last bolt on the spare tire with the tire iron, still unable to believe her bad luck. She wiped her damp brow with her sleeve, then glanced at her watch. Damn. She was late. Leaving the deflated tire on the side of the road, she tossed the tire iron into her trunk. Then she slammed it shut and hopped into the driver's seat.

"Please be there, Ramon," she implored under her breath. "Wait for me. Please wait for me." Her entreaties grew more fervent with each mile. Traffic was light this evening, affording Chloe plenty of room to maneuver on the long stretch of highway.

A wave of apprehension swept through her. *What if Ramon didn't wait for her? What if she was too late?* She floored the gas pedal, watching the speedometer creep up. Fifty. Sixty. Seventy.

Speeding was a first for law-abiding Chloe, but tonight she felt impelled to break the law. She pushed it to seventy-five, relieved her destination lay just up ahead. Then she glanced in her rearview mirror and her heart sank.

"Damn," she groaned, as she applied the brake and eased the car onto the shoulder. "Damn, damn, damn."

The pulsating red lights of the police cruiser matched the beat of her heart. She rolled down the window as the officer cautiously approached her car.

"Good evening, ma'am," he said, blinding her by shining the heavy-duty flashlight into her car. "I clocked you going seventy-two miles per hour in a fifty-mile-per-hour zone."

"I can explain." Chloe leaned toward him, desperate enough to let a little cleavage work to her advantage.

The flashlight flicked briefly down, then back up again. Judging by the implacable expression on the officer's craggy face, he was immune to cleavage. She swallowed a sigh of exasperation. She didn't have time for any more delays. Ramon would be long gone by the time she reached the Dairy Wizard. What if he didn't try to contact her again? What if he did something crazy?

"May I see your driver's license and registration, please?"

Chloe fumbled in her bag for her driver's license. "I have a family emergency."

He perked up. "A medical emergency?"

"Not yet," she muttered, seriously contemplating doing her little brother physical harm. She handed the officer her license and the registration slip.

"Chloe *D'Onofrio*," the officer exclaimed, his eyes widening. "Are you any relation to Louis D'Onofrio? Or Marco D'Onofrio? Or Ducky D'Onofrio?"

"Uh...yes, as a matter of fact, I am."

He moved back a pace, his expression suddenly wary. "Please step out of the car, Miss D'Onofrio."

With a sinking sensation, Chloe did as he instructed. She'd heard her family tell stories before about the way police reacted to the D'Onofrio name, but she'd never really believed them. Until now. Standing on the shoulder at the rear of her car, she watched as the officer did a quick search of the front and back seats. She briefly wondered if he needed a search warrant, but she didn't have time to confront him about it.

She gritted her teeth when he made her open the trunk, his hand hovering near the butt of the pistol in his belt. Just the fact that her last name was D'Onofrio made him expect trouble. Guilt by association.

After an interminable amount of time, the officer finally let her go, forgetting, in his excitement of almost nabbing a D'Onofrio, to give her a citation for speeding.

It was fifteen minutes past ten o'clock by the time Chloe reached the old, abandoned Dairy Wizard. Once a popular hangout for teenagers in the late eighties, the Dairy Wizard now sat isolated and neglected at the end of a dead-end street. One of the streetlights was out, making the large, empty parking lot even spookier than it already was.

She got out of her car and peered around the murky shadows. There was no sign of Ramon. There was no sign of anyone. A chill ran down her spine, despite the fact that it was still over eighty degrees outside. She rubbed her hands up and down her bare arms. She didn't want to stay here alone, but she couldn't leave either. Not if there was the least possibility Ramon might still show up.

As her eyes adjusted to the darkness, she moved away from her car and closer to the Dairy Wizard. She skirted an upended aluminum trash can, almost jumping out of her shoes when a black cat shot out of the can with a startled screech. She watched it run off into the thick hedge of rhododendron bushes that bordered the parking lot. It screeched again, louder this time, making the hairs prickle on the back of Chloe's neck.

She suddenly became aware of her own vulnerability. She was alone. At night. In a deserted parking lot. All five senses now on high alert, she continued toward the Dairy Wizard. She'd almost reached the plate-glass front door when she saw it. A small, pristine white note taped to the outside of the door. She'd just plucked it off when she saw a shadow move out of the corner of her eye.

Ramon.

Only it wasn't Ramon. The man who rounded the corner of the building was bigger. Broader. Bleeding.

It was Trace.

HE SHOULD HAVE turned left.

Trace pulled a handkerchief out of his back pocket and mopped up the streak of blood running down his forearm. "What the hell do you think you're doing?"

She stared at him. "Me? What are you doing here?"

"Isn't it obvious?"

She set her jaw. "Yes. And I think I should warn you that stalking is a felony."

"Stalking? You think I'm *stalking* you?"

"Call me crazy. I suppose it's just coincidence that you showed up here now?"

"Maybe I wanted an ice-cream cone."

"You're about nine years too late. The Dairy Wizard closed in '91." Her gaze flicked to the long scratch on his arm. "Besides, it looks like you're more in need of a bandage than an ice-cream cone. What happened?"

He wiped away the last of the blood with his handkerchief, then stuck it in his back pocket.

"Some wildcat got her claws into me."

Chloe arched a brow. "*Her?* How can you be so sure it was a female?"

"Because she was acting irrationally. Just like somebody else I know. Do you have any idea how dangerous it is for you to be out here alone?"

"I'm not alone. You're here."

"Only because I was smart enough to follow you."

"See," she exclaimed, stabbing one finger toward his chest, "you admit it. You've been following me."

"Damn straight. Good thing, too, considering your destination. You didn't even let a flat tire deter you."

Her eyes narrowed. "Wait a minute. You were there when I had the flat tire? Just how long have you been following me?"

"I drove up to your house just as you were pulling out of your driveway. So I decided to tag along." He took a step closer to her. "By the way, I was very impressed. Not many women I know can change a flat tire."

"You need to get out of your cave more often." She planted her hands on her hips. "And thank you so much for all your help. It took me twenty minutes to figure out how to work that stupid hoist."

"You're the one who said you don't like a man telling you what to do. I wasn't about to barge in and take over, especially since you happened to be holding a tire iron at the time." Little did she know that it had taken all his willpower to stay in his car and watch her struggle. But if he'd revealed himself, she never would have led him here. He still hadn't figured out the reason they were standing in a deserted parking lot on the outskirts of St. Louis, but he knew something was definitely up.

"And I suppose you got a good chuckle when I was stopped for speeding, too?"

His jaw tightened. "Believe me, I wasn't laughing. You were driving like a maniac. I thought only nuns drove that fast."

She blinked. "Excuse me?"

"Forget it. I'm just glad that cop slowed you down."

"He slowed me down all right. Thanks to St. Louis's finest, I missed Ramon."

He stilled. "Ramon was here?"

She sighed. "That's why he called last night. He wanted me to meet him here at ten o'clock and hand over the diamonds. He sounded…strange."

"Isn't that how he usually sounds?"

"This was different. Ramon is high-strung, but last night he sounded almost frantic."

"I'd be a little frantic, too, if I'd lost one hundred thousand dollars' worth of stolen diamonds. I'd certainly stick around long enough to see if my sister showed up with them. At the very least, I'd leave a note."

She looked up at him, her eyes widening with surprise. "A…note?"

"That's right," he confirmed. "Just like that one you've got hidden in your right hand."

She tucked her right arm behind her back. "I have no idea what you're talking about."

"Give it up, D'Onofrio. You're a lousy liar. Besides, I've been watching you ever since I parked behind that hedge. Is that note from Ramon?''

"How should I know?" she snapped. "I haven't even had time to read it yet."

"So let's read it together. There's enough light here," he said, glancing up at the mercury flood above them.

Her brows furrowed. "Why?"

"Why what?"

"Why do you care what's in the note? Why did you follow me here? Why don't you just forget you ever met me?"

"I can't," he blurted out, not wanting to admit it to himself, much less her. But it was still the truth. He couldn't stop thinking about her. Day and night, Chloe D'Onofrio filled his mind. Now she filled his senses. He could smell the subtle fragrance of her perfume. See the amber flecks in her brown eyes. Hear the beat of his own heart as he took a step closer to her and cupped her cheek in his hand, one finger gently stroking over her soft skin.

Right now, more than anything, he wanted to taste her. But this was hardly the time or the place. Not when she was still keeping secrets from him. Not when she still didn't trust him. "Show me the note, Chloe."

She moistened her lips with her tongue, her gaze never leaving his. "On one condition. No matter what it says, I call the shots. Agreed?"

He opened his mouth to argue with her when a shot rang out. It shattered his reflection in the large plate-glass window. Trace tackled Chloe, rolling so he took the brunt of the impact when they both hit the asphalt.

Another shot sounded, this bullet blasting through the big red plastic D on the Dairy Wizard sign just above their heads.

Trace held Chloe close to his chest. "Looks like someone else is calling the shots now."

CHLOE STARED at Trace, her cheeks drained of color. "Someone is trying to kill us."

"Lucky for us he's a lousy shot." He rolled away from her to upend the old picnic bench in front of them, using it as a barricade.

"He?" Chloe echoed, half sitting up. "You think it's Ramon, don't you? You actually believe my brother is shooting at us!"

Trace pulled Chloe back down. "I'm not thinking anything right now, except how to get the hell out of here."

He kept his arm firmly around her waist to stop her from moving. He could feel the tension in her muscles, see the fast beat of the pulse in her throat.

"Listen," she whispered at last.

"I don't hear anything."

"Exactly. We might be safe now. Maybe whoever was shooting at us left."

"Or maybe he's just biding his time until he can get a clear shot."

"We can make a run for my car," she whispered, "it's the closest."

"First, we need to douse the light," He looked

up at the mercury light that illuminated the stretch of pavement between the Dairy Wizard and Chloe's Taurus. "Otherwise, we'll be easy targets."

Chloe picked up a chunk of gravel. "I'll give it a try."

"Let me," he said, taking the stone out of her hand. "We don't want to be here all night."

She shrugged. "Okay, Callahan, here's your chance to impress me. Let's see if you can put out the light with one throw."

"And if I miss?"

"Then it's my turn."

He palmed the heavy stone in his hand. Taking a deep breath, he levered himself up and hurled it toward the light.

He missed.

"Forget it. This isn't going to work," he grumbled. "For one thing, I can't make an accurate throw from a kneeling position. For another, that light must be at least thirty feet high."

"Quit griping and give me some room," she whispered, picking up another stone and turning it over in her palm. She got to her knees, still hunched behind the picnic table. Then her arm whipped around like a windmill and she pitched the stone underhand up toward the light.

A loud pop sounded right before the light went out.

"I don't believe it," he muttered as she dropped back down beside him. "What a lucky shot."

"No luck about it, Callahan. In high school, I

was the starting pitcher on the fast-pitch softball team. We qualified for the state tournament."

"Now you tell me."

"You didn't give me a chance before. You just went into your Fred Flintstone caveman routine."

"Yabba-dabba-doo." He grabbed her hand. "Come on, Wilma, let's make a run for it."

They raced the short distance from the picnic table to the red Ford Taurus, Trace keeping his body between Chloe and the direction the shots had come from. She opened the driver's door and dove inside the car, lying flat across the seat. He followed right behind her, closing the car door, then landing on top of her.

"I can't breathe," she gurgled, her face pressed against the seat cushion.

Trace levered himself up on his elbows, giving her enough room to turn onto her back. He lifted his head far enough to peer out the front windshield, searching the dark shadows for some sign of the shooter.

"Get down!" she whispered urgently, grabbing his shoulders and pulling him toward her.

He sank onto her soft, voluptuous body and his breathing hitched. They fit perfectly together. And at this moment, he couldn't think of anywhere he'd rather be. Chloe D'Onofrio was brave and smart and sexy as hell. The adrenaline fueling his blood turned into something different. Something hot and molten and out of control. His heart raced and his body reacted with a will of its own.

She stared up into his face. "Kiss me."

"What?" he breathed, hardly able to believe his ears.

"Kiss me." She cradled his face in her hands. "I hate feeling scared. I want to feel...something else. I want to feel alive. Kiss me, Trace. Like you never want to stop."

With a low rumble of satisfaction, he did just as she asked. He kissed her, long and hard with no intention of stopping. He devoured her with his mouth, living for this moment alone. She kissed him back, matching his intense ferocity and serenading him with low moans of feminine desire.

At last, common sense battled its way through his dizzied senses. He lifted his head and took a deep, shuddering breath. "This is stupid. We're wasting time. We've got to get out of here."

She closed her eyes. "You're right. Get off me."

Easier said than done. But Trace finally managed to maneuver himself into a sitting position. "I'll drive. Give me the keys."

"No, I'll drive," Chloe countered, wedging herself behind him, then lunging into the driver's seat. "I'm shorter than you, it will be easier for me to hunch down behind the steering wheel."

She turned the key in the ignition before he had time to argue. Then she shifted the car into Drive and pushed the pedal to the floor. Trace jerked back as the car shot out of the parking lot.

"Is he following us?" Chloe asked, her eyes on the road.

He peered out the back window. "I don't see anyone, but keep driving."

"Where to?"

"My place."

Chloe shook her head. "All the shooter has to do is break into your car and look at your registration to get your address. And I don't think my place is safe, either."

"Then how about the police station? We can't play hide-and-seek with Ramon anymore, Chloe. Somebody just tried to kill us."

Her hands tightened on the steering wheel, but to Trace's surprise, she didn't argue with him. He waited while she struggled to come to a decision.

"Maybe you're right," she said at last. "Maybe it's time to involve the police."

CHLOE PULLED into a deserted grocery-store parking lot and turned off the ignition. Then she reached inside her purse for her cell phone. Her fingers shook as she dialed the number. Her whole body still trembled from the ordeal at the Dairy Wizard. Or from the aftereffects of Trace's kiss. She couldn't be certain which had shaken her more. She'd never been kissed like that. Ever.

Even worse, his kiss had done strange things to her. It made her feel giddy, confused, out of control. Sensations she definitely wasn't used to.

"Who are you calling?" he asked, watching her from the passenger seat.

"The police." Her hand tightened on the cell phone with the first ring.

He rubbed one hand over his jaw. "I guess I

shouldn't be surprised you have the number memorized.''

She flicked him a glance. "I guess not."

After the fourth ring, someone finally picked up on the other end. "St. Louis Police Department. How may I direct your call?"

She licked her lips. "I'd like to report a missing person."

"Your name, please?"

"Chloe D'Onofrio. My brother, Ramon D'Onofrio, is the one who is missing." She heard Trace sputter beside her, but she ignored him. "I think he may be in danger."

"And is he a juvenile?"

"No, he's twenty-two years old."

"How long has he been missing, ma'am?"

"Almost forty-eight hours." She answered a few more routine questions, then ended the phone call.

"Well?" he asked.

She stuffed the cellular back in her purse. "They want me to come down and file a missing-person report."

"That's your idea of involving the police? Filing a missing-person report? What about the fact that someone just took potshots at us? You also forgot to mention those hot diamonds hidden under your staircase. And the lousy remodeling job some creep did on your house?"

Her eyes widened.

"What about the note?"

"What note?"

She dug into her pocket. "The one on the Dairy

Wizard door. I forgot all about it." Hardly surprising, considering the circumstances. First, she'd been distracted by the shooting, then Trace's kiss. She pulled out the crumpled paper and smoothed it out on the steering wheel.

He leaned over for a closer look. "What does it say?"

As she looked at the block letters, a chill ran down her spine. Then she read the words aloud, her voice sounding much calmer than she felt. "Saturday. Same time, same place. Bring the stash or you'll never see Ramon again."

"A ransom note?" He shook his head. "That doesn't make any sense. Ramon is the one who stole the diamonds in the first place."

"You were right before," she breathed. "Someone else is involved." Then she closed her eyes. "I should have known Ramon could never pull off something this big by himself."

"And now it looks like his accomplice is holding Ramon hostage."

She nodded, then opened her eyes. "To force me to turn over the diamonds. There's only one problem."

He arched a brow. "Only one?"

"All right," she conceded, leaning back against the head rest. "Several problems. Someone shot at us. My house isn't safe anymore. You're place isn't safe, either. Ramon is in danger. And…" Her voice trailed off as her throat grew tight.

"And," he prompted.

She swallowed hard. "And I don't have the diamonds anymore."

TRACE STARED at her, his gut tightening with dread. "Please tell me you turned them over to the police."

"Not exactly."

"You didn't fence them, did you?"

"Of course not," she snapped, straightening in the seat. "Even I know you can't hock a fortune in diamonds in less than twenty-four hours."

"Then what did you do with them?"

"I mailed them."

He blinked. "You what?"

"I mailed them back to the jewelry store. I thought maybe if all the diamonds were returned, the police might drop the investigation and Ramon would be cleared."

He dropped his head back against the seat with a groan of despair. Just when he thought matters couldn't get any worse, they always did. "I don't believe it. *You mailed them.* Didn't you consider the fact that they'll check both the diamonds and the bag for fingerprints? And they'll find Ramon's. And yours." He lifted his head. "And mine."

She turned to face him. "Trace, you're talking to a D'Onofrio. We learned to wipe our fingerprints off our baby bottles. The diamonds are clean and they're in a brand-new bag. I wore gloves and wiped down each diamond. Then I wrapped the bag in an old grocery sack, printed the address in block lettering and dropped it in a mailbox five miles from my house.''

He didn't say anything, obviously still looking for a flaw in her plan. At last he said, ''All right. It might work.''

She shook her head. ''No, it won't. We have to get those diamonds back.''

''We have to go to the police,'' he countered. ''I really mean it this time, Chloe. We're talking about kidnapping here. Not to mention assault with a deadly weapon.''

''We're talking about the D'Onofrios,'' she reminded him. ''The police aren't going to bend over backward to help a D'Onofrio. In fact, they'll probably try to implicate Ramon in the shooting. And how can we possibly explain the ransom note without mentioning the diamonds?'' She shook her head. ''We have to handle this one on our own.''

''We?''

She sucked in her breath. But why should she be surprised? What man in his right mind would volunteer to become entangled in this complicated, not to mention dangerous, mess? Trace had already stuck with her longer than she'd expected. *It had been so nice.* Especially after spending so many years trying to solve the D'Onofrio family problems on her own.

Time for a reality check.

''Not we,'' she amended, as she switched on the ignition. ''This is my problem, not yours. Is there some place safe I can drop you until this all blows over? Can you stay with your aunt?''

"Blows over?" He stared at her in disbelief. "Chloe, I think you're missing the seriousness of the situation. This isn't going to just blow over. Try blow *up*."

"All right, blow up. I know you don't want to be caught in the explosion. And you certainly don't want to be around to pick up the pieces."

"How do you know what I want?"

His voice sounded low and husky, causing prickles of awareness to spread over her body. "So, what do you want?"

"I don't know." He raked one hand through his hair. "I've been confused ever since the night we met. All I know right now is that I don't want either one of us to get shot at again. And I don't want you off trying to save Ramon by yourself."

"I doubt you want to commit a Federal offense by breaking into a mailbox, either."

"Damn straight. There's got to be another way." He peered out the window, as if suddenly aware the car was moving. "Where are we going?"

"Someplace safe. Then we can decide exactly what to do."

"A hotel?"

"Not exactly."

"Then where, exactly?"

"The D'Onofrio safe house." She glanced over at him in time to see his jaw drop. "The D'Onofrios have used it for years as a place to hide out when things get a little too hot."

"A safe house," he muttered under his breath. "Unbelievable."

"Well, it's not exactly a house."

"Then what is it, exactly?"

Chloe merged onto Interstate 70, the lights of the city now in her rearview mirror.

"Years ago, my great-uncle, Paul D'Onofrio, bought a farm near Grubville to raise Angora sheep. He was actually legit."

"Imagine that."

She ignored the sarcasm. "Anyway, Uncle Paul's place provided a safe haven for some of the more...nefarious D'Onofrios. A tornado wiped out the house in '64 and Uncle Paul gave up the Angoras and moved back to the city. But he never sold the land, so the D'Onofrios still use it as a hideout."

"Don't tell me we're going to stay in a barn."

"Of course not. The hideout is actually a cave." She flashed him a wry smile. "You'll feel right at home, Fred."

8

TRACE COULDN'T BELIEVE his eyes. Chloe hadn't exaggerated. The D'Onofrio hideout really was a cave. Or more precisely, an old vegetable cellar that had been used to store food before refrigeration had come along. From the outside it looked just like the storm cellar in *The Wizard of Oz,* where everyone but Dorothy had hidden during the tornado.

Chloe had led him to an old white wooden door set in a slab of cement almost hidden among a profusion of lilac bushes. She pulled it open, then they descended down a steep flight of concrete steps into the surprisingly spacious room below. Trace could even stand at his full height of six feet, two inches without having to crouch.

"This is amazing," he said, looking around the cozy interior. A sofa sat snugly against one wall, covered with a hand-crocheted blue afghan. The floor was hard-packed dirt, covered almost wall to wall with a bright paisley area rug. The plaster walls had a fresh coat of whitewash and rows of canned goods lined the shelves near the entrance.

"The D'Onofrios have fixed it up over the years to make it more habitable." She pointed toward a folding accordion door. "My cousin Lenny even put in a bathroom that operates on an antigravity system. He's a plumber.''

"So he's legit, too?"

"Most of the time." Chloe slipped out of her shoes, then curled up on one end of the sofa. She hid a huge yawn behind her hand.

"Tired?" Trace asked, joining her on the sofa.

"I think the adrenaline is finally wearing off."

He leaned forward, resting his elbows on his knees. "We still have some decisions to make."

"I know." Her voice sounded dull and flat. "I guess I was hoping we might find Ramon here. That the ransom note was some kind of hoax. That somehow everything would work itself out and I could go back to my regularly scheduled life." She looked up at him. "But that's not going to happen, is it?"

"No, Chloe," he said gently. "That's not going to happen."

She sighed. "I don't want to think about it any more tonight. My head is already spinning. Let's talk about something else." Her mouth quirked up in a half smile. "Let's talk about you?"

"Me?" he said in surprise.

"Time to spill your deep, dark secrets, Callahan. It's only fair, since you already know most of the D'Onofrio family's."

"I already told you about my unsavory past. What else do you want to know?"

She drew up her knees and wrapped her arms around them. "Tell me about your list."

"My list?"

"Ramon told me you have a list of requirements for the perfect wife. Is that true?"

"I wouldn't exactly call them requirements," he hedged. "Just attributes I happen to find attractive in a woman." He didn't mention the attributes he currently found attractive—none of which had made his list. Deep brown eyes. A killer body. A mouth that made him burn. And he was more than ready to leap back into the fire.

"Such as?"

Trace cleared his throat and forced himself to look away from her lips. "Such as…loyalty. Family loyalty is very important to me."

She nodded. "I can't argue with that one."

"And skirts."

She blinked. "Skirts?"

"I like a woman who wears skirts. Why would any woman want to hide her legs behind a baggy pair of pants? It's a shame the government ever passed that law."

Her brows drew together in confusion. "What law?"

"In 1923, it was made legal for a woman to wear pants at any time."

She sat up on the sofa. "You actually know the year the law was passed?"

He shrugged. "It was one of the questions on a history test in high school and it just always stuck in my head. The teacher was a devout feminist."

"She must have been a great influence on you," Chloe said dryly.

"All I remember is that she had great legs."

She rolled her eyes. "So family loyalty and skirts are high on your list. Anything else?"

"She should be a great cook and enjoy cleaning, of course."

"Of course. What woman doesn't get excited over a feather duster and a whiff of Lemon Pledge?"

He frowned. "Are you being sarcastic?"

"Sorry. I don't suppose a sense of humor is on your list anywhere?"

"Actually, it is. I want a wife who smiles a lot."

"With all that cooking and cleaning, what exactly will she have to smile about?"

"A nice house," he countered. "A family who loves her. A husband who will take care of her and handle any and all problems that come up."

She tilted her head to one side.

"What century is this again?"

"Very funny. I never said she couldn't have a career, or devote herself to volunteer work if she wants to stay home and raise the kids."

"That's very generous of you, Trace. But I'm afraid the only place you'll find a woman like that is on one of those old television sitcoms."

He shifted uncomfortably on the sofa. "You're crazy."

She stared at him, her mouth falling open. "Wait a minute. That's it, isn't it?"

Heat crawled up his neck. "I don't know what you're talking about."

She laughed. "Time to confess, Callahan. You based your requirements for the ideal wife on a woman in one of those shows. I can tell by the way you're blushing.''

''Men don't blush,'' he growled, his cheeks on fire.

''Who is she?'' Chloe bounced on the sofa, her eyes sparkling with amusement. ''Mary Tyler Moore? June Cleaver? I know…Shirley Partridge!''

''Shirley Partridge? Are you nuts? She drove a psychedelic bus. I'd never marry a woman like Shirley Partridge.''

''Then who?''

He grimaced. ''You're going to keep hounding me until I tell you, aren't you?''

''That's right. I'm not one of those quiet, meek women you like so much. I want a name, Callahan.''

He set his jaw. ''Carol Brady.''

She laughed. ''*Carol Brady?* I can't believe I didn't think of her. She's perfect! She wore dresses and skirts all the time, smiled constantly, and her favorite line was, 'You're father's right, kids'.''

''Laugh all you want. But a man could do a lot worse than Carol Brady.''

''How old were you when you decided you wanted to marry her? Ten? Twelve? Twenty-five?''

He scowled at her. ''I was eleven years old at the time, and, for your information, I wanted my *dad* to marry her. Or someone just like her.''

''Because you were 'four men living all alone,''' Chloe sang, remembering one of the lines from the show's theme song.

"Something like that," he muttered, obviously embarrassed at revealing his stupid boyhood dream.

Her heart melted. For the first time since she'd met Trace Callahan, she realized she was in danger of falling in love with him. He might be opinionated and obstinate—not to mention clueless about women—but he was also the man who had stuck with her through an assault with a deadly weapon. No—make that *two* deadly weapons. He hadn't turned her brother over to the police, or abandoned her, or even questioned why she'd go to such lengths for her crazy family.

"Now it's your turn," he said, turning to Chloe.

"My turn?"

"That's right. You know about my secret crush on Carol Brady. That's blackmail material. If I don't have equal ammunition, I'll be completely at your mercy."

She swallowed at the image his words provoked. The cave suddenly seemed much smaller than before. And warmer. The night stretched before them, long and dark and intimate. She sucked in a breath, suddenly aware it was just the two of them here. Alone.

"Quit stalling," he prodded, his grin telling her he had no idea what she was thinking.

Good. For once she was glad he was clueless. Because she needed to think long and hard about these new feelings welling up inside of her. "You already know about the D'Onofrio secret hideout. You're the first outsider to be admitted, by the way. You should be honored."

He slowly shook his head. "I'm not talking about a D'Onofrio family secret. I want a secret about you. Something you've never told anyone."

Her entire life had been full of secrets. When your father was a jewel thief and your mother was an aspiring con artist, you learned to keep your mouth shut. But Trace already knew about the notorious D'Onofrio family. He wanted something more. Something just about her.

"There is one thing I've never told anyone," she said softly.

"Until now," he added with a mischievous grin.

"Until now," she agreed, finding his smile contagious. Then she took a deep breath, preparing herself to reveal something that she had buried deep in her heart seven years ago. "When I was twenty I fell madly in love."

A muscle ticked in his jaw. "I see."

"And one month later we eloped."

Trace blinked. "Oh."

She laughed aloud at his expression. "Don't look so surprised. I may not be Carol Brady, but some men don't seem to mind."

"You're a hell of a lot better than Carol Brady," he bit out.

His brisk tone surprised her. "Do you want to hear the rest of my secret or not?"

"Sure. Just spare me the honeymoon details."

"There wasn't a honeymoon. Because there wasn't a wedding. I'd neglected to tell my true love the true facts about the D'Onofrio family. But I didn't want any secrets in our marriage, so I spilled everything on the day of the wedding.''

"How did he handle it?"

"Fine. Until we got in front of the minister. Then he got a case of cold feet—or maybe a vision of his feet in cement. I tried to explain to him that just because we have Italian ancestry doesn't mean we're a part of the Mafia. But he was running down the aisle ʾy that time, so I don't think he heard me.''

"What a jerk!"

She shook her head. "No, it was my fault for not telling him sooner. He may not have wanted to live like *The Brady Bunch,* but *The Godfather* wasn't exactly his style, either.''

"Well, I still say it's his loss."

She looked up at him, surprised by his vehemence. "Thank you, Trace. I think that's the nicest thing you've said to me.''

He scowled at her. "I say nice things to you all the time.''

Her mouth dropped open. "Like what?"

"Like...you look great in skirts."

"You're hopeless." But she was far from disgusted with him. Just the opposite, in fact. She was falling hard and fast for the man.

And that was one secret Chloe definitely intended to keep to herself.

TRACE HELD HIS BREATH as Chloe's eyelids drooped and a soft sigh escaped her lips. She was asleep. *Finally.* In the last few hours, it had taken all his willpower not to take her in his arms. Not to look at her as if she were a sinful dessert and he was a starving man. Now he could watch her to his heart's content as she lay curled up on the sofa. He'd been testing himself—proving to himself that he could resist Chloe D'Onofrio.

He'd passed, but it didn't give him any satisfaction.

Moving with quiet deliberation, he picked up the afghan off the back of the sofa and gently laid it on top of her. For the first time in his life, he actually envied a blanket. He wanted to be the one on top of her. Keeping her warm—among other things.

With a silent sigh of frustration, he dragged his fingers through his hair. He'd never wanted a woman this badly. Especially a woman so completely wrong for him. He turned away from her and began to pace back and forth across the narrow room.

What was it about her that drew him?

He knew it was more than desire. He'd experienced physical attraction before, although never quite this intense. All it took was one look from her, just a touch, to set his senses whirling. Still, any man could see she was a stunning woman. Trace now realized that there was more to Chloe than great curves and a dynamite pair of legs. She had a quick wit. A stalwart spirit. A vulnerable heart.

His pacing slowed as he pondered the fact that none of those qualities were on his list. How could he possibly value skirts above a sense of humor? Incessant smiling above a keen intelligence? Vacuuming above love?

He froze. *Love?* Of course not. Impossible. Ridiculous. Still, his heart pounded in his chest as he began pacing once again. He could never love someone like Chloe. She might be wonderful, but she was completely wrong for him. She was a D'Onofrio. And he was old enough to know you didn't just marry the woman, you married the family. The thought of Ramon as his brother-in-law was almost unbearable.

Almost. Trace sank down in a beige recliner, the velour fabric worn almost threadbare on the seat and arms. He buried his face in his hands and took a deep breath. It was late and he was exhausted. This was probably not the best time to contemplate his future.

Especially with Chloe so near.

He lifted his head and looked his fill, knowing he might never see her this way again. He memorized the way her long, dark lashes fanned out on her creamy cheeks. The way her slender fingers curled around the throw pillow. He listened to her soft, somnolent breathing until the rhythm matched the beat of his heart.

Now, at this moment, he could let his imagination run wild. Pretend Chloe was his. For now. For always. Dream about watching her fall asleep every night, then awaken in his arms every morning. Tomorrow was soon enough for reality. Tomorrow Chloe would be lost to him forever.

Tomorrow he planned to report her brother to the police.

TRACE WOKE UP slowly, his muscles stiff and his right arm numb. He blinked twice, trying to orient himself to his surroundings. Then he remembered. He was in a cave with Chloe D'Onofrio. He sat up in the recliner as he inhaled the aroma of brewing coffee. A halogen light hanging from the ceiling illuminated the makeshift kitchen in the corner of the room, but Chloe was nowhere in sight.

He stood up, every muscle in his body protesting the fact that he'd used the recliner as a bed. Then he stretched his arms over his head and yawned.

The cellar door creaked open above him. "Chloe?"

"Morning, sleepyhead," she called as she climbed down the cellar steps, a grocery sack in each arm.

He hurried to take them from her. "Where have you been?"

"I couldn't stomach the thought of powdered eggs and canned sausages for breakfast, so I made a quick trip to Sully's Convenience Mart. It's only about a five-minute drive."

"I thought we were in hiding."

She shrugged. "I took a chance that Sully wasn't the one shooting at us yesterday. I like to live on the edge."

"Tell me about it," he muttered, setting the grocery sacks on the table.

"Are you always this cheerful in the morning?"

"I didn't sleep too well."

"You should have shared the sofa with me. There was plenty of room."

He might not have slept well in the rocking chair, but the thought of cuddling up next to Chloe wasn't exactly sleep-inducing, either.

He cleared his throat. "What's for breakfast?"

"Take your pick." She motioned to the assorted boxes and packages on the table. "I've got cherry Pop-Tarts, chocolate donuts and diet soda."

He grimaced. "You call that breakfast?"

"Every day," she quipped, popping the tab on her soda can.

He peeked into the grocery sack. But the only thing he found inside was the morning newspaper. "No orange juice or frozen waffles?"

"I'm sorry, dear," she teased, "it's Alice's day off."

"Very funny." He grabbed a donut out of the box, then sat down at the table with the newspaper in front of him. He'd just taken his first bite when he saw the headline. He choked, his airway constricted by donut and disbelief.

"Here," Chloe said, quickly pushing her soda toward him. "Drink this."

He washed down the donut, then took a deep breath as he slowly wiped his mouth with the back of his hand.

"Are you all right?" she asked, her eyes clouded with concern.

"No." He turned the newspaper toward her.

"I'm not all right. In fact, my life just took a decided turn for the worse."

Chloe picked up the paper, staring at the front page headline: Suspect Sought In Jewel Heist. The paper dropped onto the table as the concern in her eyes turned to panic. "*Ramon*. They're after Ramon!"

"Wrong." Trace pushed the paper towards her. "They're after *me*."

She blinked at him. "You?"

He nodded toward the front page. "Read the first paragraph."

She picked up the paper again, her forehead furrowed.

Local contractor Trace J. Callahan is being sought for questioning in the recent burglary of Choice Jewelers. Mr. Callahan was last seen on Tuesday, June 29. That evening his abandoned vehicle was found hidden near the parking lot of the Dairy Wizard on Farmingham Road. Police sources report a small ruby was discovered in the glove compartment of Callahan's vehicle. The ruby has since been identified as one of the stones stolen from the jewelry store.

She slowly lowered the paper. "A ruby? There weren't any rubies reported missing in the last newspaper article."

His jaw clenched. "Sometimes the police like to

hold back information to throw off the perpetrator and to help them weed out false confessions.''

"How do you know?"

"I have experience with the police, remember?"

She sank down into the chair across from him. "The real thief must have planted the ruby in your car the night he shot at us."

"The real thief?"

She looked up at him, then slowly shook her head. "No. It's not Ramon."

"How can you be so sure?"

She sighed. "I hate to admit it, but my brother simply isn't that smart."

"He's not exactly innocent, either. Ramon is the one who arranged the meeting last night. He not only knows about the diamonds, he wants them back."

She rubbed her fingers over her temple. "I can believe my brother broke into the jewelry store. I don't want to believe it, but I can. My father used to tell us bedtime stories about his most exciting jobs and how they ended happily—and richly—ever after. Ramon soaked up every word.''

Bedtime stories? No wonder Ramon had problems. Growing up among the D'Onofrios must have been hard enough, but to glamorize a life of crime and make it sound like a fairy tale bordered on child abuse. And Chloe had suffered, too. She'd missed most of her childhood, forced to grow up too soon when her mother went off to jail. And she was still trying to pick up the pieces.

It hit him, then, what a truly amazing woman she

was. With all her family's problems, she'd still managed to put herself through school and start her own business. The temptation to join the D'Onofrios' more lucrative, if illegal, ventures must have been almost overwhelming. Yet, she'd resisted the lure of easy money and excitement. Even after losing her mother. Her father. Her fiancé.

No doubt about it.

Chloe D'Onofrio was a truly incredible woman. She was also deluding herself if she believed Ramon wasn't up to his kneecaps in this quagmire.

"Think about it, Trace," she said, obviously seeing his skepticism reflected on his face. "You know my brother. Do you really think he could pull off something this diabolical? Frame you for a crime you didn't commit? Hold himself hostage in a ruse to get the diamonds back? Shoot at his own sister?"

"He missed, remember?"

"Barely. Besides, Ramon is scared of guns. Which always put a damper on his gangster fantasies."

"So if Ramon isn't involved, who is?"

She shook her head. "I don't know. All I do know is that if Ramon is implicated in any of this, it could blow my mother's chance for parole."

"Why should it even be a factor?"

"Because the D'Onofrio name will be in the newspapers. Again. And no doubt the reporters will dredge up all their past mishaps as well. What civic-minded parole board would put another D'Onofrio back on the street?"

He couldn't argue with her, because she was

probably right. Today, politicians got elected for their tough-on-crime stance. Especially for habitual offenders like Chloe's mother. Mrs. D'Onofrio's chances for making parole would be slim to none once it was known that her son had followed in her footsteps.

"You can't keep making excuses for Ramon," he said with quiet deliberation. "You can't keep trying to save him, or he'll never learn how to stand up on his own."

"He'll be standing in a chain gang if I don't do something!"

"You're the one who's in prison," Trace snapped, irritated with her unbending loyalty and his own feelings of helplessness. "Trapped by your brother and your mother and all those other D'Onofrios who keep you from pursuing your own dreams. You can't be their conscience forever, Chloe. You have to start taking care of yourself."

She swallowed hard. "Maybe. But if I let Ramon go to prison, I'll be...."

He reached for her hand, his irritation fading when he saw the slight tremor of her lower lip. "You'll be what?"

"I'll be...alone."

He held on tight to her hand. "You're not alone."

She gave him a watery smile. "Thanks, Fred. I take back all those things I said about you."

"What things?"

"That you're hardheaded, opinionated, bossy. They're still true," she added, "but I'm sorry I said them out loud. I should have at least included your good traits, too." She traced her thumb lightly over his knuckles. "You're handsome, honest, reliable, smart. You're also incredibly calm considering the circumstances."

Her touch made his breath catch. "Maybe I'm still in shock. Or maybe..." His voice trailed off as he stared into her eyes. They were so deliciously brown, like melted chocolate. Everything about her was delicious. His gaze fell to her lips and he suddenly knew exactly what he wanted for breakfast.

"Maybe what?" she asked, her lips parting in surprise as he suddenly stood and pulled her toward him.

"Maybe I can't think about anything except kissing you again." He bent his head and captured her mouth, savoring its sweetness. He moaned with the pleasure of a man who has finally satisfied his craving. After the long night of self-denial, he let himself fully indulge in Chloe D'Onofrio.

She tasted warm and wonderful. He wrapped his arms around her, marveling again at how perfectly she fit against him. Her hands swept through his hair, her nails lightly raking the nape of his neck. The sensation brought his entire body to full alert. He deepened the kiss, one hand trailing over the smooth curve of her hip, then gliding upward to cup her full breast.

She moaned low in her throat and that sound alone almost sent him over the edge. Her fingers tugged at the front of his shirt and somewhere in the far reaches of his mind he realized she was undoing the buttons. Now it was his turn to moan when her hand slipped inside his shirt and brushed over the hair on his chest.

He couldn't stand it anymore. More to the point, he couldn't stand up anymore. He wanted Chloe on the sofa. Under him, on top of him, it didn't make any difference. As long as she was touching him. As long as they were together.

He edged them closer to the sofa, their lips still clinging together, their hands still discovering the most exquisite places. Only one more step and all those hot, erotic dreams he'd had since meeting Chloe would finally come true.

Then he heard the cave door slam open above them, followed by the voice that gave him nightmares.

"Get your hands off my sister!"

9

CHLOE WHIRLED AROUND, slightly dizzy from the intensity of Trace's kiss. "Ramon!"

"I said get your hands off her," Ramon snapped as he limped toward them.

Chloe stepped out of Trace's arms, hastily pulling her clothing back into place. "What happened? Are you hurt?" She reached out and grabbed her brother's bony shoulders, her gaze sweeping over his rail-thin body. No blood. No broken bones. No sign of any permanent damage.

"Ouch," Ramon said, shrugging out of her grasp. "You scratched me. I hate those long fingernails."

"Sit down and tell us what happened," she insisted, practically dragging Ramon to the sofa. Her heart still beat a rapid tattoo in her chest and her mouth tingled from Trace's kiss.

Her brother always did have lousy timing.

Ramon winced and moaned all the way to the sofa, then slumped onto the cushion with an air of exhaustion. "I can't believe I made it here alive."

Trace took his time buttoning up his shirt. "You may not stay that way if you don't give us some answers."

"Me?" Ramon stuck out his chin. "I'm the one who should demand answers, Callahan. Such as— what exactly were you doing to my sister?"

Trace leveled his gaze on Chloe and the desire in his blue eyes made her stomach flip-flop. "I think that's obvious."

"I think it's disgusting." Ramon turned to Chloe. "I thought I told you to stay away from him. You never listen to me!"

"I'm listening now," she said, planting her hands on her hips. "So start talking. Who stole the diamonds? Who knocked Trace out? Who turned the house upside down? And what I'd really like to know is who decided to use Trace and me for target practice?"

Ramon rubbed his temple with his fingers. "I have a horrendous headache. And you're yelling at me."

She took a deep breath and tried to calm down. It was all happening so fast. From the moment she'd met Trace Callahan, her life and her emotions had started spinning out of control. If Ramon hadn't appeared at exactly the wrong moment, she would have followed Trace anywhere. Specifically, onto the sofa. She looked at it with longing, her body still thrumming with unfulfilled desire. Then she mentally shook herself. Her love life, or lack of one, should be the last thing on her mind right now. Her brother was here. He was safe. He needed her.

"I'm sorry I yelled at you," she said more calmly. "Would you like a soda or something to eat?"

Ramon looked up at her, his puppy-brown eyes suddenly eager. "Do you have any Fig Newtons? I've been dying for a Fig Newton."

"No, but I can run down to the store...."

"Stop coddling him," Trace interjected, a muscle knotting his jaw. "He'll survive without Fig Newtons." Then he turned to her brother. "Ramon, for once in your life, will you act like a man?"

"Trace," she scolded, "he's hurt."

Ramon scowled. "He's *never* liked me."

"Well, I happen to like your sister," Trace countered, folding his arms across his chest. "And she's been worried sick about you. So stop thinking about yourself for a change and think about her."

"All I can think about is you and her...." A fiery blush suffused Ramon's cheek. "When I saw the two of you just now..."

Chloe's own cheeks warmed at Ramon's unspoken words. "Nothing happened."

"Like hell," Trace muttered beside her.

"Really?" Ramon brightened. "That's great." He turned to Trace. "Okay. You can go home now. I'll take care of my sister."

Trace didn't move. "If you don't mind, I think I'll stick around for a while."

Ramon tipped up his chin. "And if I do mind?"

"Then I'll be happy to discuss it with you outside," Trace said, nodding toward the cellar door.

Ramon slumped back against the sofa. "All right. I'll let you stay."

"Gee, thanks."

Ramon winced as he slowly lifted his leg and

propped it on top of the coffee table. "Do you have any ice?"

"No." She bent down to examine his ankle, pushing up the elastic band of his black sweat pants and ignoring his pained groan. "It doesn't look swollen."

"It really hurts."

"What happened?" Trace asked, crossing his arms over his chest.

"I twisted it trying to escape."

Her heart clenched. "From your kidnappers?"

Ramon's straggly dark brows drew together. "Kidnappers? Where did you get a crazy idea like that?"

"From the ransom note." Trace pulled the sheet of paper out of his shirt pocket. "Are you telling us no one has been holding you against your will?"

"Of course not. I've been staying at the Pine Cone Motel on Route 30 and I got locked in the bathroom. The only way I could escape was through the window. It must have been a four-foot drop to the ground."

Chloe straightened.

"What have you been doing at the Pine Cone?"

Ramon hesitated. "You're not going to like it."

"Tell us anyway," Trace said. "We're getting used to bad news."

"I'm back with Nanette."

Chloe's mouth dropped open. "*Nanette Twigg?* I thought she was in Florida."

"She was," Ramon confirmed. "But she just couldn't stay away from the man she loves."

Trace arched a brow. "And that would be who?"

Ramon scowled. "Me."

Chloe shook her head, not certain where to begin. "Nanette is all wrong for you, Ramon."

Ramon turned mulish. "Well, I happen to think Trace Callahan is all wrong for you."

"She's a convicted felon!"

"So is he."

"She was in prison for attempted murder."

"Nobody's perfect." He sniffed. "Besides, Nan's conviction was overturned on a technicality."

She threw her arms up in the air. "That doesn't mean she's not guilty! It just means somebody made a mistake along the way and she got lucky."

"Nan deserves a little luck. She's had a rough life and her last husband made her miserable."

"Is that why she put rat poison in his oatmeal?"

"He didn't eat it," Ramon said in defense of his girlfriend. "Claimed it was too lumpy. Nan said he was the pickiest eater she ever met."

"Lucky for him," Trace quipped. "It's time to start letting your brain do your thinking, Ramon, instead of your—"

"I think," Chloe said, cutting off Trace in mid-sentence, "that we'd better start from the beginning. When did you break into Choice Jewelers?"

"As much as I hate to admit it," Ramon said with a sigh, "I didn't. Nanette did."

"Nanette did it?" Relief washed over her as she realized Ramon hadn't followed in their father's footsteps. Not yet, anyway.

"If Nanette stole the diamonds," Trace asked, "how did they end up under your staircase?"

"She hid them there," Ramon explained. "Only I didn't know it at the time. She showed up at the front door about a week ago and told me she still loved me and wanted a chance to win me back. She must have hidden the diamonds while I was upstairs changing for our date."

"Oh, Ramon," Chloe said with a groan of frustration. "She was just using you. Can't you see that?"

"Let him tell it, Chloe," Trace said, coming up to stand beside her. His hand found the back of her neck, and he gently massaged the tight muscles there. She realized then how tense she'd gotten since Ramon had started his story. She was so afraid it wasn't going to have a happy ending.

"Nanette really does love me," Ramon insisted. "In fact, it's my fault she stole the diamonds in the first place. See—" he took a deep breath "—it was my idea. My plan. We used to write letters about it back and forth when she was in prison. I suppose I was showing off in a way, trying to impress her with all my knowledge about how to be a master jewel thief. I never really meant for us to go through with it. After all, she was serving fifteen to twenty years. I thought she'd forget all about it by the time she got out."

"Only she got out sooner, and she didn't forget," Trace said softly.

Ramon shook his head, misery etched on his face. "Nope. She actually did it."

"Is she the one who hit Trace?"

He nodded. "She came to the back door that night and asked if I was home alone. I told her you were upstairs and the jerk who fired me was in the living room. She peeked around the door and almost lost it when she saw him looking at the staircase. The next thing I knew, she'd picked up the Chihuahua and bashed Callahan in the head."

"I could kill her," Chloe muttered under her breath.

"I was upset, too," Ramon replied. "She broke the Chihuahua's ear."

"She didn't do my head a lot of good, either," Trace intoned. "But go on with your story."

"Well, I freaked when I saw you lying there on the floor. I mean, you looked very dead. Then we heard Chloe at the top of the stairs and I guess we both panicked and ran."

"But not before stealing my wallet," Trace added.

"It fell out while we were shoving you under the stairs. Nanette said it might come in handy. Especially if we had to go on the lam."

"Oh, Ramon." Chloe closed her eyes in despair.

"I know." Ramon said with a sheepish glance at his sister. "But you know I don't handle a crisis very well. And Nanette was practically hysterical. That's when she told me about the diamonds. We were at the Pine Cone by then, and well, one thing led to another..."

"I think we can skip this part," Chloe said dryly.

"Anyway, I fell asleep," Ramon continued.

"Later, I found out that Nanette went back to the house to get the diamonds. Only she couldn't find them."

"Did she have to tear the house to pieces looking for them? The place is a disaster area."

Ramon shrugged. "I guess she panicked again. I mean, she was pretty paranoid by that point. She was even worried about the letters she'd sent me from prison. I told her I'd saved every one."

"Could they implicate her in the robbery?" Trace asked.

"Well, yeah. I mean, she asked a lot of questions. And she mentioned in one of her letters that Choice Jewelers seemed like an easy mark because of its location."

"No wonder your room was the worst," Chloe murmured, as all the pieces started to come together. "She was looking for those letters as well as the diamonds."

"All I know is Nanette came back to the Pine Cone empty-handed. I couldn't calm her down until I promised to call Chloe and ask her to meet us and give back the diamonds."

"Then what happened?"

"We went to bed. The next morning, Nanette went out to buy us breakfast and I went to the bathroom."

"And..." she prompted.

Ramon's gaze dropped to the floor. "And I couldn't get out of the bathroom. The door had jammed somehow. Nanette never came back and I was stuck in there overnight. I finally escaped this morning and came here.''

''Why here?''

''I thought Nan might be here.''

She couldn't believe it. ''You told Nanette about the D'Onofrio safe house? That's a family secret. How could you tell her?''

Ramon scowled. ''Because I wanted her to have someplace safe to hide if the heat got turned up. Besides, what's Callahan doing here if it's such a big family secret?''

''That's different.''

''How?''

Because I love him. But she didn't say the words. Ramon thought he was in love, too. Maybe they were both wrong. She was too confused to think clearly at the moment. ''It just is. Anyway, she's not here.''

''Then where is she? I have to find her. I'm worried about her.''

Chloe reached for his hand. ''The police are the ones who have to find her. And you should be worried about yourself. I just hope they don't charge you as an accessory.''

He paled. ''The police.''

''That's right, Ramon,'' Trace said, his icy tone sending a chill through Chloe. ''We're turning you in.''

TRACE SQUARED his shoulders, preparing himself for a fight. But Ramon didn't argue with him. He looked almost resigned, even relieved.

Chloe, however, was another matter.

"We?" she echoed, turning on Trace. "Can't *we* at least discuss it first?"

"Okay, forget we," Trace said. "I mean me. Ramon, let's go."

"I don't think I can walk," Ramon said, wincing as he set his foot on the floor.

"That's all right. I can haul you out of here over my shoulder."

"I can walk." Ramon stood up and moved with amazing speed toward the concrete steps.

"Wait just a minute." Chloe grabbed Trace's arm as Ramon headed up the stairs. "We may be in a cave, but that doesn't mean you can go into your Fred Flintstone routine again. Ramon hasn't even answered all our questions yet."

"That's because he doesn't know the answers. Or he doesn't want to admit them."

Her mouth thinned. "Because of Nanette."

"She must be quite a number."

Chloe shivered. "I've never met her. She was my mother's cellmate for a few months last year. It was Mom's first and last attempt to play matchmaker."

"That's best left to the experts."

Chloe arched a brow. "Like Madame Sophia?"

"Maybe." His gaze locked with hers and that familiar hunger gnawed away at his insides. She looked rumpled and distraught and utterly gorgeous. He could definitely get used to looking at Chloe D'Onofrio across the breakfast table every morning. But he had no intention of looking at her through a bulletproof partition in a prison visitor's room. "But at the moment I'm a wanted man."

"In more ways than one," she murmured, following her brother up the concrete steps.

CHLOE SAT in the back seat of the Taurus, trying to talk some sense into her brother. An arduous, if not impossible task. To her surprise, Trace hadn't said a word from the driver's seat for the last twenty minutes. Unfortunately, neither had Ramon.

She'd been carrying on a one-way conversation with her brother for the entire trip, trying to convince him that Nanette was trouble, not his true love. She wasn't even sure he heard her. Ramon sat in mute silence, his eyes bright with the glow of martyrdom.

The car slowed to a stop, then Trace cut the engine. Chloe looked out the window, surprised to see her house looming before them. "What are we doing here? I thought we were headed for the police station."

"Your brother will have the best chance to make a deal if he cooperates fully with the authorities," Trace replied. "I thought if he brought Nanette's letters with him to the police station as documented evidence of her involvement, he might score some points."

"I don't want to score points," Ramon said, finally breaking his silence. "I want to take the rap for the woman I love."

She swallowed a groan. She should have known. One of Ramon's favorite stories as a child had been about their Great-Uncle Teddy. He'd lived on the right side of the law, sliding his toe over the line only a few times. Then he'd met Rose Thornton, con artist extraordinaire. She had more scams than scruples. But she finally got caught. Then Uncle Teddy stepped in to take the rap for her. It was the D'Onofrio family's greatest tragic romance. Also, its greatest irony. The D'Onofrio who had served the longest prison sentence was also the only one who hadn't been guilty.

Panic welled up inside of her. "Ramon, you can't…"

Ramon's excited exclamation cut off his sister in midsentence.

"She's here!" He popped the car door open, then bounded to the porch, where a husky blonde wound her arms around his neck and gave him a torrid kiss.

"This isn't good," Trace said from the front seat.

"We have to do something," she said, watching in bemused amazement as the kiss went on…and on…and on.

Trace opened the driver's door. "Okay, you take your brother, I'll take the blonde."

Chloe joined him out on the street. "Forget it, Fred. That woman has big breasts and she knows how to use them. You wouldn't stand a chance. I'll take the bimbo, you take my brother."

"That's absolutely ridiculous." He followed her up the sidewalk. "Breasts have no effect on me."

She shot him a skeptical glance over her shoulder. "Remember the first night we met? You almost went into a coma. Sometimes cleavage can have that effect on a man."

"Not just any cleavage. In case you didn't know it, Chloe, you happen to be pretty spectacular. Above the neck, as well as below."

By the time they reached the front porch, the young lovers had disappeared inside. Chloe turned to Trace. "Right now I feel more scared than spectacular. But hold that thought, will you?"

His gaze locked on her chest. "I'm sorry, did you say something?"

"Very funny." Then she took a deep breath. "What's the plan?"

"We take them both in." He stepped up to the door, leaning over to give her a swift, sweet kiss. "Then we continue what we started this morning."

He opened the door before she had a chance to disagree. Or agree. Or say anything. He was making unilateral decisions again, but at this point she rather liked his take charge attitude. He made it all sound so easy.

Then she saw what lay beyond the door and knew it wouldn't be easy at all.

TRACE STARED at the bottle blonde standing in front of him. But it wasn't her breasts that held his attention.

It was the .38 Special in her hand.

He shifted in front of Chloe to shield her from the barrel of the gun. "You must be Nanette."

"Don't move," she ordered. Cool deliberation

shone in her silvery-gray eyes. One look told Trace she was devoid of both passion and compassion. Nanette wasn't a woman, she was an icicle.

"We want the diamonds," Nanette said. "Don't we, Ramon?"

Ramon stood behind her, his Adam's apple bobbing in his throat and his face pasty-white. "You promised no guns, sweetheart. Remember?"

"Don't wimp out on me, Ramon. We've come too far to leave empty-handed now."

"Forget the diamonds," Ramon implored. "We've still got each other."

Nanette snorted. "You've always been able to crack me up." She waved the gun toward the open door. "Is that your sister?"

Ramon cleared his throat, then made the introductions. "Nan, this is my sister, Chloe. Chloe, this is Nanette Twigg."

Nanette dismissed Chloe with a disdainful glance, then slid her wintry gaze over Trace. It made his blood run cold. "Not bad. Your sister has good taste." A wry smile creased her thin lips. "Must run in the family."

"Thanks, sweetheart," Ramon murmured, his cheeks flushed with love. Then he looked up at his sister. "Isn't she something?"

Chloe couldn't believe her brother. "Your *girl-friend* is holding us at gunpoint!"

"I'm his fiancée," Nanette informed her. "The engagement is back on."

Ramon grinned. "We're getting married in Mexico. It's so beautiful there—a great place for a honeymoon. I've got some travel brochures up in my room if you want to see them."

"Ramon," Nanette said between clenched teeth, "shut your mouth. We can't tell them where we're going. We can't tell anybody."

"Now, Nanette," Trace said, his gaze trained on the gun, "is that any way to talk to your fiancé?"

"I'll talk to him any way I want."

Ramon's brow furrowed. "You mean my own sister can't come to the wedding?"

Nanette snorted. "Some sister. You just told me she's ready to turn you over to the cops."

Ramon glared at Trace. "It was his idea. I was going to take the rap for you, baby."

"No need," Nanette said with a smile. "Callahan's going to take the rap for both of us."

Chloe sucked in her breath. "What's that supposed to mean?"

"It means your brother's been worried about you, Chloe. He doesn't like you hanging around such a loser. So I've taken care of *his* little problem and *my* little problem all at the same time."

Chloe's fingers curled lightly around Trace's biceps. "I still don't understand."

Trace fixed his gaze on Nanette. *That's right, Chloe, keep her talking. Distract her.*

"Your boyfriend's going down for the jewel heist." Malicious amusement gleamed in Nanette's eyes. "The cops are already looking for him. It should just be a matter of time before they collar him and bring him in.''

"But they don't have any evidence against him.''

"Don't you read the newspapers? The cops found a ruby in his car. Pretty incriminating, if you ask me.''

Ramon tapped her on the shoulder. "Uh...Nan, I never really agreed to anything like that.''

"I did it for you, darling,'' Nanette replied, neither her attention nor her gun hand ever wavering. "You wanted Callahan out of your sister's life, didn't you?''

"Well, yeah, but...''

"With Callahan behind bars, you don't have to worry about your sister and I don't have to worry about the cops tailing us. We can start our marriage off right.''

Ramon looked from his sister to his fiancée and back again. "I've got to think about this for a minute.''

"There's nothing to think about,'' Nanette snapped. "It's already done. I even went back to the jewelry store and dropped Callahan's wallet in the parking lot for good measure. That will place him at the scene of the crime. And didn't you tell me he has a record?''

Ramon nodded, looking completely bewildered now. "Yeah. So?''

"So they'll nail him good. He'll be in prison forever.'' She smiled. "And we'll be in Mexico living happily ever after.''

"You're forgetting one thing," Trace said, wanting to rattle her.

Nanette arched a penciled brow. "What?"

"You don't have the diamonds."

Chloe's hand tightened on his arm as an angry flush mottled Nanette's cheeks. "So give them to me. Now."

"Gee, I'd love to, but I don't have them on me."

Nanette cocked the gun. "I'm counting to three, Callahan...."

"Forget it." Chloe stepped in front of Trace. "You can't have the diamonds and you can't have my brother. I'd rather see Ramon behind bars than trapped for the rest of his life with someone like you."

Trace yanked Chloe back behind him, his heart pounding hard in his chest. For the longest seconds of his life, the gun had been aimed straight at her chest. If he'd been uncertain about his feelings before, he definitely wasn't now. He was absolutely furious at her. And almost beside himself with fear and love.

"Stop moving!" Nanette screeched, jerking the gun at them.

"All right," Trace said in a low, soothing voice. "We won't move anymore. You're all right. You're fine."

"I'm not fine. I want my diamonds." She held the gun higher. "I may have missed at the Dairy Wizard, but I guarantee you I won't miss at this range."

Ramon turned on Nanette, his eyes wide. "You mean it's true? You shot at my sister?"

"I shot over her head. I just wanted to scare her."

"It worked," Chloe muttered.

"Scare her?" A muscle knotted Ramon's jaw. "*Scare her?* Why? She's never done anything to you."

Trace saw his chance. He might not be close enough to reach for the gun, but Ramon was in the perfect position to grab it. "A man doesn't let anyone threaten his family," Trace said, desperately hoping Ramon would listen to him.

"Shut up," Nanette snarled.

Trace ignored her. "Can you really love a woman who would try to hurt your sister?"

"Nanette is the girl of my dreams," Ramon muttered, closing his eyes. "But this is a nightmare."

"This is reality," Trace said softly. "Sometimes our dreams can overtake our common sense. Make us want something that doesn't exist. Nanette doesn't really love you. She's using you. Open your eyes, Ramon. See for yourself."

Three heartbeats later, Ramon finally opened his eyes. He looked at Nanette with the gun in her hand, her mouth pressed into a firm, determined line. Then he turned to see his sister, partially shielded behind Trace's body.

"I love you, Ramon," Chloe whispered. "No matter what happens."

The confusion disappeared from Ramon's eyes

and determination took its place. He turned back to Nanette, and for the first time, Trace saw the potential of the man in front of him.

Ramon took a deep breath, then held out his hand.

"Give me the gun."

"Are you crazy?" Nanette whipped her hair over her shoulder. "Don't listen to him. He's just trying to trick you. I'm the only one you can trust. The only one who really loves you."

"It's over, Nan," Ramon said gently, reaching for the gun.

She spun on him, her eyes wild with fury. "It's over for you!" Then she shot him.

Chloe screamed as Ramon grabbed his thigh, then crumpled onto the carpet. Blood soaked through his faded jeans.

Nanette whirled back around to face Trace and Chloe. "Now maybe you'll quit fooling around. I want those damn diamonds and I want them right now!"

She practically screamed the last words and Trace knew she was on the edge of losing control. Ramon lay behind her, still clutching his leg. Then he looked up and made eye contact with Trace.

At that moment, Trace knew exactly what Ramon was thinking. That probably should have scared him, but he didn't take time to consider the implications. Instead, he nodded imperceptibly at Ramon, then cleared his throat to get Nanette's full attention. "All right. We'll give you the diamonds."

Her thin shoulders relaxed a fraction. "Finally. Where are they?"

"Right in plain sight," he improvised, watching Ramon out of the corner of his eye. "We hid them in the chandelier."

In the same moment Nanette looked up at the ceiling, Ramon rolled toward her ankles, flipping her backward over his prostrate body. She hit the floor hard, a shot ringing out as the impact knocked the gun from her hand.

Trace dove for it while Chloe scrambled toward her brother. He reached the gun just as Nanette got back on her feet. "Hold it right there," he ordered, rising to his feet to face her, his back to the front door.

"Damn you!" Nanette screeched, her face livid. But she didn't move.

"Trace," Chloe gasped, her face ashen as she cradled her unconscious brother in her arms. "I think he's dead."

"He's not dead," he reassured her gently. "He just fainted. He did the same thing after he dropped that saw on my foot."

Nanette uttered a small cry, catching Trace's attention once more. Her eyes widened and her mouth began to tremble as she worked up some hiccuping sobs. Big, crystal tears spilled over her cheeks as she held up her hands. "Please don't shoot me! I don't have your diamonds. I swear I don't. Please don't hurt me anymore.''

Trace's brow furrowed at her bizarre words. Maybe the woman had finally gone over the edge. Then he felt the warm breeze at his back and glanced over his shoulder at the front door.

It was standing wide open.

And there was a policeman crouched in the doorway, his legs spread wide apart and his gun at the ready. ''Drop your weapon,'' he said. ''You're under arrest.''

10

"WHY WON'T YOU believe me?"

Chloe sat in the tiny interview room of the St. Louis Police Department. "Trace Callahan did not steal those diamonds!"

Sergeant Clemens, a middle-aged woman with unsettling cobalt-blue eyes, folded her hands on top of the table. "Miss D'Onofrio, even you have to admit your story is a bit far-fetched. Diamonds under the staircase? Assault by Chihuahua?" Sergeant Clemens looked down at her notepad. "And let's not forget the shoot-out at the Dairy Wizard."

"It's all true! Ask Trace if you don't believe me."

"I already have. Now I'd like to ask you a few more questions."

Chloe fought back an urge to scream. She'd been answering questions for the last two hours. At least the officer had assured her that Ramon was out of danger and recovering at Sisters of Mercy Hospital. Unfortunately, he'd been heavily sedated and couldn't give a statement to the police. Not that the cops seemed overly eager to believe any D'Onofrio. She just hoped Trace was having better luck.

After this fiasco, she'd be lucky if he ever wanted to see her again.

The sergeant flipped to a clean page in her notepad. "When you discovered the diamonds under the staircase, why didn't you contact the police?"

Chloe swallowed a sigh of impatience. She'd been over this story three times already. "I was afraid my brother might be...involved. I wanted to find him first and give him a chance to explain."

"And tampering with evidence didn't concern you or Mr. Callahan?"

"No...I mean, yes. Of course it did. Trace wanted to turn the diamonds over to the police immediately. But I convinced him to wait...."

"Was this before or after you kissed him?"

Chloe blinked. "What?"

The sergeant consulted her notes. "According to Mr. Callahan, you kissed him shortly after he discovered the diamonds under the staircase."

"That wasn't a kiss...really. I was giving him mouth-to-mouth resuscitation."

"I see," the sergeant replied, scribbling notes onto her pad.

"No, I don't think you do," Chloe countered. "Trace found the diamonds and got hit on the head. I thought he was dead and gave him mouth-to-mouth. Only I found out he wasn't dead. In fact, I found out he was a damn good kisser. But that doesn't have anything to do with everything that happened later."

Sergeant Clemens arched a shaggy brow. "Anything else he's *damn good* at?"

Chloe frowned. "Is this a criminal investigation or an audition for *The Love Connection?*"

"I'm just trying to establish the nature of your relationship."

She swallowed.

"How did Trace describe it?"

"I prefer to ask the questions, Miss D'Onofrio. That way I can determine if your story matches that of the suspect."

"We're...friends." She hesitated. "Well, not really friends, we haven't known each other that long. The night we found the diamonds was our first date." *And no doubt their last.* "Actually, it was more like a fake date."

The sergeant's stubby pencil paused in midair. "A *fake* date?"

"It's rather complicated," Chloe explained, wishing she'd kept her mouth shut.

"Why am I not surprised?" Sergeant Clemens sat forward in her chair. "But I'd still like to hear about it."

"It all started when I met Madame Sophia," Chloe began. Then she told her about the coffee grounds and how she'd coerced Trace into rehiring her brother. "So you see," she said with a sigh, "it's really all my fault. I'm the one who got Trace into this mess."

Sergeant Clemens stared thoughtfully at her.

"I just have one more question, Miss D'Onofrio."

"What is it?" she asked wearily.

"Are you in love with Trace Callahan?"

This time she didn't hesitate at all. "Yes."

"IT'S ALL MY FAULT," Trace said at the conclusion of his second interview with Sergeant Clemens. He leaned back in the metal folding chair in the interrogation room, watching as the sergeant jotted a few lines in her notepad.

At last she looked up at him. "Your fault? Is this a confession?"

He scowled. "No. I already told you Nanette is to blame for the robbery, and the shooting, and for locking Ramon in the bathroom. She's also the one who clobbered me with the Chihuahua."

Sergeant Clemens nodded. "Her story does have some inconsistencies."

"The woman is a consummate liar. Just look at how she conned Ramon into thinking she was the girl of his dreams." He shook his head. "The poor guy actually thought he was in love."

"Maybe it was for real."

Trace shook his head. "Nanette didn't respect him. She didn't care about his needs or wants. She just wanted to use him to fulfill her own fantasies. Love is about compromise. It's about sharing everything—dreams, hope, loss. But most of all, it's about wanting the very best for the one you love, and wanting to the be the very best for her."

She smiled. "You sound like an expert."

"I certainly wasn't a week ago." He took a deep breath. "But I'm working on it."

The door opened and a uniformed police officer stuck his head in. "Hey, Sarge, a call just came in from Choice Jewelers. It's the damnedest thing. They just got all those stolen diamonds back in the mail.''

Sergeant Clemens turned back to Trace. "And here Ms. Twigg swore you had them in your possession.''

"And Chloe and I told you she mailed them two days ago.''

"Looks like you may be off the hook, Mr. Callahan.'' She stood and headed toward the door. Then she hesitated, finally turning back around to face him. "I understand your aunt owns Café Romeo.''

"That's right,'' he said, confused by the sudden change of topic.

Sergeant Clemens cleared her throat. "I'm recently divorced and it's been hell trying to meet decent, single men my age. Do you really believe Madame Sophia can find my perfect match?''

"Yes,'' Trace said, with all the conviction of a true convert. "I do.''

TWO WEEKS LATER, Chloe sat nervously in her chair waiting for the parole hearing to begin. She'd taken the red-eye flight from Cincinnati the night before, leaving Ramon to the care of the counselors at the innovative Oracle Clinic, where he was in recovery from his gunshot wound and his emotional problems. In the week she'd spent in Cincinnati, she could already see a change in him, a maturity that she'd never glimpsed before. Maybe because she'd always treated him as if he were still a little boy.

The police had agreed not to press any charges against Ramon in exchange for him turning state's evidence against Nanette. Surprisingly, it had been Ramon's idea to seek counseling. For the first time, she actually had hope that her brother might be able to lead a happy, normal life.

More hope than she had for herself. She'd only seen Trace briefly after they were released from custody, and then in the company of Sergeant Clemens. He'd looked awful, with the heavy shadow of a beard stubbling his cheeks and dark circles under his eyes. And she'd barely been able to keep from throwing her arms around him.

She wished now she'd given in to her impulse, since it was the last time she'd seen him. She knew he was working overtime to complete the work on Café Romeo, but whenever she showed up at the coffeehouse with fabric swatches or a new idea for the decor, he'd conveniently disappear. It was obvious he was avoiding her.

They had talked a few times on the telephone, when she'd called him about the design plans for the new addition to the café. But their conversations had been stilted and filled with long, tense silences.

Chloe sighed. Absence had certainly made her heart grow fonder, but she'd bet that he'd been reveling in his D'Onofrio-free days.

And could she really blame him?

A flurry of movement at the door made her look up. The three members of the parole board entered the room and seated themselves at the head table. She twisted her fingers together as she studied them, the two men and one woman who held the fate of her mother in their hands.

Eileen D'Onofrio sat with her lawyer at the conference table, looking remarkably cool and poised for a woman teetering on the brink of freedom. Her hair was drawn neatly back in a matronly bun, making her look older than her forty-eight years.

"I believe we're ready to begin," said the head of parole board, who was seated at the center of the table. He was an older man with a receding hairline, and wore a black-and-white Three Stooges tie and a pair of bifocals perched on the end of his nose. The nameplate in front of him read Walter Sullivan. The other two members of the board were identified as Edna Evans and Ricardo Lopez.

She swallowed hard as the social worker stood up to give her report. For the most part, it was positive, although there was concern about Eileen D'Onofrio's ability to secure employment, given her age. The fact that her prior work experience had mostly consisted of illegal activities didn't help much, either.

"Well, that didn't go too well," Chloe murmured under her breath, when the social worker finally resumed her seat.

The head of the parole board shuffled through the papers in the file folder in front of him. "Is there anyone present who wishes to be heard on this matter?"

"I do." Chloe stood up and took a deep breath, mentally rehearsing the speech she'd perfected over the last year—including her promise to provide housing for her mother and help her look for a job. She only hoped they didn't ask for too many details, since she'd just put the house on the market to pay for Ramon's treatment. Hopefully, she could gloss over that little obstacle and simply plead with the parole board to give Eileen D'Onofrio one more chance.

Mr. Sullivan leaned forward.

"Please state your name and your relationship to Mrs. D'Onofrio."

"My name is Chloe D'Onofrio and I'm her daughter."

He sat back in his chair. "Proceed, Ms. D'Onofrio."

She gripped the oak railing in front of her to steady herself. "I'm here to reassure the board that I will do everything in my power to help my mother reestablish herself in society."

"Are you in a financial position to support Mrs. D'Onofrio?" Edna Evans asked.

"Well...almost. I've recently started my own business, so I'm optimistic about my financial future." Chloe suppressed a grimace, wishing she didn't sound like an advertisement for a savings and loan. "And I'm determined to help her find employment."

Edna arched a skeptical brow. "But will you have time to do so when you're also trying to get a business off the ground?"

"I'll make the time," Chloe promised. "I'll do whatever I have to do."

Ricardo Lopez looked her up and down. "Are you married or single, Ms. D'Onofrio?"

"Single," she replied, suddenly wary. Maybe she needed to rephrase her last remark. She'd do whatever she had to do, *within reason,* to help her mother. But she'd definitely draw the line at dating, or even worse, sleeping with Lopez.

"Won't living with your mother put a damper on your social life?" he asked.

She gave him her best look-but-don't-touch smile. "I don't have a social life, so that isn't a problem."

"Do I understand that you own a house?" Mr. Sullivan asked, looking at the report.

"Well…temporarily." But before she could explain further, the double doors to the hearing room burst open and Madame Sophia flew into the room, the tails of her purple caftan floating behind her.

Chloe blinked. *What was Madame Sophia doing here?* Then her heart skipped a beat when she saw Trace Callahan following in his aunt's wake. The dove-gray suit he wore emphasized his broad shoulders and his sapphire-blue tie matched the color of his eyes.

Damn, he was gorgeous.

Trace met her gaze and her breathing hitched. Her hand tightened on the oak rail while her mind raced to find an explanation for his sudden appearance. She refused to believe the worst—that he'd come to wreak his revenge by sabotaging her mother's parole hearing. Still, he'd never expressed his outrage at everything that had happened to him, including the fact that he'd actually become a suspect in a robbery and been taken into custody.

And what about his aunt? She couldn't be too happy about it, either. Although it was hard to tell by her expression. At the moment, she just looked very determined.

Chloe watched Madame Sophia parade right up to the head table, the bracelets on her arm jingling with each step.

"Am I too late?" Sophie asked, gasping for breath.

Walter Sullivan's brows rose at the sight of her. "I assume you wish to make a statement."

"I certainly do."

Chloe was aware that Trace had taken a seat across the aisle from her. From the way her neck burned, she knew he was still looking at her.

"I'm Madame Sophia, the proprietor of Café Romeo, where I brew up perfect coffee and perfect couples." Then she winked at the head of the parole board. "Nice to see you again, Mr. Sullivan. How is your new bride?"

Mr. Sullivan emitted a nervous cough. "She's fine, wonderful, in fact. It's nice to see you again, Madame Sophia. But I, uh, have to wonder just what you're doing here."

Sophie glanced around the room. "This is the parole hearing for Eileen D'Onofrio, isn't it?"

"Yes. Yes, it is," Mr. Sullivan replied. "Are you acquainted with Mrs. D'Onofrio?"

"Heavens, no. I've never met her before in my life. But her son has been an employee of mine for the last three years. I believe you met him during your first visit to Café Romeo. Didn't he spill a cup of café mocha on your lap?''

Mr. Sullivan shifted uncomfortably in his chair. "Yes, now that you mention it, I do remember him. I believe his name was Ramon."

Sophie beamed. "That's right. Ramon D'Onofrio. You've probably seen his name in the newspapers recently."

Chloe swallowed a groan. This was not helping. But how could she stop her? Especially when it appeared that Madame Sophia and the head of the parole board were on friendly terms.

"Yes." Mr. Sullivan pulled the lengthy article from his file. "I have it right here. Says Ramon D'Onofrio was involved in the break-in at Choice Jewelers."

"That's right," Madame Sophia chimed. "His sister, Chloe D'Onofrio, was tangled up in it, too, but the papers barely mentioned her at all."

Chloe closed her eyes, wishing she could sink right through the floor.

Mr. Sullivan set down the paper. "The D'Onofrios certainly are an…active family."

"Didn't we just hold a hearing for a Kit D'Onofrio last week?" asked a fellow board member.

Mr. Sullivan nodded. "A niece of Mrs. D'Onofrio. She's the one who called us fat, pathetic morons after we denied her parole."

"That's right," said Edna Evans, scowling at Eileen. "I certainly do remember her."

Chloe gave up all hope. Not only would her mother not get parole this time, she'd be lucky if they didn't make a recommendation to extend her sentence. Hot tears burned in her eyes, but she blinked them back. She'd become too used to disappointment over the years to fall apart now.

Mr. Sullivan steepled his fingers under his double chin. "Naturally, we cannot allow our feelings for Ms. Kit D'Onofrio to prejudice our decision regarding Mrs. Eileen D'Onofrio."

"Naturally," Madame Sophia echoed. "And I'm sure the fact that I'm offering Mrs. D'Onofrio a full-time job at Café Romeo will make your decision much easier."

"What kind of job?" Mr. Sullivan asked.

"Anything she wants," Madame Sophia replied. "I'm expanding my business, so I've got several openings at the moment. Waitress, hostess, bookkeeper, you name it. I also have excellent insurance benefits for my staff, thanks to my nephew Noah Callahan. And another nephew, Jake Callahan, recently started a retirement plan for my full-time employees."

Chloe held her breath, almost unable to believe what she was hearing. Then she looked at Trace and saw the love shining in those incredible blue eyes. She swallowed hard.

Could it really be possible?

Nothing had ever turned out the way she'd wanted. Could one of her dreams finally be coming true?

"Well," Mr. Sullivan said, "it seems the matter

of Mrs. D'Onofrio's employment is settled. Now, back to the matter of housing." His gaze fastened on Chloe. "Would you care to elaborate on what you meant by *temporarily?*"

Her throat was so tight it ached. "I put my house on the market yesterday."

"And I took it off the market today," Trace said, rising to his feet.

She turned to look at him, feeling slightly dizzy. "What do you mean?"

He walked over to her. "I mean I made an offer on your house two hours ago. A very generous offer, according to the real-estate agent."

Now she was not only dizzy, but thoroughly confused. "You want...my house?"

"Among other things," he murmured softly. Then he turned toward the parole board. "Since I no longer need my condominium, I'll be subleasing it to Eileen D'Onofrio at the rate of one dollar a month. At least until she can afford to pay the full lease."

"That's incredibly generous," Lopez remarked. "But who exactly are you and how are you acquainted with Mrs. D'Onofrio?"

"I'm Trace Callahan," he replied, "and I'm her future son-in-law."

Chloe's mouth dropped open. "What did you say?"

He smiled. "Oops, I'm doing it again, aren't I?" He turned to the parole board. "I have this habit of telling Chloe what to do instead of asking her. I'm going to have to work on it."

"No time like the present," Madame Sophia said, beaming at both of them.

"Right as always, Aunt Sophie." Trace got down on one knee.

Chloe looked at him in amazement, then over at her mother. Eileen gazed at them with happy tears shining in her eyes.

He took her hand. "Chloe D'Onofrio, will you do the me the honor of making me the happiest man on earth by becoming my wife?"

She was so stunned she couldn't speak. Her mouth was working but no words would come out.

He obviously took her silence as uncertainty, because his expression grew more serious. "I know I can tend to be a little chauvinistic."

His attempt at humility made her laugh. "A little?" she teased, finally finding her voice.

"And some of my ideas about women and marriage are a little antiquated."

She grinned. "You'd fit right in at the Neanderthal Club."

His fingers gently squeezed hers. "And it's true we haven't known each other very long. But it's also true that I love you. I just hope you'll give me a chance to sweep you off your feet. Or at least let me sweep *for* you—I've been working on it. I can do the dishes, too. I only broke three glasses last time. And I finally figured out how to use the vacuum cleaner. Although it didn't work too well picking up the leaves on my deck."

"Oh, Trace," she said, laughter and love bubbling up inside her.

"That's why I've been avoiding you for the last two weeks, even though it's been sheer torture. I needed to prove to myself that I could change. That I could be worthy of a woman like you."

"What if I don't want you to change?" she asked softly.

"Then you can take me for better or for worse, although I promise to keep working on the worse parts." His grin turned playful. "And there are some better parts you haven't even seen yet."

Chloe smiled as she gave him a slow, lingering once-over. "What exactly are you offering, Mr. Callahan?"

He stood up and took a step closer to her. "Myself."

"That's an intriguing proposition. I think I'll take you up on it—say for the next fifty years?"

"Sixty," he countered, drawing her into his arms.

"You've got a deal," she whispered, then let him seal it with a kiss.

He did it thoroughly, leaving no doubt in her mind about the depth of his love. She responded with equal fervor, savoring the taste of his mouth as well as the growl of desire deep in his throat.

The sound of applause finally broke through to them, and Trace lifted his head, a silly grin on his face. "Thanks, Aunt Sophie."

Madame Sophia dabbed at her eyes with her sleeve. "My pleasure, Trace." Then she turned to the parole board. "Free cappuccinos for everyone at Café Romeo! My treat."

Mr. Sullivan cleared his throat. "We do have the matter of Mrs. D'Onofrio's parole to settle first." He glanced at his fellow board members, who were both smiling. "But somehow I don't think it will take long to make our decision." He winked at Madame Sophia. "Save me a chocolate biscotto."

Chloe clung to Trace's hand, almost afraid to hope. She'd already been given so much today. Could she possibly have her mother back, too?

She soon found out the answer. Her first reaction was to throw herself into Trace's arms. Her second was to invite her mother to the wedding.

Epilogue

"Do you have any idea what time it is?" Jake asked, pacing nervously back and forth in the tiny anteroom off the main chapel.

Trace leaned against a bookshelf and folded his arms across his chest. "It's almost time to make Chloe my bride. Did I ever thank you and Nina for letting us make it a double wedding?"

"There won't be a double wedding if the best man doesn't show up soon. I'm just glad we were smart enough not to let him hold the rings for us."

Trace straightened up. "I thought Noah was downstairs."

Jake shook his head. "I just talked to the minister. He hasn't seen him yet. And I'm starting to worry."

"He's probably just got a case of cold feet. You know how Noah feels about weddings."

"Well my feet aren't cold," Jake countered. "Just the opposite. I'm ready to proceed straight to the honeymoon." He adjusted his cummerbund. "Speaking of honeymoons, where are you and Chloe going?"

"Chloe's family has a little place in the country. It's the perfect spot—very private." It was also underground, but that fact was a D'Onofrio family secret. And Trace Callahan would be a member of the D'Onofrio family in exactly— He glanced at his watch. "Jake, look at the time!"

"I've been looking at it for the last hour. My wedding is supposed to start in five minutes."

"So is mine." Trace walked over to the window. "So where is our best man?"

"That's what I want to know. Noah might be a little irresponsible, but it isn't like him to be late for something this important."

The door to the anteroom opened and they both turned to see Aunt Sophie framed in the doorway. She wore a gold caftan laced with sparkly silver thread and a pair of gold silk slippers. "Are you both ready to live happily ever after?"

"Not exactly," Trace replied. "We're missing our best man."

"I'm afraid Noah isn't going to make it to the ceremony," Sophie informed them. "He just ran into his perfect match in the parking lot, so he's a little...tied up right now."

"Uh oh," Jake muttered under his breath.

She smiled. "I hope you don't mind if I stand in as best man. Or should I say best aunt?"

"The very best," Trace replied, kissing his Aunt Sophie on the cheek. She received an identical kiss from Jake. "We'd love to have you stand up for us. Right, Jake?"

Jake nodded. "Right. And the sooner the better."

The strains of the Wedding March sifted through the open door. "That's our cue," Trace said, as he and Jake each offered Sophie their arm. She whooped with delight as they lifted her right off the floor in their haste to get to the door.

"This is the only way to travel," Aunt Sophie said, the melodic jingle of her bracelets mingling with her laughter.

Jake looked over their aunt's head at Trace. "Should we be worried about our little brother?"

"Definitely." Trace grinned. "But not until after the honeymoon."

* * * * *

*Find out how Noah Callahan meets
his perfect match in*

BEAUTY AND THE BACHELOR,

*Harlequin Duets #29
on sale June 2000.*

KAY DAVID

Too Hot
for Comfort

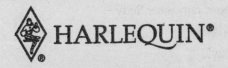

HARLEQUIN®

TORONTO • NEW YORK • LONDON
AMSTERDAM • PARIS • SYDNEY • HAMBURG
STOCKHOLM • ATHENS • TOKYO • MILAN • MADRID
PRAGUE • WARSAW • BUDAPEST • AUCKLAND

Dear Reader,

I travel frequently in my personal life and as a result often find myself stuck in airports. The idea for Too Hot for Comfort came to me in just such a situation. Last year, while sitting in a bar in the Miami International Airport, waiting for a midnight flight to Bolivia, I was idly watching a television talk show and wishing I were somewhere else. And then it struck me.

How do those talk-show hosts on TV and radio handle the weird and wacky calls they must get? Larry King never gets flustered...Jerry Springer can handle anything...Oprah always has an answer. How do they do it?

By the time my flight was called, I had my notebook in hand and this story half plotted. Somewhere over Central America, my characters came to life and began to fall in love. By the time we flew over Bogota, Sally and Jake knew their love was doomed. Hearts always triumph, however, and touching down in Santa Cruz, eight hours later, theirs was a love story—a funny love story—that would prove once and for all that love can be found in the most unexpected places.

I hope you enjoy reading Too Hot for Comfort as much as I enjoyed creating it. And next time you call into a talk show, remember Sally....

Best wishes,

Kay David

To my wonderful husband, Pieter. I love you.

1

"GO AHEAD, CALLER. You're on the air!"

"I...I—well, I've never done this kind of thing before. Called in to a radio show. I'm kinda nervous."

"That's all right. We're all friends here at KHRD. What's your question?"

"Well, um... I—I don't exactly know how to put it."

Sally Beaumont grinned at the woman standing beside her, Linda Javin, her best friend and coproducer. They were in the soundproof engineer's room next to the broadcast booth and they could see Mary Margaret Henley from where they stood as she spoke into the mike. Mary Margaret had come to the station dressed for her part—a radio star. She wore a fake Chanel suit she'd gotten in Dallas and full makeup, including her favorite shade of lavender eye shadow. She'd informed Sally and Linda right off the bat that it made her eyes look like Elizabeth Taylor's. Her hair was sprayed and teased until it could have stood up and walked out of the booth on its own had it not been anchored so firmly to Mary Margaret's head by an enormous set of headphones.

"You go ahead now, caller. We all want to hear your question."

Caller sounded like "collar" and *hear* had come out as "here a." Mary Margaret had more than a Texas accent. She had a *west* Texas accent and no word had only one syllable, no matter how it was spelled. Her intonation had given Sally pause but in the end, she'd decided it didn't really matter. Mary Margaret was known for miles. She was the best cook this side of Amarillo and Sally had been thrilled to snag the woman for her latest brainchild—a call-in talk show about cooking.

Too Hot for Comfort was bound to be a hit—the women of Comfort, Texas, had little to do during the blistering summer months besides cook, clean house, and corral their children who had been freed from school. They kept the radio blaring the whole blessed day so the audience was a built-in one for sure.

It was going to be the hit that got Sally out of town.

Mary Margaret glanced toward Linda and Sally and smiled royally as she spoke into the microphone. "We've all been 'round the kitchen more than once here, honey, you just go on ahead and ask your question. Don't be shy.''

Encouraged by the familiar and friendly voice, the caller spoke again, this time in a rush. ''Well, you see, my husband wants to do something I'm not real sure about.'' She dropped her voice. ''Something naughty. It kinda sounds like fun...but I've haven't let anyone spank me since I was five years old. He says he wants to be my sugar daddy and make me his honey bunny.'' She giggled. ''What do you think? Should we try it?''

Linda gasped loudly while Sally stared dumbly through the glass. Mary Margaret sat perfectly still, her face a frozen mask. The caller couldn't have possibly said what Sally thought she'd said, so why didn't Mary Margaret answer her? Why didn't she tell her how to whip egg whites into a frothy cloud? Why didn't she explain the difference between chop and mince?

The caller spoke again, and this time she sounded more assured than she had at first, almost chatty. ''Well, I told him I wouldn't wear the diaper—no way—but I might not mind the other if I got to return the favor, you know what I mean?''

Silence. Utter, total silence.

From a primitive level devoted to survival, Sally's brain issued a call to arms, and she jumped in front of the window to gesture wildly at Mary

Margaret. "Answer her, for God's sake," Sally screamed. "Say something. Say anything!" But the woman had gone deaf, dumb *and* blind. She ignored Sally's wild gyrations and sat paralyzed with some emotion Sally could only guess at.

"You better get in there and resuscitate her." Linda shot Sally a frantic look. "I think she's died and gone to cooking heaven."

Mary Margaret's tinted cheeks *were* white and her eyes had begun to roll back in her head. It took Sally only a moment to decide what to do. She couldn't embarrass the caller and tell her she'd mistaken a cooking show for a sex show. The explanation would only make things worse. She had to get the woman off the phone as soon as possible and that meant only one thing: answering her. Sally grabbed the microphone in the engineering booth and spoke, her voice more composed and self-assured than she expected, her heart pounding inside her chest. "Well, caller, if this is something you both want to try and no one's going to get hurt by it, why not? I say spank and let spank!"

The woman on the phone let loose an audible breath. "Really? You—you don't think this is too weird?"

Weird? Everything in Comfort was weird and Sally ought to know. She had lived there her whole life, except for four years—four glorious years—in Houston when she'd attended the university there.

"I think you're really cooking!" she choked out. "Thanks so much for calling and now we're going to hear from our sponsor—"

With her pulse thundering, she punched the kill button, cued up a commercial for Johnny's LP and Feed then jerked open the door to the booth. "Mary Margaret! Get a grip! You've got to think on your feet here."

The woman's shaded eyes took in Sally's face as if she were a visitor who'd suddenly dropped in from a different universe. "Did you heah that question? What kind of cookin' question is that?"

"She obviously made a mistake and thought the show was about something else. You have to be prepared for a few nut cases."

"Y-you told me you screened these calls!"

Sally felt her face flame. She and Linda had been so excited they'd forgotten they were supposed to be doing that very thing. "We do but—"

Linda's voice reached the booth with sudden urgency. "Back in ten, Sally!"

Ignoring Linda, Mary Margaret stared accusingly at Sally. "Well, then what kinda screening was that?"

"We—we goofed up, Mary Margaret. I'm sorry. Please—"

"Back in five!"

"Well, I'm not doing this. No siree!" Ripping off the headset, the woman rose from the padded chair, grabbed her handbag and clutched it to her chest. "I don't talk about S.E.X." She spelled out the word, couldn't even say it. "Especially to strangers—*especially* to strangers who want...who want to spank each other!" Full of indignant self-respect, she brushed past Sally in a haze of Jungle Gardenia and fled from the room.

Suddenly speechless, Sally looked toward Linda. She was holding up three fingers and folding them down, a second at a time. With her heart in her throat, Sally raced from the booth at the very last second and punched the tape back in. Johnny's LP was going to get a bonus today. As the commercial started over, Sally stared at her friend in dismay. "This is a disaster!"

"I know." Linda shook her head. "I'm sorry, Sally. I should have been doing my job instead of standing there watching, but good Lord Almighty! What on earth made that woman think the show was about sex?"

"No one knew what it was about!" Sally moaned. "Rita only gave us four thirty-second promos in the past four weeks. It could have been about car repair for all anyone knew."

Linda wore a hopeless expression. "Well, what are we going to do?"

"You're going to get your butt in there and start answering questions."

Both women turned abruptly as Rita March spoke. The station manager was a tall and imposing woman. Very imposing. And very tall. Few people argued when she pronounced something, and none of her employees dared voice anything but agreement. She stared down at Sally with frosty blue eyes and an even chillier demeanor. Sally had two seconds to wonder if she'd heard her complaint about the advertising, then Rita spoke again.

"You lined up five new sponsors for this show and I won't have them listening to dead air. What's *on* the air is bad enough. I can only imagine the phone calls I'm going to be getting. Get in there and fix this."

She knew better, but this was a desperate situation. Sally dared to argue. "Rita—this is a cooking show. I—I don't know how to cook."

"It *was* a cooking show. Now it's a sex show, thanks to that idiot whose bum is going to be red tonight. Turn on that mike and start talking about S.E.X. Tomorrow we'll kill it." The rest of the message went unspoken but it was just as clear. *And you, too…* She added a final zinger. "You *do* know something about sex, don't you?"

Behind them, Linda snickered. Sally sent her a baleful glare. "It's been a while, but I think I can manage it."

"Then you're on. Come to my office as soon as this disaster is over."

With a sinking heart, Sally watched her boss disappear down the hall while behind her Linda spoke again, her voice almost machinelike. "Back in five," she said.

Sally had only one thought.

What would her father say? Lamon Beaumont was the minister of the only Methodist church in town and he would not appreciate this turn of events. No way.

She leapt into the booth and grabbed the headphones just as Linda pointed her finger and mouthed the words "And now!"

"You're on, caller," Sally's mouth was so dry the words seemed to stick inside. She forced them out, remembering the first time in college she'd run a broadcast. *They don't know you're nervous,* her professor had said. *They can't see you. Just talk.* "What's on your mind?"

This time the caller was a man. Sally prayed for a question about garlic or chopped liver or how to boil an egg—anything but sex. God wasn't listening, though.

She hoped her father wasn't, either.

"Well, uh, there's this widow woman who lives down the road from me, and well, uh, we've kissed a time or two and I think she's ready to move on."

"And?"

"Well...do you know anything 'bout them condoms that glow in the dark?"

"SHERIFF, SHERIFF—you just gotta listen to this. You ain't gonna believe it. Turn your radio on."

The woman's voice was high and strident, and Jake Nolte turned immediately, even though she wasn't addressing him. He wasn't the sheriff, he wasn't an officer, he wasn't anything anymore but a retired cop. It was a strange feeling and he still wasn't used to it.

Jake's best friend, Bob MacAroy, who was the sheriff, looked at his dispatcher poised in the doorway. She was what Jake's daddy would have called a "full-figured woman." The two main reasons for that were bouncing up and down beneath the straining buttons of her uniform shirt as she jumped from one foot to the other. She seemed extremely upset, her bright eyes bugging outward, her face a shade of red Jake hadn't seen in a long time. The women he knew back in Houston didn't blush. About anything.

"What *is* it, Darlene? Can't you see I'm in a meeting and—"

"I know, Sheriff, I know." She shot an apologetic glance in Jake's direction, her chest heaving, her breath so short she could hardly speak. "I'm real sorry, but I think you ought to hear this! It...it's disgraceful! We might need to do something about it—go down to the station or something."

Bob lifted his hands in a gesture of defeat. Then he swung his chair around to flip on the radio resting on the credenza behind him. He hadn't asked the dispatcher which frequency to tune in and Jake knew why as he remembered where he was. A town the size of Comfort was lucky to have one station much less two. Bob didn't have to ask.

The voice blared out as clearly as if the speaker was in the next room. Bob picked up his coffee and took a sip.

"I'm just awondering about these condom things. I'm not shooting blanks and she's fifty— just a young 'un still. I wouldn't want anything happening here, but I'm not crazy about putting something between me and her. I like to really feel my women, ya know?"

The swallow of coffee Bob had just taken spurted out in an arch across his desk and landed wetly on a stack of neatly typed reports. Darlene wasn't going to like *that*, Jake thought idly. Bob started to laugh. "Shit-fire! That's Elmer Holley, down at the gas station! What the hell…?"

Darlene's mouth pursed into a tiny circle. "Sheriff! Watch your mouth. There's a lady present, don't ya know?"

"I know, Darlene, I know, and I am very sorry. Please forgive me. It's just that…" He glanced toward Jake then back at the radio. "I—I can't believe old Elmer—"

"Shh—" She tilted her head. "Listen to this."

The woman's voice that answered was rich and lush with an unconventional gravelly tone to it. Full of self-assuredness and definitely in control, the voice made Jake think of warm sheets and even warmer bodies. For a second he imagined what she must look like. Curvy, he was sure, with long, silky hair that hung down a slim, elegant back. Her eyes would be smoky, dark with promise.

"You've brought up a really important issue, caller. Condoms aren't just for birth control anymore, and everyone needs to practice safe sex. STDs are everywhere—"

"S T whats?"

"STDs—sexually transmitted diseases— There's some nasty bugs running around these days and even if you haven't been sexually active in awhile—

"In awhile! It's been a coon's age!"

"That doesn't matter. One of the fastest growing segments of the AIDS population is the elderly. You need to protect yourself. Always."

The man spoke again, this time more subdued. "Well, thanks. I—I never thought about that."

"You should," the woman answered. "We all need to, regardless of our age or sexual preferences. Thanks for calling." A slight pause came over the air, then the sexy voice resumed. "This is KHRD, broadcasting from downtown Comfort. You've been listening to *Too Hot For Comfort*." For the first time since she'd begun to speak, she stammered slightly. "This is S-Sally Beaumont saying goodbye for today." Music immediately filled the tiny office as Bob swung his chair around and shook his head.

"Boy, oh, boy. Sally Beaumont! I can't believe it."

"Well, aren't you gonna do something?" Darlene put her hands on her hips. They were well-padded. Her holster would never fall down on its own.

Bob looked at the dispatcher with patient exasperation. Jake had seen the same expression a thousand times when they'd both been cops back in Houston, on the street as partners. "Haven't you heard of the First Amendment, Darlene? The right to free speech?"

"But that's pornography!"

Bob's brown eyes went flat and dark and Jake knew what was coming. Darlene had stepped over the line.

"No. *That is not pornography.*" Bob spoke each word slowly and distinctly, as if to make sure she got his point. "Now, if you don't mind, I'd like to finish my conversation with the lieutenant, here. Please shut the door and don't disturb us any more."

With an audible huff, the woman closed the door. Jake looked at Bob and spoke for the very first time, saying only one word. "Pornography?"

Bob shrugged, a disgusted frown now marring his forehead. "It's a conservative town, Jake. What can I say? Darlene's not alone. This is going to raise some eyebrows, that's for sure. I never would have thought little Sally Beaumont would do something like that..."

Jake thought of the voice. The sexy, dark voice. His image didn't match with someone Bob would refer to as "little" Sally Beaumont. His curiosity got the better of him. "Why is that?"

"Well for one thing, her daddy's the local preacher. They live in town but Sally lives out by the lake—'bout five minutes from my place, as a matter of fact. I wouldn't think of Sally as an expert at sex. She was a good girl back in school."

Jake raised his eyebrows. "A good girl, huh? Guess that means you tried and she turned you down?"

Bob looked indignant. "She's younger than us, for God's sake. A lot younger. Twenty-something."

Jake kept his face neutral. Twenty-something might sound too young for Bob—he'd been married fifteen years to the same woman—but to Jake it sounded just right. Women that young weren't interested in commitments. They liked excitement, entertainment. If he'd been interested, which he wasn't, he might have considered looking into the body that went with the voice. He wasn't interested, though. Not one bit.

"Besides, this is the Bible Belt, Jake, remember? Folks around here don't talk about stuff like that."

Jake started to point out that some of them obviously did, but instead he just shook his head. "It's been a while since I've been here, guess I forgot." His fingers tightened on the scarred wooden arms of the chair where he sat as second thoughts assailed him. "You know, Bob, this might not be such a good place for me after all. I'm not the kind of guy who's gonna fit into a town like this—"

"Not fit in? Hell, you'd fit in anywhere so don't give me that garbage, Nolte. Besides, where else would you go? What else would you do? My cabin out at the lake's been empty for months and you've got to land somewhere. At least until you decide what else you want to do.''

Decide what else he wanted to do? There wasn't a decision to be made. As if his body were agreeing, a vague pain began to ache up and down Jake's right leg. His fingers went automatically to the small indented knot on his upper thigh. A few inches higher and to the left and he wouldn't have had to worry about Elmer's problem ever again. Or any other problem, for that matter. The drug dealer's shot had missed Jake's femoral artery, but barely. Tired of his job and his life, he'd left Houston. Now he wanted to do exactly…nothing.

He realized Bob was speaking again. ''—and Debbie has some friends she wants to introduce you to. They're nice women. You'll have a good time—''

Jake rose slowly. ''I didn't come here for a good time, Bob.''

''Well, I know that, buddy, but it wouldn't kill you to go out some night with us, now, would it? Make some friends, drink some beer, relax a little?''

Jake reached for the keys to Bob's cabin he'd laid on the desk when Jake had first come in. ''It wouldn't kill me,'' he agreed, ''but making friends isn't why I came to Comfort. I want peace and quiet. I want to fish and mind my own business. I

want to get the big city out of my system, Bob."
He stared down at his old friend. "Peace and quiet,
buddy. That's all I want."

SALLY CRAWLED from the broadcast booth down
the hall to Rita's office. At least it felt as if she
were crawling. Her shoulders couldn't have gotten
any lower or her ego, either. *Too Hot for Comfort*
was going to sink her. It *had* been a good idea, she
told herself. It really had. Obviously she should
have picked another name—Cooking in Comfort or
In the Kitchen in Comfort. Anything that would
have made it more clear it was a *cooking* show.
The setup had been great, though, regardless. The
concept *could* have worked. It *could* have gotten
her noticed.

All Sally had ever wanted to do was get out of
Comfort. From the moment she'd returned after college, that had been her single thought. Looking
back on the situation, she wondered where her brain
had been when she'd accepted the job at KHRD.
Sure, times had been tough and jobs in radio or
television had been almost nonexistent, but she
could have looked some more.

She passed the coffeepot and the two ad men,
Sonny LaBouef and Frank Francis, who never left
its side. They eyed her as she walked by and began
to snigger. When she was almost at the end of the

hall, Sonny called out. "Hey, Sal—I got me a date tonight with a girl who has some handcuffs. Should I take her a whip and chain or some flowers?"

Frank, the straight man, cracked up at Sonny's erudite humor.

Sally ignored them both, remembering instead the look on her parents' faces six years ago when she'd told them about the job offer—right there in Comfort. They'd been so proud, so happy. She'd felt the weight of their smiles, and every time she'd considered turning down the position to go farther afield, all she could think of was their resulting disappointment if she'd said no. She was their only child and ever since she'd been old enough to understand what that meant, she'd carried the responsibility of their happiness on her shoulders.

And now here she was, six years later. She hadn't moved on, she hadn't married, she hadn't done a thing. All of her old friends had families of their own—children, dogs, gardens. The ones who didn't sent her E-mail from exotic places like New York and Los Angeles where they had fabulous jobs and wore designer clothing. All she had was a piddling little job at a dying radio station and now she was going to lose that.

Squaring her shoulders the best she could, she opened the door to Rita's office and went inside.

2

RITA'S SECRETARY, Tiffany Jackson, looked up as Sally came into the office. The woman didn't say a word. She didn't have to. Her tight, prissy look said it all. *I'm happy as hell you're about to get fired.*

In the twelfth grade, Ross Martin had asked Sally to the prom instead of Tiffany, and she'd never forgiven Sally for this transgression. Sally told herself she should feel sorry for her if this was all Tiffany had to worry about, but charity came hard when she continually made life difficult for Sally.

"Rita's busy. You'll have to wait." Tiffany's voice was as satisfied as her expression.

Sally nodded and sat down on the couch near the door. After a few minutes, she felt the bottle-blonde's stare, but refused to look at her.

After another five minutes, Sally couldn't stand it any longer. She raised her eyes and met Tiffany's gaze. There was something besides her usual smugness in her glare, but Sally wasn't too sure what it was. For one long moment they stared at each other, then Tiffany spoke.

"How come you know so much about sex?"

Speechlessly, Sally looked at the secretary. "Wh—what?"

"You answered all those questions everyone had and you never even stumbled. I was listening." She narrowed her eyes. "You learn all that stuff while you lived in Houston or did you know it before then?"

...*like in the twelfth grade?* If she hadn't been about to lose her job, Sally would have laughed out loud. Here was the answer Tiffany had been searching for since high school; *this* was why Ross Martin had picked Sally instead of Tiffany. All those years ago, Sally had obviously known the *Kama Sutra* and where to buy sparkly condoms.

Before Sally could answer, the door to Rita's office came open. She stood in the opening, filling it up, and looked at Sally. "Let's get this over with," she said ominously.

Sally jumped up and followed her boss into her office, closing the door behind her.

"Sit down."

Sally did so gratefully. Her knees were rubbery and her stomach was fighting the jelly doughnut she'd eaten to celebrate the morning's show. Obviously consumed before the show had begun.

Instead of saying anything, Rita went to the wide
tinted window behind her desk. She stood there,
with her back to Sally, and stared out without saying a word.

Her beige suit blended in with the dusty land-
scape outside the glass. Summer had just begun, but
the heat had been with them for a good month. The
parking lot shimmered in the hot Texas sun and
little waves of glimmering light rippled across the
surface for as far as Sally could see. Beyond the
baking cars and steaming asphalt, the pin oaks already looked parched and worn. In the planter beside the window, the lantana had tried to stay perky,
but the pink blossoms wore an air of defeat.

Sally felt the same way.

Rita turned around slowly and looked at her. Her
question was the last one Sally expected. "You got
some pretty strange questions out there. How *did*
you know all those answers?"

"They weren't that weird," Sally answered without thinking. "At least not to me. I worked a teen
hot line when I lived in Houston, and before I could
start taking calls, I had to go through sixty hours
of training. Ninety-nine percent of the questions
were about sex. It's mostly common-sense stuff
anyway."

Rita nodded slowly. "But you didn't get rattled.

You handled yourself well at the mike. Why did you go the producer route?''

"I like the behind-the-scenes work." Sally paused, the words still stinging as she remembered them. "And one of my professors said my voice sounded like rocks being shook up in a bag. He said it'd never work on the air."

Rita raised her eyebrows then walked around the edge of her desk and sat down in one of the chairs beside Sally. "Well, he was wrong. Your voice is wonderful. It's unique and sexy. It's perfect, as a matter of fact."

Sally stared at her dumbly. Personally, she'd never thought there was anything wrong with her voice, but she'd had no desire to be the star, unlike most of her classmates. She'd wanted to get into the nitty-gritty. Plan what the station did. Run the place. But a "perfect" voice? Perfect for what?

"Perfect for what?" she asked.

"Perfect for a show about sex."

Sally thought of Mary Margaret. She knew now how the woman had felt. Stunned. Unable to move. "Wh—what do you mean?"

"I mean the phones have been going crazy since the show was aired—"

"I'll just bet they have—"

Rita shook her head. "It was neck and neck— positive and negative. And we only lost one spon-

sor. The others loved it, especially Johnny's LP."
She leaned closer to where Sally sat. "The nega-
tives don't matter, Sally. We got calls, don't you
see? People were listening. They'll be talking about
this for days. They'll be talking...and they'll be listening."

Sally shook her head. "I—I don't think I understand, Rita."

"You have a hit on your hands, girl. A major
hit."

"But...but this is a cooking show... And Mary
Margaret ran out of here—"

"Forget cooking and forget Mary Margaret. *Too
Hot for Comfort* is no longer about cooking. It's all
about sex and you're going to handle it personally."

Sally was shaking her head before Rita could finish. "I don't think..."

"There's nothing to think about, Sally. We've
been taking sponsors all morning. Ed's Drug Emporium—you can imagine why they want in—and
Lucy's Secrets, too. You know, that lingerie store
out on the highway? Carl Park's Auto Shop, too,
for some strange reason..."

"Rita, I—I can't host a show like that. I'm not
a disc jockey, I don't know how to talk to people."

"That's ridiculous, of course you do. You proved
it this morning." She stared at Sally. "You obvi-

ously feel comfortable with the topic and you know something about it. What's the problem?''

Sally hesitated, then she spoke quietly. ''My father would die... I can't embarrass him like that.''

Rita leaned back in her chair and put her hands together, the fingertips touching. She didn't say anything for a moment, then finally she spoke. ''You're twenty-eight, Sally. You want to leave Comfort. This show *could* be an opportunity for you to get noticed. Austin, San Antone—they like to think we're hicks out here and maybe we are— but the point is, it only takes one station to hear this, pick it up and play it. Whether they laugh at us or not, we don't give a shit. All we want is for them to buy it...then you're on your way.'' She paused. ''Are you willing to give up the best chance you've had in years to leave here because of your father?''

Her mind in a turmoil, Sally couldn't say no and she couldn't say yes. She couldn't say anything. Rita was telling the truth, but...

Rita leaned forward and reached for a file on the desk, clearly dismissing Sally for the time being. ''You think about it,'' she said quietly. ''The show's supposed to air again two days from now. I'll obviously need an answer before then.''

JAKE GLANCED at the hand-drawn map one more time, then angled his pickup down the dirt road on his right. It was a good thing Bob was the sheriff because he never would have made it as the local cartographer. Comfort wasn't too complicated, though, and once past the outskirts of town, things got even simpler. You went south, you hit Mexico. You went north, you ended up in Oklahoma. Comfort's one and only body of water—Lake Merriweather—was smack in between the two, about twenty miles out of town. Bob's cabin was on the eastern side of the lake and the sunsets were almost as good as the fishing. He'd invited Jake up a lot when they'd still been together on the force in Houston, but Jake had come only once. Sandra didn't like him going somewhere on his weekends off and after she'd left him, he hadn't had the energy or the desire to make the long drive up from Houston.

But now he was here.

He pulled up in front of the small frame house and killed the engine. Immediate and total quiet enveloped him, along with the scent of something he assumed was fresh air off the lake. It'd been so long since he'd smelled anything but smog, diesel and other big-city fumes, he wasn't too sure. As he walked down the gravel path toward the cabin, pine trees brushed at him and a squirrel, perched on a nearby rock, chattered at him.

Ten minutes later he had his stuff stowed in the cabin and his first chilled beer in his hand. Wandering to the back porch, he sat down in the rocker and looked out over the lake, taking a deep draft of the cold beer as he stared out over the pristine blue water.

"This is it," he said out loud. "This is retirement, Nolte. Whaddya do now?"

He waited, but the answer didn't come—only the sunset. He watched the red sphere dip into the lake, extinguishing the light and heat, then he rose and went back inside. Dinner was a ham sandwich and another beer, then he climbed into bed and turned out the light. Sleep came fast and hard, but when the phone rang, the sound brought him into instant awareness. Without even thinking, he reached across the unfamiliar bed, picked up the receiver and growled "Nolte."

"Jake, it's Bob. Got a problem, man."

For half a second, Jake thought he was in Houston, five years past. Bob's phone calls back then had always started just that way, but a moment later, Jake remembered where he was and suddenly the call didn't make any sense. "What's going on?"

"I got two deputies. One's wife is having a baby in Kerrville, and the other one's on a call over in Sisterdale, little town east of here."

Jake glanced at the bedside clock with bleary eyes. "You called me at two in the morning to tell me this?"

"No, I called you at two in the morning to tell you somebody just threw a big-ass rock into Sally Beaumont's living-room window. You're five minutes away. Could you drive over and calm her down? I'll be there as fast as I can."

Jake was already reaching for his pants, the urgency of Bob's voice making him move fast. "I'm on my way," he said. "Just give me some directions."

SHE'D BEEN HALF ASLEEP, half awake when the sound of breaking glass had brought Sally to full awareness. She'd wanted to duck under the bed and tell herself it was a bad dream, but with her heart in her throat, she climbed out, grabbed the baseball bat she kept nearby and tiptoed into the living room.

The huge picture window that faced the lake had been shattered, and the glass that remained in the frame pointed upward with gaping sharp teeth. Bits and pieces of it lay shining brightly on the floor, the moonlight hitting the shards and making them sparkle like diamonds someone had carelessly scattered. In the center of the broken glass was a rock.

And tied to the rock was a piece of paper.

She'd picked it up and untied the string with trembling fingers, knowing already she wasn't about to read a message of good cheer.

Decent people don't listen to smut!

The letters had been printed in a childish scrawl, an obvious attempt to disguise the handwriting. Sally had taken a deep breath and told herself it was nothing. She would have forgotten about it, cleaned up the mess and gone back to bed, but then she'd seen the other side of the missive.

Shut up or we'll quiet you for good.

And that's when she picked up the phone and called the sheriff.

The man standing before her nodded thoughtfully as Sally finished her narrative.

"You weren't hurt?"

Sally looked up at him and tried not to stare, but that was impossible so she just gave up and looked. Jake Nolte was not the most handsome man she'd ever seen, but there was definitely *something* about him. Something that pulled her gaze and refused to let go. The electric blue eyes? No, they were intriguing but that wasn't it. The coal-black hair still a little messy from his sleep? No, it wasn't that, although she wouldn't mind running her fingers through those dark strands....

He bent over to pick up something off the floor

and she couldn't help but notice how well his jeans fit. As attractive as he was in that department, his body wasn't what held her gaze, either. As he straightened and she looked at him again, she decided whatever was holding her interest had nothing to do with his physical attributes, but instead was something about his attitude. He'd been around and seen it all; his air was one of weary acceptance that said nothing surprised him.

But underneath he still cared.

She gave herself a mental shake. All this and she'd known the guy less than five minutes? She really was losing it.

"I—I was in bed," she said, finally answering his question. "In the other room."

"Bob said you sounded shook up."

"I was," she confessed. "It's not every day I get a rock through the window...but then again, it's not every day I talk about S.E.X. on the radio."

He looked at her strangely as she spelled out the word. "Sounds like that's what this is about, but are there any other possibilities?"

"Not that I can think of."

"Got any enemies?"

She shook her head.

"No angry ex-husband? No angry ex-boyfriend?"

"No angry ex-anything."

He had picked up the note from the rock with her eyebrow tweezers and had put it in a plastic bag from her kitchen. He held the bag up now, their eyes meeting over it, his so blue they almost seemed to glow. "This pretty much explains it, but it never hurts to check."

"S—sure," she answered. A little voice in the back of her head was telling her he'd wanted to know if she had a boyfriend, but then logic took over. He was being a cop, that's all. Doing his job, even though it wasn't really his job, as he'd explained when she'd opened her front door.

He walked over to the window and began to examine the broken glass. Then he lifted his gaze to the lake. "Could have come by water." He turned. "Did you hear a boat? See any lights?"

"No. I was pretty much asleep. The breaking glass woke me. By the time I got here, I'm sure they were long gone."

The lean lines of his body were outlined from the light shining in off the porch. He had to be over six feet, with not an ounce of anything but muscle on his frame. She could only imagine what it would be like to be a bad guy and see him looming in front of you. Not fun, she concluded.

Sitting on a nearby chair, she forced herself to concentrate on the real reason he was there. "It's the radio show, I know it is. This town is so small—

minded, nothing would surprise me in that department. Their brains don't go past the city-limit sign.''

"If you feel that way, why don't you move?"

She looked up at him, those blue eyes capturing her gaze and holding it. "I have family here."

Before he could ask her more, the doorbell rang. She started to get up, but he held out one hand and stopped her. "Let me," he said, his voice deep and authoritative. "You stay here."

She nodded, then as he walked toward the hallway, she noticed, for the first time, the small bulge in the waistband at the back of his pants. His shirt was not tucked in and she hadn't realized why until this moment. He had a gun.

He put his hand behind him, on the weapon, and looked out the window of her front door. Immediately relaxing, he grinned and turned the handle. "What kind of response time you got down here?" Jake asked. "You'd be fired back in Houston for taking this long."

"Yeah, yeah…"

Hearing Bob MacAroy's voice, Sally rose and came toward the entry just as the sheriff stepped inside and shut the door behind him.

"Hey there, Sally. Sorry for the delay." He glanced at Jake, then back at her. "Hope you don't mind I sent Jake over. I wanted to get someone here as fast as I could. He was close.''

Sally let her gaze go to the tall, silent man standing beside Bob. ''I didn't mind,'' she said slowly. ''I didn't mind at all.''

Bob walked into the living room, glass crunching beneath his feet. He studied the mess as Jake came up behind him and handed him the note. ''This was tied to the rock. Miss Beaumont handled it but you might be able to lift some other prints if you're lucky.''

The sheriff nodded. ''I'll send it off to Austin. It'll take a while, but you never know. Those DPS boys are pretty good.''

He turned around and began to ask Sally the same questions Jake had. Somehow it wasn't quite as interesting answering them the second time around...or maybe it wasn't quite as interesting because Bob was asking them now and not Jake. When Bob had told her he was sending Jake Nolte he'd explained they'd been partners in Houston and Jake was staying at his lake house for a while.

She wondered now what was going on. Why was he at Bob's cabin? Was it just a vacation? How long was ''a while?'' Everyone in town knew how particular Bob was about his fishing cabin. He guarded it as if it held gold instead of old lures and beat-up furniture. They must be close friends.

Bob's voice brought her attention back to the moment. "I called Junior down at the glass and mirror shop but Betty Lou answered and said he couldn't get here till in the morning. Said he was sleeping at his mother's house...she's down with a bad back again and he was staying with her." Bob sent a look toward the open window, then his gaze returned to her. "Would you like to come over to the house? You could sleep in Brittany's room. She's got bunk beds."

Sally smiled at the offer, then thought twice about Bob's daughter's room. The ten-year-old had made it a shrine to 'N Sync. It'd be easier to sleep at home with a broken window, than to have that band looking down at her as she tried to snooze. "Thanks, Bob, but I don't think I'll even go back to bed. I appreciate it, though."

"You sure? You aren't scared?"

"This is Comfort, remember? Somebody's just making their opinion known, that's all."

"Yeah, but this is a helluva way to do it."

Footsteps sounded and they both turned to see Jake Nolte reenter the room. "Maybe you could go stay with your family for a few days," he said. "Until things settle down."

"No." She spoke quickly, without even thinking. "I don't want to do that. I'll stay here. I'll be fine, I'm sure."

The blue eyes studied her, then he nodded slowly as if he understood everything she wasn't saying. That her parents would take her in, but the cost would be her privacy and independence—two things she valued above all. That she didn't want to embarrass her father any more than she already had. That it would just...complicate her life even more.

"Well, I'm down the road if you need me." Jake Nolte ducked his head in Bob's direction, then he walked out the front door without another word.

3

AFTER NAILING UP a piece of plywood over the open window, Bob MacAroy left. By the time Sally got dressed and had her first cup of coffee, the sun was rising over the lake. She stood on her porch, where Jake Nolte had been an hour earlier, and stared out over the water. It was as blue and remote as his eyes and once again, she wondered what kind of man he was. There was something awfully intriguing about him. Immediately she analyzed her reaction—she analyzed everything and planned everything—and she began to question herself. Was it him or just the fact that he wasn't from Comfort? She'd had a few near misses with guys in town—had almost let Max Swinford put a diamond on her hand—but at the last moment she always thought about what it would mean to marry a man from Comfort.

Staying there. Forever.

She swigged down the rest of her coffee, then turned and went inside, the thought bringing her full circle. Rita had told her the show could be her ticket out of here, but as Sally thought about the price, she still wasn't sure she was ready to pay it. She was surprised her parents hadn't called already, but yesterday had been her mother's bridge day and her father had probably been too busy. Summer in Comfort meant only one thing to him—Vacation Bible School. For two weeks, he'd have a church full of kids and nothing else would matter. She'd forgotten about that yesterday during the broadcast, otherwise she wouldn't have been so worried. He never listened to the radio when VBS was about to start. He didn't have the time.

Which might make this morning the perfect opportunity, she thought suddenly. She could go to the house and discuss the show with her mother. Maybe feel her out about it first. She was always the easy one.

Grabbing her briefcase, Sally left the house, locking the door behind her. She passed Bob's cabin five minutes later and turned her head automatically to look down the dusty drive. She caught a quick glimpse of a red pickup truck, but nothing more amid the oaks. If Jake Nolte was human, he'd probably gone back to bed, she surmised. The thought was all her poor brain needed. Instantly the image of the tall cop, tangled in the sheets, shot into her mind. Bare-chested with his hair tousled and his smile inviting...his appearance—even if it was imaginary—made her throat tighten and her heart race. He wouldn't be alone in bed, of course. She would be lying beside him, one leg thrown over his with possessive sensuality. The picture played out, with Sally reaching over for him, her hand trailing over his chest. She shook her head, as if to dispel the vision, but stubbornly it refused to leave. Only after she parked in her parents' driveway, did the fantasy finally disappear.

REBECCA BEAUMONT met her daughter on the doorstep of the house where Sally had grown up. She held a pink mixing bowl with a plastic spoon sticking out of it, and in the bright Texas sun, her mother's white hair gleamed. "I was in the kitchen when I saw you pull in the driveway," Rebecca said with a smile. "What a treat! You almost never visit before work!" She held up the bowl. "I'm making French toast. Want some?"

Sally's mouth watered, then she thought again. "Is Dad here?" she said cautiously.

"No, no. He's left already. I got hungry and thought 'why not?' I can fix French toast just for me, can't I?"

Sally smiled and nodded, more relief than she'd expected flooding her. "French toast sounds great. I'll share it with you."

They stepped into the cool dim hallway, heading

for the kitchen, Rebecca chattering all the way. Sally let her talk, but through the effervescence she thought she sensed a nervous thread, unusual for her mother. By the time the toast was ready and they'd sat down at the table, Sally was sure Rebecca *had* heard the broadcast—but she was waiting for Sally to speak first.

The bite of crispy toast and sweet maple syrup Sally had just taken turned to dust in her mouth. Swallowing painfully, she put down her fork and faced her mother. "Mom, I came by for a reason this morning. I—I wanted to know if you heard the—"

"I heard the show," her mother said. "Dorothy called and canceled bridge yesterday because her shingles were acting up so I stayed home." Rebecca Beaumont placed her own fork down on the pristine white place mat beneath her plate. Her voice and features stayed neutral. "I heard it all."

Sally sat nervously, her stomach churning. "Did Daddy?"

"No. He didn't actually hear it. I—I told him about it and I'm sure he'll learn more today."

Sally didn't need more explanation; she knew what her mother was talking about. The Comfort phone lines were probably smoking, they were so busy.

Sally waited for her mother to say more, but she

didn't. What thoughts were running through her head? How to tell Sally she'd been disowned? How to tell her what a disappointment she was?

Finally Rebecca spoke, a delicate pink blush staining her soft cheeks as the words began. "Sally, sweetheart, I—I was wondering...not that I need any or anything but...do condoms really come with sparkles now?"

Sally stared at her mother. In the background of her mind, she heard music. It sounded like the theme from *The Twilight Zone*.

"Sally?"

"Uh, yeah...I'm here."

Her mother stared at her expectantly. "Well?"

"Um, yes, Mom, they do. With sparkles and glitter and ribs and everything else you can imagine—and some things you can't." Before she could say more, her mother spoke again.

"And that other woman—the one who wanted her boyfriend to tie her up? Do a lot of young folks go in for that sort of thing?"

The conversation was taking such an unreal air that Sally imagined herself floating up from the chair and looking down on the two of them from the white plastic light fixture her father had installed when she'd been in the fifth grade. Unbelievably, her mother didn't appear upset, only curious. What was going on? What alien had taken over her mother's body?

"Do they use that yellow kind of rope you get down at the hardware store or do they use something special?"

"You—you can use anything you like," Sally said without thinking, her brain spinning. "Velvet rope, scarves, chains... I don't think there's too many rules as far as bondage is concerned."

"Bondage...hmmm."

Just hearing the word come from her mother's lips was too much. Sally stood up abruptly and took her plate to the kitchen sink. What was happening? Why was her mother asking these questions instead of telling Sally how she'd ruined their lives? Taking a deep breath, Sally turned and faced her mother. "The program—it—it didn't upset you?"

Rebecca looked surprised. "Upset me? Heavens no. I wasn't upset, honey. Why should I be? Sex education is a wonderful thing and for a lot of years your father has been considering just such a thing at the church. He simply didn't know what to do or how to do it. I think your program is wonderfully educational. We're proud of you. Really we are!"

Sally's mouth actually fell open. Her mother's words were so unexpected, she couldn't control herself. "Are you crazy? You think it's an educational program?"

Her mother nodded solemnly. "Well, of course, darling. What else could it be? People have questions. They need answers. We know you worked on the hot line in college. This is just the same only it's being broadcast. You're helping many more people."

"And this is how Daddy feels, too?"

"Well...yes. He was a little concerned at first, but after I explained it to him, he understood. How hard you'd worked on the program and how much you wanted to help people. How you felt it would be good for your career. After that, he wasn't upset."

"How much I wanted to help people! Mom! You knew that show was supposed to be about cooking, not sex!"

"Oh, I don't think so." Rebecca spoke slowly, her gaze meeting Sally's from across the kitchen, the lingering homey smell of French toast in the air between them. "I distinctly remember you telling me something quite different—and once I explained that to your father, he wasn't upset at all."

Stunned, Sally gripped the edge of the sink and stared at her mother. She didn't understand. She'd expected her mother to be horrified and her father clutching his chest. Instead, Rebecca Beaumont was helping her daughter, actually paving the way and smoothing things over with her father before they'd even had a chance to get rough. "A-are you sure?" *Are you sure this is okay and neither of you are going to get hurt?*

"Absolutely." Rebecca Beaumont met her daughter's startled and confused gaze without hesitation, a steady thoughtful look on her face that contained a message that went beyond the words she spoke. "I think *Too Hot For Comfort* is a public service this town has needed for a very long time. We're proud of you, Sally. Very proud." Suddenly her eyes began to twinkle. "In fact, I can't wait to hear the next installment."

AFTER REACHING WORK, Sally suffered the jokes and snide remarks everyone on staff seemed determined to make at her expense. She got more than one or two ugly looks, as well. The receptionist, Loretta Smith, a blue-rinsed member of Sally's father's church, leaned over at the coffee machine and whispered, "How could you? Your poor father..." Loretta's best friend at the station, Pearl Westbrook down in typing, echoed Loretta's sentiments. At the lunch counter, she made a point of bringing her tray to Sally's table and then turning on her heel to walk in the other direction. It would have been funny...if Sally hadn't gotten a rock through her window at 2:00 a.m.

Linda could hardly believe it when Sally told her

about the rock and the message. "Who would do something like that?"

"Who knows?" Sally answered, shaking her head. She pushed a fork through the salad she'd selected, feeling so confused she hardly knew which end was up. She'd been totally prepared for her parent's reproach, but they were supporting her. What was going on? And then there was Jake Nolte. At the oddest moments he kept popping into her head. She told Linda about his and Bob's arrival last night.

"Whoa, whoa..." Linda held up one hand. "Jake Nolte. Is he the hunk staying out at Bob's place?"

Sally looked at her in amazement. "You know him?"

"Not really, but Debbie told me he was coming. She said she might try and fix me up with him." Linda leaned closer. "What do you think? Should I go for it?"

Something that felt curiously like jealousy poked Sally in the ribs. "I don't know," she said stiffly. "He seems rather remote to me."

Linda stared at her for a few seconds then burst out laughing, her eyes twinkling. "*Raather remote?* Oh, baby! You've already got your little paws out for him, don't you?"

"That's not true!"

"Oh, puleeze.... You're so easy to get a rise out of, it's hardly even fun." Linda leaned over the table. "If you like the guy, tell Debbie. The only reason she didn't ask you in the first place is that you never seem interested, Sally. You've turned down everyone's attempts to match you up with someone."

"I'm usually *not* interested," she said, toying with a piece of lettuce. Looking up, she grinned, "But I might be willing to make an exception this time."

Linda rolled her eyes. "Then call her, for God's sake. They're having a barbecue out there at the camp on Saturday." She started to say more, but suddenly fell silent. Sally looked up in time to see Rita approaching. The station manager stopped at their table and stared at Sally.

"I understand you had some problems out at your place last night."

Sally nodded. She wasn't surprised Rita knew.

"If your insurance won't cover it, the station will pay for the glass. I've already told Bubba to send us the bill." She leaned down. "This should make your decision a little easier."

"What do you mean?"

"If you don't go back on the air, they win." Rita's eyes were like flint. "This is your chance to prove what you're worth, Sally. Don't let some idiot with a rock make up your mind for you. I'll expect you in my office tomorrow morning, giving me the answer I want to hear.'' Her steely gaze pierced Sally's a second longer, then she turned around and walked away.

Watching the station manager leave, Linda and Sally sat in silence. Linda spoke only after Rita disappeared through the lunchroom doors. "I wonder what she paid him?"

Sally frowned. "Paid who?"

Linda smiled. "The guy with the rock."

JAKE ANGLED HIS pickup truck into the parking spot directly in front of Brookshire Brother's Groceries. When he'd arrived in town last night, he'd only bought the necessities—cold beer, frozen pizzas, sandwich stuff—but now he was going to have to do some major shopping. More beer, of course, a pound of hamburger and maybe some eggs. And another few pizzas, too. He climbed from the truck and made his way into the store, his eye on a dark-headed woman in front of him. For a second, he thought it was Sally Beaumont, then he realized his mistake when the woman turned. Sally was much slimmer and wore her hair smooth and short. Last night, he'd watched the silky brown curtain swing against her neck as she'd answered his questions;

every so often she had tucked it behind her ears with slim, pale fingers.

He grabbed a cart from a jumbled line and pushed it into the fruit section with more vigor than necessary. Sally Beaumont hadn't been at all what he'd expected. When she'd opened the door to her house, he'd been more than surprised. Her voice definitely didn't match the rest of her. The curves he'd imagined were more gentle than voluptuous; the sexy, smoldering eyes he'd conjured had turned out to be brown—soft and huge with lashes so long they brushed her cheeks when she lowered her eyes. She'd looked innocent and naive. It was hard to reconcile that gravelly, sexy voice with the slim young woman who'd greeted him.

He threw a couple of tomatoes in the cart and pushed it down the next aisle. What in the hell was he doing thinking of Sally Beaumont anyway? She was young—a career woman concerned with nothing but her job. There was no ''ex-anything'' she'd told him, and to back up her point, her house had contained no photos of her with friends, no outward signs of any hobby, nothing to show that she thought of anything but work. The magazines on her coffee table had been trade journals and the books reference guides. No novels for Sally Beaumont. No novels and no old boyfriends.

He reached the end of the second aisle without

picking up a thing. Sally still on his mind, he headed to the dairy counter for the eggs, barely missing an old lady with two bags of cat food in her arms. He hadn't been interested in a woman since Sandra had left him, their divorce a cold and short-lived contest. She'd been a career woman, too. A mortgage banker. They'd met in a cop bar and had gotten married six weeks later. He didn't really know why, except the sex had been great. Everything else had been the pits. After five miserable years, they'd gone their separate ways.

Thinking of Sandra was like stepping into a cold shower. All thoughts of dating anyone else, including Sally, went out the window. Jake finished his shopping, went through the checkout, grabbed up the white plastic bags and headed outside.

Sally Beaumont was leaning against the fender of his pickup.

WHEN JAKE CAME OUT of Brookshire Brothers carrying his groceries, Sally's breath caught in her throat and a funny twist of something warm started in her stomach. *Whoa there, girl. Slow down, take it easy!* The words of warning sounded inside her head but her body wasn't listening. Actually, the rest of her hadn't listened too well, either. When she'd seen the shiny red pickup, her brain had ordered her to keep going, but her hands had turned the steering wheel and swung her car into the asphalt lot to park. Then her fingers had unlocked the door, her legs had jumped out, and here she was, leaning against his vehicle, her heart doing a rhumba.

His blue eyes seemed to warm as they took her in, but it could have just been her imagination. "Hi, there." His voice was deep and sexy.

"Hi, yourself," she answered. She nodded to the grocery bags, seeing the beer through the plastic. "Got a liquid diet going?"

He unlocked his truck and dumped the bags on the seat. "You can't fish without beer. It's a rule."

"So that's why my daddy's never caught anything! He always takes orange juice."

"There's exceptions for preachers. Maybe he's just a bad fisherman." Jake closed the car door then looked at her more closely. "You talk to him about your show? You seemed pretty worried last night about what he'd think."

"I spoke with my mom." Sally shook her head. "To say the conversation was bizarre would not do it justice."

"They're mad?"

"No—just the opposite...."

She found herself about to explain more, then broke off abruptly. "God, I didn't come here to bore you with all this...."

"You're not boring me. I asked, remember?"

She looked up into his eyes. She hadn't imagined it. They *were* warmer now, the light blue had darkened into a deep sapphire. She nodded slowly. "I— I guess I just don't understand it."

"And that bothers you. You're the kind of woman who likes to analyze it all, understand why people do what they do."

She looked at him in amazement. "How did you know that?"

He smiled. She hadn't noticed until now how full and perfect his lips were. "I'm not a mind reader— it's just obvious. You've clearly given it a lot of thought already." He shrugged, his wide shoulders moving easily beneath the black T-shirt stretching across his chest. "Why? would be my question. Just accept it. They're happy, you're happy—I'm sure your show will do great. Just go for it and don't worry about why."

"Is that what you do?" she asked.

"Generally speaking, yeah. Doesn't pay to do much else. Can't change fate, right?"

She nodded slowly. Maybe he was right. Maybe she examined things *too* closely sometimes. If her parents had accepted the show, and Rita obviously wanted her to do it, then Sally should be thrilled. It could be her ticket out of Comfort—just as Rita had said. So why wasn't she jumping up and down?

They stood together in the hot sunlight, then slowly, Sally realized Jake was staring at her. She blinked and came out of her thoughts. "I only stopped to say thank you," she said. "You left this morning before I had a chance. I appreciate you coming over before Bob got there."

He put a thumb to the cap perched on his head. *Big Johnson* was stitched across the top. "No problem. It was the quickest thing to do."

"You were a cop in Houston...with Bob?"

"That's right. Twenty years on the force."

"Now what?"

"Now I'm retired." He nodded toward his groceries. "Fishing and drinking. That's my job now."

Sally spoke without thinking. "Retired! You're too young to retire."

He grinned again. "Thanks for the compliment. Unfortunately, you're wrong. I'm almost forty, and that's ancient if you're a cop. Especially a cop with a bum leg."

Her eyes dropped without thinking. "A bum leg?"

His hand went to his upper thigh. "Long story. It seemed like a good time to leave. While I still could."

She started to ask what had happened, then stopped. It was none of her business, was it? And besides, why did she even care? She wasn't looking for a relationship here—she'd only stopped to thank the man, not start up a lifelong commitment.

"You have any more problems, feel free to call, though. I may be retired, but I can still shoot straight."

She smiled. "I'll do that. Hopefully, we won't need the shooting part. I think they just wanted to scare me, that's all."

"You never can tell. Keep my number close."

A few minutes later, he drove away. Sally watched the pickup disappear down the dusty street. She'd been halfway hoping he'd say something about the barbecue Linda had mentioned, but he hadn't. Under a little cloud of disappointment, she turned and headed for the grocery store.

IN HIS REARVIEW MIRROR, Jake watched Sally's figure grow smaller and smaller. There was something about her... She was itching to get away from her life as she knew it, but underneath, he suspected, she was not really as sure as she appeared. The whiskey-rough voice and confident attitude were one thing, but there was a vulnerability behind those soft brown eyes that you didn't notice unless you took the time.

Shaking his head, he aimed the pickup out of town and told himself he didn't *have* the time. Didn't *want* to have the time. A woman like Sally

Beaumont was the last kind of complication he needed. He was on the downswing, ready to kick back and let life roll past him. She was just the opposite—anxious to get out there and see what life was all about. Besides, her new show probably *would* launch her and she'd be outta Comfort like a rocket. She couldn't start a long-term relationship with anyone, much less him.

For some reason, the image of her shattered living-room window came into his mind, bringing with it an uncomfortable thought. Sally was ready to move on for sure, but whoever had thrown that rock might not let her.

4

BY THE TIME Sally got home that evening, Bubba had come and gone. The picture window was as perfect as it had been before, the view of the lake it framed just as soothing and relaxing. Sally tugged off her suit and her panty hose and slipped on a pair of shorts and a T-shirt. Clutching a handful of catfish feed, she padded barefoot down to the water as she did every evening. The dock was long, but by the time she reached the end the water was already roiling with silver flashes and long whiskers that were bobbing up and down with greedy enthusiasm. She flung the food into the water then sat down to watch. The pellets floated for only a few seconds then disappeared, gobbled up by the eager fish.

After seeing Jake, she'd stopped by the church on her way home and talked to her father. He hadn't had much time, but he'd sat down with her, his attitude as caring and gentle as it always was.

"You *aren't* angry?" she'd asked.

"No, honey. Your mother and I have always been proud of you—you know that."

"Except for that time with your new Buick..."

He smiled. "Well, there *was* that time," he acknowledged.

"I thought the show would embarrass you."

His brown eyes crinkled. "Embarrass me?"

"You know...at the church."

He shook his head. "It could get tricky, but if anyone says anything, I'll just point out the need for sex education. Did you know we had four girls at Comfort High get pregnant last year? Four girls! When you were in high school, there was only one...in four years. Our young people need to know more about sex and if your radio talk show can do that, then I say more power to you."

Sally felt a sweep of guilt come over her. He was making her sound like some kind of crusading angel. "Dad...you know the show isn't *exactly* educational...."

In the light streaming through his office window, she thought she saw a twinkle in his eyes, but once again, Sally didn't trust herself to know that for sure.

"People are calling you and asking questions, right?"

"Well, yes...but—"

"And they need this information? It's not readily available anywhere else?"

"Well, maybe...but—"

"Then it's educational, Sally. It's educational and a public service. If Elmer Holley doesn't know how to find glow-in-the-dark condoms by himself, believe me, you're helping society by leading him in the right direction."

Sally couldn't help herself. She started to giggle, then her father joined her and soon they were laughing out loud—*too* loud for where they were, in a preacher's study.

When they quieted back down, she wiped the tears from her eyes and stared at her dad. "I thought—"

"I know what you thought, honey, but you thought wrong. Your mother and I are grown adults." His eyes did twinkle now. "And we've known about sex for quite a long time."

"That's not what I meant... Your job, your position..."

He dropped his gaze and put his hands on the top of his desk. For a minute, they both stared at those hands, pale and flecked with brown spots. When he spoke, his voice held regret. "This town is full of mighty good people, Sally Anne, but I've got to tell you, it's not the Comfort I knew when I was younger. The narrow-mindedness I've been seeing lately is beginning to bother me.''

For the second time that day, Sally felt her mouth drop open. She'd never heard her father criticize anything or anyone in Comfort. They hadn't had a talk like this in quite a while, either, she realized a moment later.

The door burst open a second after that, a tiny redheaded boy standing on the threshold. "It's Story Time!'' he yelled. "We want to hear about Moses and the Ten Combatants.''

Her father stood, then shot a glance toward her and shrugged. "A new version, I guess.''

Sally grinned at the recollection. Looking into the lake water, she thought about her meeting tomorrow with Rita. She'd say yes to doing the show, she knew. There was nothing standing in her way now…unless you counted the rock.

And, of course, Sally didn't.

SALLY WAS ALMOST READY for bed when the phone rang. It startled her, scared her actually, and she found her heart racing. Maybe the rock had upset her more than she wanted to admit.

Debbie MacAroy's friendly voice answered Sally's tentative hello. "Sally! This is Debbie! How ya doing?''

Debbie ran the local beauty shop and everything

she said seemed to end with an exclamation point. When she'd first come to Comfort with Bob, after years in Houston, she'd had to relearn how to do hair. In central Texas, your hair wasn't fixed until it stood out from your head at least six inches and was lacquered to a high polish so it could withstand the wind. To Debbie's credit, she'd learned fast. Lots of teasing, lots of spray...and plenty of gossip.

"I'm just fine, Debbie." Sally tried to make her voice sound casual, but her heart hadn't slowed a bit. In fact, it had speeded up. Had Debbie called about the barbecue? Childishly, behind her back, Sally crossed her fingers. "How you doing?"

"We're great! In fact, we're having a party! To introduce a new friend of Bob's around. Well, heck, it's Jake—I'm forgettin' you met him the other night. It's a surprise! He doesn't know a thing about it, but we're all showing up at the cabin on Saturday at noon! Won't that be a hoot! Bring some potato salad and a cooler of soda! Okay? See ya then!"

Sally hung up the phone slowly, a grin spreading over her face. That explained everything, she thought. He hadn't even known about the party....

"AND FIVE ... four ... three ... two ... you're on!" Linda pointed to Sally, isolated in the broadcast booth.

Sally's mouth was so dry she couldn't have spit

if her life depended on it, but somehow she managed to get the words out.

"Good afternoon, Comfort. This is Sally Beaumont with *Too Hot for Comfort,* and we're here for your questions. The lines are ready so we'll take callers as they come."

After her meeting with Rita, who'd been thrilled but not surprised by Sally's capitulation, they'd agreed to try and corral the questions by targeting certain topics each day. The station manager had actually liked Rebecca Beaumont's take on the show, too. That it was educational. "Maybe that'll keep out some of the bigger nut cases..." Rita had said.

"Today's subject is sex and alternative lifestyles." Sally took a deep breath. "Any thoughts out there on that?"

While Sally was still speaking, Linda held up her forefinger. A signal to pick up line one. Already! She flashed her other fingers three times. There were calls waiting, too! Sally suddenly wanted to crawl under the desk, but she punched the first button on the phone and answered. "Hi, caller. What's on your mind?"

"What's with this topic business?" It was a man speaking and he sounded cranky. "I got a question and it ain't about alternative life whatevers."

"Okay, then." Sally's heart thudded. "What is your question?"

"I wanna know how many times a week is normal?"

"How many times what is normal?"

"What the hell do you think? This ain't a show about plowing, is it? How many times a week should two people have sex?"

"I—I don't think there's an absolute rule on that, sir. Whatever feels comfortable to both partners is normal."

"Well, gol-darned, what kinda answer is that? How many times a week do *you* do it?"

Outside, in the engineer's booth, Linda doubled over with laughter. She was holding up her hand, making a circle out of her thumb and forefinger.

Sally held up a finger of her own—Linda was *supposed* to be screening calls—then returned to business. "I believe the national average is six times a month, sir. I think that works out to about one-and-a-half times a week."

"How in the hell do you have half-sex?"

"It's just a figure," Sally said hopelessly. "An average number!"

"All right, then. Thass good enough, I guess!" He slammed the phone down so hard Sally's ear rang.

She looked out into the booth. Still all she could

see of Linda was her hand. She held up two fingers, and Sally punched the second phone line.

"Hi, caller. You're on *Too Hot for Comfort*. What's your question?"

"Am I on?"

"You're on."

"Well…I…I like to be on top and my husband likes to be there, too. We're gettin' into some awful fights about who gets to be on top. Have you got any suggestions?"

What the hell had happened to alternative lifestyles? Sally wondered if her mother was listening. Was *this* as educational as she'd thought it would be?

"Why don't you try some different positions?" Sally offered. "Something where you're both on top."

"Both…on top? Wh—what do you mean?"

"Lie facing each other. That way neither of you loses. How's that?"

"Ohhh, that sounds kinda interestin'."

"Well, good, I'm glad I helped. And this may help even more… Now we're going to hear from our latest sponsor, Lucy's Secrets. If your love life is flagging, Lucy's got a secret for you. Come on out to Highway 69, and she'll help you select the lingerie that'll do the trick.…" Sally pointed to Linda who'd finally managed to get back in her chair. She cued the music and Sally relaxed back in her own seat.

She had only a moment's rest, though, before the next round of questions began. And they didn't end. When the show's hour was up, the phone lines were still flashing. Sally randomly selected one final call, her mind twirling, her brain exhausted.

"Hi, caller. You're on the air. What's your question?"

The voice was tentative and shy. Young, probably a teenager, she imagined, but she couldn't tell if it was a boy or a girl. "It's about your topic," the caller said. "You know, alternative life-styles."

"Yes, go on."

"Well, I'm just wondering how...well, how you know if you want one or not."

"Some people don't think it's a matter of wanting one. Gender identity—which is basically what we're talking about—is something you're born with, they think. You know—like blue eyes or black hair. A strong chin or wide shoulders." As soon as the words were out, she thought of Jake. She shook her head and continued. "Some people believe you're naturally attracted to one sex or the other and that's just how it is. You meet someone, you fall in love with them—it doesn't matter which sex they are."

"Can you change it? That attraction, I mean?"

"Some believe you can," she said carefully. "Some people don't. Are you having some questions about your own identity?"

"No! Nuh-uh. Absolutely not. I—I know what I like. It—it's a friend of mine, you know. I'm asking for him—um—her."

Sally's heart swelled in sympathy. The poor kid was obviously confused and trying desperately to deny it. "I understand. The important thing to tell your friend is that sometimes it takes a while to sort things like this out. Your friend might be confused now, but that's only because when we're young everything's confusing. As we grow older, we sort things out."

"Yeah, right." The caller sounded relieved. "Wow, thanks, man. That really makes sense, too. I mean, what's the rush, right? Got the rest of my life—uh, his life—I mean her life…to decide. Thanks."

Linda cued up the show's canned ending and with a weary sigh, Sally stood, rolling her shoulders. A second later, Rita opened the door. "Damn good show, Sally."

Sally arched her back. "You think?"

"I know!" Rita was usually faint with her praise and Sally couldn't believe her ears. She held up her thumb. "Damn good."

SATURDAY MORNING dawned hot and hotter. Jake slipped on a pair of shorts and his cap and headed for the lake. It was time to do some serious fishing.

With a full cooler and a brimming bait bucket, he climbed into Bob's rattletrap flat-bottomed boat and navigated to the center of the lake. Five minutes later, he had his rod and reel in one hand and a cold Corona in the other. He sat back against the seat in the boat and gave a contented sigh. It just didn't get much better than this.

As soon as he closed his eyes, of course, Sally Beaumont invaded his mind. Leaning up against his pickup truck, those soft brown eyes looking into his. He shook his head. God, she was a good-looking woman. And that voice! Yesterday afternoon, he'd listened to the show—along with everyone else in Comfort, he was sure—and once again, her gravelly voice had made him think of things he shouldn't. Like her underwear. Would it match her voice or her appearance? Prim and proper or lacy and see-through? K-Mart or Lucy's out on Highway 69?

He let the fantasy build, and two hours later—with one helluva dream rattling around in his head—he woke up. Sweaty, sunburned and horny beyond belief, there was only one way to handle it—well, two actually—but one that was acceptable right now. He stood up, peeled off his shorts and jumped into the lake. The water was shockingly cold and it took away his breath—and all evidence of his thoughts of Sally. He swam in circles around the boat for fifteen minutes, then he climbed back in and headed toward the cabin, the little engine behind the boat put-putting with all the force of a sewing machine. A few minutes later, reaching the dock, he jumped from the boat, grabbed his clothes and his tackle box and started up the slope toward the house.

By the time he heard the voices, it was too late. He couldn't do a thing.

Debbie MacAroy was the first one to see him.

"Hey, Jake! Wow! You been fishing or what?" As if in afterthought, she spoke again, explaining why there were fifty strangers behind her, all staring at him in surprise. "Hey! We're having a party for you! To introduce you to everybody! Guess they're going to get to know you real good, huh?" She burst out laughing.

Jake smiled weakly and wished he had more in his hand than a ragged pair of shorts and a plastic box. Thank God he'd bought an extra large one.

"Hey there, Debbie," he said with as much dignity as he could muster. "I wasn't expecting a party or I wouldn't have dressed this casually."

Bob ambled over and joined Debbie. He had two beers in his hands. He held one out to Jake, a mock expression of apology on his face. "I brought this to you, but seeing as how you got your hands full, maybe it ought to wait, huh?"

Jake gritted his teeth. "Think you could help me out here, pal? Get me a towel or something?"

Ignoring Jake's question, Bob glanced down, then back up. "You always fish in the buff? What 'bout them 'skeeters? Don't they getcha?"

"It was hot. I went swimming. I thought I'd just come back up here, shower and then dress. Like I said...I wasn't expecting a party."

From the corner of Jake's eye, he caught a movement and when he saw who it was, he groaned. Sally Beaumont. Great. Just great. She had on white shorts and a tight sleeveless T-shirt, with a long-sleeved shirt tied around her waist. Her legs seemed to go on forever. She was trying hard not to grin but as she reached Bob and Debbie's side, she couldn't hold it back a minute longer. She started to giggle, her eyes crinkling in the corners, her laughter as sexy and deep as her voice. "Hello, Jake! We're having a barbecue at your place today. Guess Debbie forgot to tell you, huh?"

Seeing her grin and hearing that sexy laugh, Jake suddenly couldn't do anything but smile himself. "Hell, no, I knew about it. This is how we dress for barbecues in Houston. Didn't you know?"

Her eyes met his. They were gleaming, still, but

the expression had shifted minutely. "Can't say as I knew that," she drawled. "Sounds kinda interesting, though. What happens if you drop sauce somewhere you shouldn't?"

"Well, that depends…"

Her eyes were definitely gleaming now. He was sure of it. "On what?"

"On where it lands and how good a friend you are with the one sitting next to you."

Before Sally could answer, Debbie leaned over and handed Jake a bath towel. He hadn't even realized she'd left as he'd been talking to Sally. "Here ya are, Jake! Cover yourself up and go on inside and change! We'll set up the tables and get things going out here."

His eyes never leaving Sally's, Jake took the towel and draped it around his waist. It was hard going with the tackle box in his hands as well, but he couldn't very well drop one for the other. She kept her gaze on his until he got the towel around him, then she lowered her stare to the blue-and-white striped cotton. Lazily, she brought her eyes back to his face and grinned, then she turned around and walked away.

"OH. MY. GOD. Did you see that butt?" Linda held a can of beer and a rib, her eyes huge. "Did you see it, Sally? The man is perfect. I mean perfect."

Sally sipped her own beer. "Yes. I saw it and yes, it's perfect." Her voice was glum.

Linda looked at her with a puzzled expression. "What *is* your problem? He was eyeing you like you were the last piece of apple pie, and if I'm not mistaken those weren't just casual looks you were sending him, either."

"He's *retired,* Linda! He's in Comfort to fish and drink beer. I don't want a man like that! I'm leaving here as soon as I can, remember?"

"Oh, yeah, right! I forgot there for a minute. You hate your home town and everything in it. That's why you've lived here for six years and haven't left..."

The words hit hard. Sally gave her friend a sharp look. "If you've got something to say, let's hear it. Don't be shy."

Linda took a bite of her rib. "All right," she said, speaking around a mouthful of barbecue. "How's this for honesty? I think you're using your parents as an excuse to stay here. I think you actually do love Comfort and all the nuts that live here and if you did leave, you'd probably be back within a week." She waved the rib in Sally's face. "*That's* what I really think."

"Well, you think wrong," Sally shot back. "Besides, who died and made you the expert psychologist around here?"

Linda grinned. "The same one who died and made you the sex expert!"

Feigning outrage, Sally flounced away and headed toward the buffet. Deep inside she was afraid Linda might be right. In fact, she'd been wondering about this herself, but today Sally wasn't going to think about it. Today, she just wanted barbecue and beer and nothing more stressful than looking at Jake. Who did have the perfect butt and the perfect everything else as far as she could see— which hadn't been far enough. Damn, that tackle box had been big!

Just as she reached the table, the man in question reached her side. He held an empty plate and was about to fill it up. He grinned and held out his hands. "Does this look better?"

No. He now had on blue-jean cutoffs and a black T-shirt, the muscular chest covered, the buff biceps hidden. "Let's just say it's more appropriate," she answered. "How's that?"

He nodded. "Grab a plate, then I want you to tell me about these people hanging around on my lawn."

Sally did as he ordered and together they took heaping platters to a small table someone had set up under the pin oak tree. Jake sat closer to her than she would have sat to him, but she didn't mind. The hard feel of his thigh next to hers was definitely not unpleasant, and sometime between being naked and getting clothed, he'd added a light aftershave, too. Something that smelled really clean and soapy.

"Okay," he said as they settled in. "Tell me who these folks are."

She nodded her head toward the edge of the house. "Well, that's my mom and dad right over there. Did you meet them?"

"No, thank God. I think they came late. Didn't get to see my emergence from the lake."

Sally smiled. "The two women with them are Loretta Smith and Pearl Westbrook. They work at the station. I'm sure they're bending Daddy's ear about how sinful my program is. They couldn't wait until tomorrow after church."

Jake nodded. "And how about them?" He pointed toward another group with his beer can. "They look interesting. That woman in the middle is mighty overdressed. And how does she get her hair to stand up like that?"

It hadn't been necessary for him to point. Sally knew exactly who he meant. "That's Mary Margaret Henley. She's Bob's aunt, twice-removed, and she's currently unhappy with me, too. She was the cooking expert I hired to do the show and when the first question came in, you would have thought I'd stabbed her with a meat carver. She was not pleased.''

"You had no control over the callers...."

"Explain that to her, please." Sally shook her head. "She had plans to be the Martha Stewart of the air waves, but obviously that didn't work out. She left in a huff and hasn't spoken to me since."

Sally pointed discreetly to Rita March and Linda. They were standing by the dessert table, nibbling cookies with Ricky Carter. Obnoxious and pushy, the man had clearly barged in—they would never have invited him to join them. "And that's my boss and my best friend. Rita and Linda, with Ricky Carter. He's a recent hire at the station." She laughed. "Linda thinks Rita paid someone to throw the rock through my window so I'd get my back up and stay and do the program. She's a nut." Still chuckling, she sent a glance at Jake's profile. He was studying Rita as she pointed them out, she realized all at once, and it wasn't just a casual interest. "Linda didn't mean it," she said suddenly. "It was a joke. Rita wouldn't do something like that."

He turned, his laser eyes drilling hers. "Are you sure?"

Was she sure? All at once, Sally sobered and considered the question. Rita *would* do whatever it took to make the station successful. She was tough and playing in what was basically a man's field.

Still… "I don't think she'd do something to hurt me."

"The rock didn't hurt you. You were sleeping. Anyone looking into the window could see you weren't around."

Pulling in her bottom lip, Sally shook her head slowly. "It's not Rita's style. She's more straightforward. She told me exactly what she thought about doing the program right up front. She doesn't hold back."

"What about your friend, Linda? Any reason for her to do it?"

"Oh, God, no. Linda's even more up-front." Sally shook her head. "No. No way."

"Then who?" Wiping his mouth on a red, white and blue paper napkin, Jake leaned back and looked at her.

"How about Pearl and Loretta? They're sure I'm meant for hell."

Jake stared at the two women. "Either one of them own a boat?"

"Pearl's husband is a big fisherman. He's got a twin-engine Stinger that'll cross the lake in five minutes. I think I would have heard it, though. It's louder than hell."

"But you said you were sleeping."

She shrugged.

"Anyone else? How about the famous Mary Margaret?"

Sally burst out laughing. "Are you kidding? She wouldn't risk getting her shoes dirty just to toss a rock through my window. Although, I guess she could throw it. Look at those arms. They're made for rolling dough, aren't they?"

They both stared at the overdressed, fussy-looking woman and began to laugh. A few minutes after that, Bob and Debbie came and joined them, Bob explaining to Jake who the rest of the people were, Debbie and Sally occasionally joining in.

By the time dusk had begun to fall, most of the guests had left. Bob and Debbie went last, Bob carrying Brittany in his arms, her shirt smeared with barbecue sauce, one of her tennis shoes missing in action.

"You look for that shoe, now, Jake. Those things cost a fortune these days!" Walking to her car, Debbie spoke, her own arms full of plastic containers. "They still halfway fit her, too!"

Jake promised to look for the shoe, then turned to Sally as Bob and Debbie drove away a moment later. "Do you have to leave now? We could have a nightcap...I've got some Amaretto."

In the full moonlight, his stare was almost magnetic. Somewhere out near the lake, a hoot-owl cried. Sally shivered and suddenly she understood what her father meant when he preached on temptation. "I think it'd be best for me to get on home."

Jake reached out and trailed a finger down her cheek, tucking her hair behind her ear. "Why would that be best?" he said. "I don't think a drink would hurt things, would it?"

"No. Probably not. But..."

He waited.

"But I—I've got to get up early in the morning and go into the station. I need to catch up on my regular work. Since I started the show, everything else got dropped...."

It was such a patent excuse, there was obviously nothing else he could say. For a second she thought he might argue—hoped he might argue?—then he dipped his head in acquiescence. "All right, then. Guess you know best."

They turned and walked toward her car, Sally already regretting her words, but not knowing exactly how to change them. She opened her mouth to try, then stopped abruptly and gasped. Jake instantly tensed.

"What is it?"

She pointed to her car without a word. All four tires were flat.

Flat and slashed to ribbons.

5

"GO INSIDE." Jake's voice was grim. He didn't really think whoever had slashed Sally's tires was still there, but he didn't want to have to worry about her and look around, too. "Right now. Lock the door and stay there till I come in."

She turned and ran soundlessly back to the cabin. When he heard the door slam shut, Jake began to circle the car slowly. The moonlight was almost as bright as day. In the silvery expanse he could see footprints all the way around the automobile, but none stood out from the rest. Boots, tennis shoes, even someone wearing high heels. Anyone from the party could have done the damage—or actually, anyone could have come up the driveway and done it while they were eating. He looked more closely at the car. It was spotless. No handprints on the side, no muddy hints at all. He stood back and shook his head. Malicious mischief or another warning? A fluttering motion caught his eye and he saw a piece of paper tucked under one of the windshield wipers. Using just the edge of his fingers, he plucked the note out and read it, the printed letters easy to see in the bright light pouring over his shoulder.

THIS IS YOUR SECOND WARNING. COMFORT DON'T NEED SMUT!

With the letter in his hand, Jake went inside. Sally was standing in the center of Bob's small living room, in the glow of a single lamp. She was licking her lips and trying not to look nervous. Her hands gave her away, though; they were twisted together, her long fingers knotted. She darted a quick look at the paper he held and reached out for it.

He managed to yank it back at the very last second. "No—we might get some prints off it!"

She looked startled, but nodded. "Wh—what does it say?"

He held it out and she read it. When she finished, she lifted her eyes to his and said simply. "Oh, shit."

"Yeah, that just about sums it up." He shook his head. "What kind of idiot would get this riled up about a damned talk show? I just don't understand it."

"That's Comfort," she said, slowly sinking into a tattered recliner.

"I've got to call Bob. He'll need to hear about this."

Bob answered on the second ring and listened silently as Jake described the situation.

"I'll drop off Debbie and Brittany and come right back—"

"There's no reason to do that. The car's not going anywhere and I already checked it out as well as you would. Just come out in the morning. I can give you the note then. You ever get any prints off the first one?"

"Oh, hell no. That's gonna take weeks. Might speed things up now, since we got a second one."

They talked for a few more minutes, then Jake hung up. When he went back into the living room, Sally looked at him. She seemed more angry than worried. "I can't believe this," she steamed. "What in the hell is this nut trying to accomplish?"

Jake sat down on the sofa, the old springs complaining under his weight. "You're assuming logical thought there, Sally. Whoever's doing this might not think like you or me." She nodded silently, then he spoke again. "Does it scare you?"

For a second, she played with a gold necklace around her neck. "Kinda."

"Want to stay here?"

Her fingers stilled and she met his gaze. "I—I don't think so."

"Why not?"

She paused, then allowed her big brown eyes to

focus on his. Her voice was an unintentional sexy growl. "It might be more dangerous for me here."

"I could sleep on the couch."

"But we both know you wouldn't."

They stared at each other. She was right, and Jake *did* know it. He didn't really give a damn, though. It was inevitable, wasn't it? From the day he'd heard her voice, he'd known what the outcome would be. Known what he *wanted* it to be.

She rose slowly. "Could you just give me a ride home? I think that'd be the smartest thing."

He stood, too, his gaze locking on hers from across the room. "Do you always do the smartest thing?"

Her mouth parted slightly and she took a deep breath. He could see her chest rise and fall beneath the T-shirt. "Not always, but in this case, I think I'd better. Don't you?"

He didn't answer; he couldn't. He turned and got his keys, then walked outside to his truck, her footsteps echoing behind his a second later.

When Jake pulled up to Sally's house a few minutes later, she was still numb. Numb, and scared, and more confused than she'd ever been in her life. Sally Beaumont was not a woman who moved fast—on anything—and she'd been so tempted to say yes and spend the night with Jake, that it shocked her.

He made her want to do reckless things.

He got out of the truck and came over to her side of the vehicle, then opened her door and held out his hand to help her. She took his warm fingers in hers and slid from the cab, but he didn't move away. Instead, he looked down at her and took a step closer.

Most of his face was in the shadow thrown off by the huge pecan tree that took up half her front yard. She couldn't see his expression, but she could feel the tension in his body. It radiated toward her and enveloped her like some kind of electrical field. She felt trapped.

"I should go inside first," he said. "Just to check out your house. Then I'll leave. I promise."

"Okay," she answered. "That's fine."

But neither of them moved.

Ever so slowly, he raised his hands and placed them on either side of her face. His touch was hot. His fingers stayed still for just a second, then he slid his right palm underneath her hair and behind her neck where he cupped the curve of her head. He tilted her back until her eyes were looking straight into his.

She thought for a moment he was going to say something, but then suddenly he seemed to change his mind. His eyes shifted and so did his expression and a moment later, he lowered his head and began to kiss her.

His lips were fuller and more demanding than she'd expected. When his mouth pressed against hers and his tongue slid forward, she realized he wasn't the kind of man who simply kissed a woman; he had expectations. He wanted what he was giving returned—in spades.

She hesitated, and then it seemed impossible to do anything but kiss him back. Her hands went around his waist and he dropped his to her back, and they moved closer, their lips never parting.

A tingle she hadn't felt in a very long time—if ever—started somewhere in the vicinity of Sally's gut and moved upward. A warmth spread with it, the kind of warmth that starts slow but grows quickly. She wanted Jake. Wanted him naked in her bed, her legs wrapped around him, their hands tangled together, their bodies sweaty and gleaming in the moonlight trapped in the sheets.

His hands slid downward. Her shorts were short and she could feel his fingers as they moved lower to brush exposed flesh. She groaned and he responded, pulling her closer to cup the weight of her bottom, his touch even more insistent, his fingers edging inward.

They stayed that way for a moment, Sally almost

dizzy. Finally, she gasped and pulled back, some shred of common sense finally awakening inside her.

"This—this isn't what I—I planned on," she managed.

He looked down at her, his eyes dark and heavy-lidded, his lips full. "You don't have to plan everything."

"Oh yes, I do."

"Why?"

"I—I've always been that way."

"Then maybe it's time for change, Sally." He said her name with a rumble. She felt it all the way down her body, which responded automatically. *Yes!*

"No." She shook her head. "Pl-planning is best. That way there are no surprises."

"There's always going to be surprises, darlin'. That's life." He tightened his arms around her and she thought he was going to kiss her again. But he didn't. He released her and made her wait on the porch while he checked out her house. It was fine, of course, and he left a few minutes later, promising to help with the car the next day. She went to bed, but she didn't go to sleep.

BOB ARRIVED at the cabin early the next morning, earlier than Jake would have liked. He hadn't gotten a lick of sleep; he'd tossed and turned and dreamed of brown eyes all night long. Finally he'd just gotten up, but he wasn't ready for company—not Bob's, anyway.

The screen door squeaked as Bob pushed it open. "You home?"

"Back here. In the bathroom."

Bob's heavy steps rattled the ancient wood floor. He stopped in the door to the bath, his eyes catching Jake's in the cloudy mirror as he scraped the razor over his cheeks.

"I saw the car," he said. "Helluva mess, huh?"

Jake nodded. "Somebody's mad. They could have just let the air out of the tires and accomplished the same goal."

Bob leaned against the doorway. "Any ideas?"

Jake told him about the three women he and Sally had discussed; Pearl, Loretta and Mary Margaret. Bob shook his head and laughed. "All the usual suspects, right?"

Jake grinned in response. "You got any better ones?"

Bob sobered. "As a matter of fact, I might. I stopped at the station this morning and did something I should have done when the rock went through her window. I called a buddy of mine in DPS and had him run all the names of everyone at

KHRD through their computer. It keeps track of all charges filed, whether they go to trial or not."

Jake's hand froze, the razor poised between the sink and his face. "And?"

"There's a new guy down at the station—an electrical engineer by the name of Ricky Carter—"

"He was here yesterday. At the party."

Bob nodded. "Yeah, well, he had a party of his own last year in San Antone. Seems he was arrested and charged with assault. He got unhappy with his girlfriend and took a baseball bat to her lawn ornaments."

Jake turned around slowly and stared at Bob. "Let me get this straight." He paused. "You found a guy that beat up a ceramic gnome?"

Bob nodded seriously, then arched one eyebrow. "*Seven* gnomes. And Snow White, too. There were crime scene photos." He closed his eyes and seemed to shudder. "It wasn't pretty, Nolte, I'm here to tell ya."

"And the reason you think this gnome killer could be behind Sally's problem is…?"

"The guy took the bat to his girlfriend's car after that…and then he tried to get her. He told the arresting office he'd overheard her talking about sex with some of her buddies and he didn't want her talking like that."

Jake dropped the towel he'd been using to wipe his face. "And Rita March still hired him?"

"She didn't know about it. The girlfriend dropped the charges and he didn't put them on his employment application. I called Rita this morning. She went to the office and checked."

"Sounds promising."

"Yeah." Jake paused. "And there's more... Seems like Mr. Carter asked Sally out when he first moved here three months ago. She turned him down and he was not happy about it. Wrote her some E-mail, telling her what a great thing she was passing up. Sally showed it to Rita, but they both decided to blow it off at the time."

"You think he could be behind the rock and the tires?"

"He might be using the situation just to harass her. Stranger things have happened."

They moved into the kitchen. Jake poured two cups of coffee from the pot he'd brewed earlier. "You tell Sally all this?"

"Not yet." Bob sipped from the cup and grimaced. "Damn! This tastes like sh—"

Jake spoke casually, ignoring the coffee critique. "I'm going over there this afternoon. I'll tell her for you. That way you can go on home..."

Bob met Jake's eyes across the scarred kitchen

counter. "*You're* going to see Sally this afternoon? Why?"

"I offered to help with the car. You know, see to the tires, all that."

Bob's gaze was speculative. "Elmer down at the Exxon usually handles that sort of thing pretty well."

Jake shrugged. "I offered and she accepted. Maybe she didn't want someone who uses glow-in-the-dark condoms messing with her car."

"How does she know *you* don't use 'em?"

Jake lifted his coffee mug and smiled over the rim. "How do you know she doesn't?"

SALLY KNEW HER MOTHER would call when she didn't show up at church that morning so she saved Rebecca the trouble. She phoned her first and gave her a rundown on what had happened to the car and the window.

Her mother was shocked. "Oh, dear. This is terrible. Maybe you should move in with us for awhile. It's not safe out there all by yourself at the lake."

Her answer was exactly what Sally expected, and somehow it made her feel better even as it exasperated her. "Mother, I'm fine. And besides, Jake can get here in five minutes." As soon as she spoke his name, Sally bit her tongue. What was she thinking? If her greatest goal was getting out of town, her mother's was getting Sally married.

"Jake? You mean, Bob's friend. That nice young man at the barbecue yesterday."

Sally closed her eyes. "That's him."

"Well..." Pause. "Are you...seeing him?"

Sally thought of Jake's emergence from the lake. She held back a giggle and dodged the question. "He's...um...helping Bob—with the case."

It took Sally another ten minutes to convince her mother she was fine, then they hung up. And Sally stared aimlessly at the wall over the couch. On a normal weekend after church, she'd drive down to the station, but without a car, she couldn't go into the office and without going into the office, she didn't know what to do. All at once, she realized how much she depended on her work to keep her busy. She had nothing else.

She wandered out to the porch and sat down on the swing. It faced the lake, and as she touched the floor with her toe to set the chair in motion, she let her mind return to the two topics it couldn't seem to leave alone: Who could be doing these bad things to her, and how attracted she was finding herself to Jake Nolte.

Strangely enough, she really wasn't too concerned about the rock or the car. No one in Comfort would want to seriously harm her; they were just trying to let her know they weren't happy. She had thought briefly of canceling the show, but she knew she wouldn't. *Too Hot For Comfort* had the potential to be a hit, and she enjoyed doing it.

No, the main thing on her mind was Jake. Every time she got around him, she felt itchy and hot— as if she were wearing a wool sweater that was too tight. He made it hard for her to breathe and even harder for her to concentrate...on anything but him.

By midafternoon, Sally was about to go nuts. She talked to Linda six times on the phone, she ate almost a whole jar of peanut butter, and she flipped through all the channels on the television set too many times to count. She was bound and determined not to call Jake, though. When the car was ready, he'd show up.

An hour later, he did.

Sally stood in the shade of her front porch and watched him pull into her driveway. He killed the engine of his pickup and climbed out, the hot afternoon sun highlighting his coal-black hair and making it gleam. He had on gold-rimmed sunglasses, jeans and a T-shirt. He walked slowly up to her porch, stopping just short of the steps.

"Your car's ready," he said. "I drove over to Kerrville to the discount place and got you four new tires. Elmer put them on for you. The car's at his shop now so I'll take you on over and you can pick it up.''

Sally had never thought of tires as a topic for romance, but the fact that he'd driven all that way just to save her some money... "You didn't have to do that,'' she said. "But I sure do appreciate it.''

"I didn't mind. I figured you'd pay me back...one way or another.''

Did everything the man say have sexual overtones...or was it just her? "I—I will pay you back. My purse is inside. I'll write you a check.''

He took two more steps to come up on the porch where she was holding the screen door. Taking off his glasses, he looked at her. "Actually, I was hoping for something more than a check.''

Her heart began to thud inside her chest.

"It's awful hot,'' he said. "How 'bout a glass of something cold and wet?''

Her legs went weak, and she smiled faintly. "Sure. I—I think I can manage that.'' She held the door open wider and he brushed past her. Or at least he started to. He stopped halfway through the door and looked down at her. His eyelashes were way too long and dark, she thought suddenly, her mouth going dry at his closeness. A man shouldn't be allowed to have eyelashes like that. It wasn't fair.

"Was your night all right?'' he asked. "No unwanted visitors?''

Only you in my dreams. "I—it was fine. Went right to sleep and never even woke up once."

His eyes pierced hers. She was lying like a big dog and he knew it. "Good," he said slowly. "I'm glad. Me, too."

Sally swallowed hard. A lump had lodged in her throat and she was having a hard time breathing. Finally, he stepped past her and entered the living room. Even though he'd been inside before, she hadn't quite realized at that time how much he seemed to fill up the space.

He nodded toward the picture window, but his eyes never left hers. "Got your glass repaired."

"Yes."

"Nice view."

"Thanks."

They met an instant later somewhere in the middle of the room. Sally wasn't sure who moved first, but it didn't seem to matter. All she knew was that one moment she was standing there, wishing he'd kiss her, and the next moment he was, his arms wrapped tightly around her, her breasts pushing against his chest. He murmured something deep and low in his throat. She didn't know what it was, and she didn't really care. All she could think about was his mouth on hers...his firm, wide lips, his warm insistent tongue, his hands...his hands that were everywhere at once.

They held on to each other as if to let go would court disaster. Finally, one of them came up for air. Stunned, Sally leaned back in the circle of Jake's arms and looked up at him.

"Wh-what's going on?"

"I think that's called kissing."

She shook her head. "That's not like any kissing I've ever encountered before."

"Then I guess you haven't been kissing the right guy."

Her heart flipped over. Twice. Then she reluctantly stepped back from him, breaking the embrace. "Jake—I—I don't know how to tell you this, but I'm not looking for a relationship right now."

"Good," he said. "Neither am I."

She blinked. "You aren't?"

He shook his head.

"But…" His words left her confused, a little disappointed, maybe even a little angry.

"Every kiss doesn't mean something cosmic, Sally. Sometimes a kiss really is just a kiss. Don't analyze it, okay? Just sit back and enjoy the ride."

"Sometimes a kiss is just a kiss." She repeated the words, as if trying them out.

"That's right." He took up the space she'd put between them, then bent over and brushed the corner of her mouth with his lips. It was just a simple touch, not even sexual, but it sparked something deep inside her, and suddenly she wasn't so sure he wasn't lying.

Sometimes a kiss is just a kiss...

She looked up at him, into those deep blue eyes, her mind spinning like the reels down at the station. *Yeah,* she thought suddenly, *and sometimes it's a helluva lot more.*

6

"I JUST DON'T KNOW how to describe it." Sally looked at Linda helplessly. "I've never felt this way before."

They were sitting at the Dairy Queen eating lunch. Well, Linda was eating. Sally was poking at the taco salad she'd ordered and trying to describe her feelings. They'd already discussed the astonishing news Jake had told her about Ricky Carter and they'd moved on to something more interesting— Jake himself.

"You're really falling for this guy, aren't you?" Linda had wonder in her voice. "Man, after all these years...I can't believe it."

"I am not *falling* for anyone! I just...I just find him very appealing, that's all. And it's purely physical." The last came as an afterthought, then Sally realized it was true. She didn't really know anything about Jake beyond the barest of backgrounds. "I don't even know the guy."

"What's it worth to you to know more?" Linda speared a cherry tomato from Sally's bowl and waved the fork over the table in a grandiose gesture. "I might be able to help you out."

"What do you mean?"

She popped the whole tomato into her mouth and spoke around it. "Debbie told me all about him. I got the goods."

Sally wanted to act disinterested, but there was no way she could. Not after Sunday afternoon. Not after *that* kiss. She leaned across the table. "Give it up."

"Well, he grew up in Houston and lived there all his life. He's divorced. Was married five years. Her name was Sandra and she was a witch with a 'b.' Hated the fact he was a cop and gave him a hard time about everything. They went their separate ways and she hooked up with a computer salesman from Spokane."

Sally waved her hand. "Go on, go on..."

"Obviously they had no kids, but according to Debbie, he loves children. He's Brittany's godfather and always gives her incredible presents for her birthday and at Christmas. When he and Bob were partners back in Houston, he used to do volunteer work on his days off at a downtown shelter for homeless kids."

"Why'd he leave Houston?"

Linda squeezed more dressing out of a plastic container onto her salad, then answered. "He was shot during a robbery and after he recovered, he decided he'd had enough. He retired and moved here.''

Shot! Sally was stunned. My God, no wonder he wanted nothing more than peace and quiet. Who wouldn't?

''HI, CALLER, you're on the air. What's your question?''

''It's my boyfriend. He's...um...pressuring me, ya know? To...you know...do the nasty. I don't...you know...know what to do 'cause I ain't too interested in becoming a mama.''

Sally moved closer to the mike. Finally a question she could handle. The morning's show had been a tough one, the topic—methods of birth control—ignored as always. She'd answered questions on everything from her mother's favorite—bondage—to Viagra, and quite a few points in between. She and Linda had started handing out imaginary ribbons to the ''Winner of the Day.'' Qualifications for getting the award varied, but it had begun to boil down to the weirdest caller. Today's choice would be an easy one. It'd have to be the one guy with the heifer... Oh, yeah. There was definitely some serious sexual dysfunction going on there.

''How old are you, caller?''

"I'm thirteen and I—I don't live 'round Comfort. I'm from…um somewhere else."

"Well, you're smart to be thinking about the consequences of having sex so young. Being a parent is a scary thing, especially for someone who isn't ready."

"Yeah, yeah, I know. But…" The voice grew tentative and then died out.

Sally wanted to reach through the mike and give the poor girl a hug. "You probably think you're going to lose him, right?"

"He told me if I didn't give him what he wanted, there were plenty of girls who would, you know? And I don't wanna lose my boyfriend. I…I don't got nobody else."

"Do you have a mom and dad at home?"

The voice turned sullen. "Yeah, kinda. My mom…and a stepdad."

"Can you talk to them about this?"

"Oh, sure! Right! I can see that happening.…"

Sally felt the pressure build behind her eyes. This kid was all alone and facing serious stuff. "What if you relented and gave your boyfriend what he wanted? Is that a guarantee he'd stay?"

Silence came over the line. "I—I don't know. I hadn't thought about it."

"Well, let's think about it now. You could have

sex with him, and that still doesn't mean he'd be there forever, right?''

The answer was slow in coming, but it came. ''Yeah. He could bug out anytime.''

''That's right.''

''So...what you're saying is giving in to him don't mean I'll get what I want. It just means he'll get what he wants.''

Sally held a long breath then expelled it quietly. ''That's exactly right. He'd get everything—and you might end up with a disease or a baby. The first thing you said was you didn't want to be a mama. Becoming a parent is something everyone having sex should think about long and hard. You're very smart to be considering it now...before it's too late.'' Sally started to click off, then she stopped. ''Call me back, okay? Let me know what happens.''

''Yeah...yeah, I might do that. And thanks...''

WHEN SALLY came to the front door of the office later that evening, Jake was leaning against the fender of *her* car, waiting for her just as she had waited for him that day at the grocery store. She paused before stepping outside to watch him for a moment. Though he wore his sunglasses, she could tell his eyes were sweeping the parking lot, from one side to the other, slowly, thoroughly. He appeared to be looking for something or someone other than her.

He had on pressed slacks and a white pullover shirt with short sleeves that showed off his growing tan and taut biceps. His body language was interesting; he was alert, tense, but leaning against her fender as if he didn't have a care in the world. She opened the door and headed for where he stood.

As she approached, he smiled appreciatively. "Hi, there!"

"Hi, yourself." She was suddenly glad she'd worn her best suit to work that day. It was white with blue trim and she had on white pumps that went with it. "What's going on?"

"I was in the neighborhood and realized I was hungry. How about driving over to Medina with me? I hear there's a good steak house there."

She answered without thinking. It was the only way she could; if she thought about it, she would have said no, and she really didn't want to do that. "A steak sounds great."

They walked to his pickup side by side. She glanced up at him. "Did you hear the show?"

"Never miss it."

"What'd you think?"

He opened the car door for her and helped her inside. She sat down, then looked at him expectantly. "I think you gave some damn good advice," he said. "Especially to that last kid—the thirteen-year-old." He shook his head. "She's under some kind of pressure. I really felt sorry for her."

"I did, too." In the evening dusk, they looked at each other and something seemed to pass between them. A shared concern for kids who were alone, for kids who had questions but no answers and no one to turn to for help.

He closed the door and walked around to his side of the truck. A moment later they were pulling away from the station and heading toward the highway.

"When I came out of the station…"

"Yeah?" His voice was noncommittal.

"You seemed to be looking for someone."

"I was." He glanced at her then back at the road. "You."

"No one else?"

He glanced over at her again. They were driving west, into the sun. Behind his glasses she could see nothing but a glare. "I was looking for Ricky Carter," he confessed after a second.

She tensed. "Did Bob hear something else about him?"

Jake shook his head. "No, no. Nothing like that." He let the words die out and silence built inside the cab.

It hit her a second later. "You were hoping he'd

see you...waiting for me.'' Her voice held surprise and amazement.

He shrugged and said nothing.

A ribbon of warmth curled inside her chest. He wanted to protect her, keep her safe. No one had ever done that kind of thing for her before. Of course, she'd never needed it before, either, but it instantly made her feel wonderful.

...*sometimes a kiss is just a kiss...*

Sure, it was...

JAKE PULLED UP in front of the restaurant, parked, then opened Sally's door. Five minutes later they were sitting in a darkened booth, menus the size of the Houston phone book in their hands. He took one quick glance, then set the tome down. She studied hers for almost two full minutes. He watched her perfect face as she read each selection, considered it, then rejected it. In a way, it was amusing...and in another way it was scary. Had she studied him that carefully, too?

He didn't know why he cared—except that her lips were so damn soft and her curves so damn appealing that when they weren't together, he couldn't get either of them out of his brain. She was smart, too, smart and funny and caring. Before coming to Comfort, he didn't think women like Sally existed anymore. The ones he'd dated after

Sandra had been just like Sandra: hard, selfish and egotistical.

Sally finally put down the menu then looked at him from across the table. There was a small red candle in the center between them and the flame of it danced in the breeze from an overhead fan. Her brown eyes gleamed in the light.

"I found out something about you today," she said slowly.

"And that was?"

"That you worked with kids back in Houston. Homeless kids. Is that true?"

"Yeah, it's true. Debbie been flapping her mouth?"

"Nothing's a secret in Comfort. You ought to know that by now." She put her arms on the table and stared at him. "Why that? Why homeless kids?"

"I saw too many youngsters living on the streets in Houston. I'd take them to the shelters every night, and one thing just led to another. Before I knew it, I was spending my Saturdays down there, too."

"Did you enjoy working with them?"

He thought carefully then answered. "I don't know that 'enjoy' is the right word. I felt like I was able to do some good, and when I was there, I didn't think about my own problems, as pitiful as they were in comparison. In a way it was selfish of me—I did it to help myself as much as the kids.''

The waitress came, took their orders, then left. Sally reached for a piece of bread from the basket the woman had placed in the center of the table.

"That's how it always works," she said, tearing the roll into smaller, dainty pieces. "You never do some good that a little bit doesn't rub off on you. That's to be expected."

"Is that what's happening to you?"

She lifted her eyes. "What do you mean?"

"With the show. Are you getting something good out of that?"

"I had no altruistic motives for that show, believe me. I want out of Comfort and a hit could be the way that happens."

"But you're helping people."

She waved her hand in the air, bread crumbs flying. "I don't know..."

"Well, I know. And so does that teenager who called today." He pursed his lips and made a kissing sound. "And so does that guy who's in love with his heifer. He definitely needed some help and I'm sure the cow's appreciative, too!"

She burst out laughing and shook her head. "You think? Bovine intervention? God, I am a friend to man and animals, alike! Who'da thought it?"

Their drinks came and over the cold draft beer,

Jake spoke slowly. "Tell me about your parents," he said. "When I suggested you stay with them that first day you seemed real reluctant. How come? I thought you had the perfect childhood growing up here."

She took a long swallow of her drink, her throat moving so seductively in the candlelight, he couldn't take his eyes off her. She put the glass down carefully and spoke. "I'm an only child. My parents love me dearly and I love them. But sometimes they smother me. They're very conservative and very careful and I've been the focus of their lives since the day I was born." She played with a napkin on the table. "Because they've always been so involved in my life, I've always felt...I don't know...almost responsible for them, in a way. Like I have to do really well, you know...so they're happy."

"Is that why you came back to Comfort after college?"

"I knew it would please them," she confessed, "but jobs were scarce. When I found this one, I knew I should grab it."

Jake couldn't help himself; he reached across the table and took her hand in his. "You aren't really responsible for them. You know that, don't you?"

"I know. But I love them and I wanted to do the

right thing." She shook her head. "They'll live in Comfort forever. I just hope I don't."

OVER DESSERT, he asked her about her plans. "Why do you want to leave Comfort so much? It doesn't seem all that bad to me."

She leaned back against the booth, her fingers still wrapped around her coffee mug. It'd been a fantastic evening. They'd eaten so much she felt stuffed and they had talked about everything under the sun. At his question, she tensed, though, and she didn't exactly know why.

"I'm tired of living in a place where everyone knows your business. You can't sneeze without someone down the street saying 'God bless you.'"

He raised one dark eyebrow. "There's worse things they can say."

"I know, I know." She leaned closer to him. "Here's a perfect example, though. Mabel Slider and her first cousin are sitting one table over. By sunrise tomorrow, everyone in Comfort will know we were here and that we shared a piece of apple pie for dessert. Doesn't that bug you?"

"Not really. Now if you'd wanted lime pie, yeah, but apple—"

She swung a mock fist in his direction and grazed the brick wall of his shoulder. He caught her fingers with his and held them fast. She could almost feel the burn of Mabel's stare.

Her voice came out breathless. "And now they'll know we were holding hands."

He brought her fingers up to his lips and kissed them one by one. "And what will they say after that...?"

Her breath came fast and in shortened gulps. "That they were sure the hand-holding was followed by a night of wild debauchery. I already have that reputation, you know. After all, I'm the S.E.X. expert."

"It seems a real shame they have to make that up. Can't we at least give them a little something to base it all on?" Without waiting for her to answer, he suddenly leaned across the table and pressed his lips against hers in a gentle but insistent kiss. He tasted of coffee and apple pie and desire. The room dissolved into a haze of nothingness and she melted under the promise of his mouth.

When he pulled back a second later, she was breathing even harder than she had been before. They got up and left, walking past Mabel's table without another glance, their eyes locked on each other, one thing on their minds.

7

SHE WASN'T SURE where Jake was taking them, but after they got in the truck and drove off into the darkness, Sally didn't care. She was sitting close to him in the pickup, and he'd draped his arm over her legs, pulling her even closer. His thigh was pressed against her own, and a tense awareness filled the cab. He wanted to make love to her.

She wanted him, too.

He reached over and turned on the radio. The soft, sexy voice of the nighttime DJ—Dee Loving—wafted out. At six foot four, with a ragged goatee and tattoos up and down his arms, he looked more like a Hell's Angel than a nighttime disc jockey, but his program was one of the most popular at the station. There were a lot of lonely people in Comfort after ten o'clock. They constantly called with requests for forlorn songs and dedicated them to lovers long gone. Sally didn't listen often; it made her sad. She closed her eyes now, though, and let the music wash over her. The sound of the song mingled with the warmth coming from Jake's body and the smell of his aftershave. For just one second, Sally let herself wonder what it might be like if they were having a relationship. A *real* relationship…the kind that led to the altar and children and PTA and all the stuff that went with being a family.

It was a curious sensation. She'd never allowed herself to seriously contemplate that idea with any other man. Why now? Why Jake? Sure, he was handsome and sexy and smart and he could melt her with a kiss, but she had things to do, places to go. She couldn't let him get in the way of that, could she? Without being really conscious of what she was doing, Sally began to examine the situation from every angle she could think of, her analyzing mind picking it apart and putting it back together a thousand different ways.

The next thing she knew, the truck was slowing and had stopped. She looked around and realized they were on the west side of the lake. It was spread out in front of them, and the water shone like a mirror, the reflection of the summer moon a wavery silver disk that seemed to float on top. Jake rolled down both the windows then turned off the engine. The sweet smell of pine immediately came into the cab, along with the kind of sudden silence that only a summer night can hold. Complete and utter quiet. After a bit, the stillness faded and was replaced by crickets and owls and a soft wind dancing through the leaves.

Jake turned to her, his arm along the back of the seat, his fingers curling softly around her shoulder. "I found this spot the other night," he said, leaning closer. "I got lost, made a wrong turn. After I figured out where I was, I wanted you to see it, too."

His breath was warm against her cheek. Sally was sure he could hear her heart, it was pounding so fast and so loudly. "It is beautiful," she said.

"Do you know where we are?" He leaned closer and nuzzled her ear. His lips were soft, but his cheeks were rough. The combination of the two sensations—a feathery touch and a scratchy rasp—was almost more than she could bear.

"N-not exactly."

"Look straight ahead." His voice was a low growl, sexy and deep. "Across the lake."

She didn't want to look at anything; she wanted to turn and face him then rip off all his clothes, but she took a deep breath and did as he instructed. In the distant black, all she could see were two twinkling lights. They looked as if they were side by side, but she knew better. The span between them was distorted by their position across the water.

"It's your house," he said quietly. "Your house and Bob's cabin. You didn't know you could see them from this road?"

She shook her head. "I had no idea."

He eased a finger down her cheek. The touch was soft and barely there, but she felt it. Oh, boy, did she feel it! The warmth of his skin, the barest scrape of his nail, the tiniest hint of what might come. All her senses seemed heightened, on alert.

"You can walk all the way around the lake from here and get to our backyards without a soul seeing you. I went that way the other night," he said. "And I saw you through your window. You really should close your drapes at night."

"I—I don't have drapes."

In the moonlight his eyes gleamed. "Do you understand what I'm saying, Sally? Whoever threw that rock through your window could have easily parked in this spot, hiked around the lake, then tossed the rock and run back here. They didn't have to come down your drive or even approach in a boat."

She nodded and looked back across the water. Her porch light twinkled in the distance then seemed to flicker and go out. It was only the wind, moving limbs and leaves between her house and where she sat, but for a second, her heart stuttered.

Jake took her chin between his thumb and finger and turned her to face him again. "There's someone out there—some kind of nut—who doesn't approve of what you're doing, and it's beginning to make me nervous.''

Sally's pulse hammered, but that was because of Jake's closeness, not his words. "No one would hurt me here in Comfort," she said.

"You don't know that for sure."

"Jake, please…the most serious crime we've had in the past five years was when Royce Lee's barn was torched. Royce only had his '57 Chevy inside, but that car was his pride and joy. It took Bob a day to figure out Royce had a girlfriend *and* a wife and they'd found out about each other. They wanted to teach him a lesson. One of 'em poured the gasoline and the other lit the match.''

Jake chuckled, but his eyes weren't laughing. "I hear what you're saying, babe, but this could be more serious. People who get riled up about stuff like this don't always have a good handle on reality and that makes them unpredictable. It could be a rock through the window today but tomorrow it could be a shot from a .22. I don't want that happening to you.'' He paused then tightened his fingers around her shoulder. "I brought you here so you could see what I was talking about. I want you to get some drapes and I want you to be careful.''

"Anything else?''

He looked thoughtful for a moment, a slight frown marring his forehead before it cleared and his eyes captured hers. "As a matter of fact, yes. There is one more thing…"

"What's that?"

He pulled her toward him and lowered his head, his mouth almost covering hers. "Just this," he murmured. "Just this…"

SHE'D BEEN EXPECTING him to kiss her, but Sally still wasn't prepared. Just as before, his mouth felt soft and demanding, yet this time, there was even more to the kiss. She wouldn't have thought it possible, but he seemed to want an even deeper response from her than he had before. His hands were warmer, his tongue slicker, his murmurs more determined. She responded before she could even think about it.

They kissed for one long moment, then Jake pushed her gently away. Startled, she looked at him, then she realized what he was doing when he moved closer to her and out from under the steering wheel. With his hands on her shoulders he turned her around then pulled her into his lap. The position was even more intimate, and Sally's breath caught in her throat as he began to slowly unbutton her jacket. Through the haze of her growing desire, she wondered about the sanity of what they were doing. Two grown-ups, sitting in a car, making out like teenagers. It seemed preposterous, but it felt absolutely delicious. She wasn't about to stop it from happening.

Instead, she concentrated on the moment. The cool breeze as it came into the truck and caressed her skin. Her exposed bra that shone in the moonlight. Jake's hands as they covered the delicate cups a moment later. He groaned and bent his head to kiss the slope of her breasts, then he dipped lower, his mouth replacing his hands as he gently sucked her nipples through the lace.

She groaned and arched her back, the wet feel of his tongue a teasing torment. Holding the weight of each breast, he brought them closer and buried his face between them. Again she felt the contrast of his warm soft hands and his face, stubbled and rough. In the morning, she'd have reminders of his beard, but now—at this moment—nothing mattered but getting closer to him.

She reached for his shirt and slowly began to unbutton it. When it fell open, she slipped her hands inside and let them slide over his chest. It was hard and firm and she pressed herself against him, even the barrier of her bra too much. As if sensing her thoughts, Jake reached around and undid the clasp. She slipped out of her jacket, then he helped her shed it all before pulling her closer. Skin to skin, they held on to each other in the cab of the truck, Sally's heart thundering, nothing more important to her now than feeling Jake, kissing Jake, wanting Jake.

With one arm wrapped around her, he slid his hand under her skirt and started to kiss her again, his lips so perfectly melded to hers, Sally wondered why she'd ever bothered to kiss anyone else. This was what it was all about, she wondered with part of her brain. This was what they talked about in the movies, what you read about in the books—this was it! She was so deep into the feeling of his hands, his mouth, his touch, it took more than a second to realize something was wrong—terribly wrong—and by then it was too late.

The cab of the truck filled with blinding light and a deep, disembodied voice spoke from out of the darkness. "Excuse me for interrupting folks, but could you please step out of the car and let me see some ID?"

JAKE'S FIRST IMPULSE was to reach under the seat and pull out his .45; then he remembered where he was. This was Comfort, not Houston. The guy with the flashlight wasn't someone out to rob them—he was wearing a uniform and had his own gun on his hip, even though he barely looked old enough to shave.

Holding a hand above his eyes to keep the glare

out, Jake shielded Sally with his chest and spoke to the kid. "How 'bout dousing the light there, son?"

"Please step out of the vehicle, sir."

Bob had trained 'em well.

"Go ahead," Sally whispered at his back. "I—I think I'm decent."

Jake eased open the door and stepped outside. "My wallet's in my pocket," he said. "I'm going to reach inside and get it."

The black metal flashlight beamed a steady path between them. "That's fine."

Jake removed the folded leather wallet slowly, then opened it to his Texas driver's license. He handed it to the young officer.

A second later, the kid gulped; Jake could actually hear him. "Y-You're Jake Nolte? Sheriff Mac's friend?"

"That's me."

"Hot damn, sir, I'm sorry! I—I didn't know. Sheriff told us to keep an eye on this spot and that's what I was doing. I saw your truck with the lights off and everything, and I didn't even think it might be you. Golly, sir, I'm sorry. I—"

"It's okay, son." Jake took his ID back and slipped it into his wallet. "You're doing your job and that's what you're supposed to be doing. I guess you radioed in before you got out of the cruiser?"

"Oh, yessir! That's SOP."

Jake nodded wearily. Great, just great! Bob would never let him live this one down. Never in a thousand years...

The deputy touched his fingers to his cap and started backing up. "Well, you two have a nice night now." He nodded in the direction of Jake's back. "See you later, Sally Anne. Take care."

A faint voice came from behind Jake. "See ya later, Billy Ray. You watch out, too."

Jake stood still until the officer got back into his car and drove away. He then turned slowly and looked at Sally. She was standing barefoot in the pine needles, her hair twisted and mussed. He'd kissed off all her lipstick and she'd buttoned her jacket wrong; it hung lopsided with a teasing gap right in the front that allowed him a tiny glimpse of bare breast.

"Want to start over?"

She shook her head. "I think we'd better get home. I have a clean record—I want to keep it that way."

SALLY WATCHED Jake's taillights disappear down the driveway. He'd walked her to the door, checked out her house, then finally let her go inside. But not before he'd kissed her once...and then once again.

Touching her swollen lips with her fingertips, she

closed the front door and locked it. What was happening to her? What was Jake doing to her?

"Turning my life upside down," she answered out loud in the empty silence of her home. "He's turning it upside down and inside out."

Dangling her pumps in one hand and her purse in the other, she walked into the kitchen where she dropped both things on the countertop and opened the refrigerator door. She reached inside for the milk, opened it and drank straight from the white plastic jug. She had to get a grip on her life. Things at the station were just about to break—she could feel it—and when they did, she didn't want her thinking clouded with images of Jake Nolte and his bright blue eyes.

The light in the refrigerator cast a ghostly shadow against the kitchen's cabinets. She stared at it in the darkness. Her plan didn't include him...or his kisses...or the deep ache she was feeling right now inside her, the ache that had started the minute he'd picked her up outside the station and taken her away.

So what was she going to do?

She replaced the milk carton and shut the refrigerator door. Leaning against it, she closed her eyes and thought. Thought of his fingers against her throat and the feel of his chest under her hand. She thought of the chances she had of ever finding another man who could kiss her like Jake. She thought of her show and where it might take her.

After a moment, she turned and walked through the darkened house to her bedroom. She stripped off her clothes and fell into bed…and wished he was lying beside her.

RITA CALLED SALLY into her office bright and early Monday morning. When Sally passed by her desk, Tiffany's eyes were so narrow and suspicious, she knew immediately word had spread. Mabel had done her duty and told everyone she could that she'd seen Sally and Jake at the restaurant. Actually, Sally had already guessed as much. In church on Sunday morning, she'd gotten a few stares, but she'd thought it was because of the show. She hadn't suspected Mabel was *that* efficient.

Without saying a word, Sally smiled sweetly at Tiffany and went into the inner sanctum.

Rita took off her reading glasses as Sally came in and pointed to one of the chairs in front of her desk. "Have a seat. I just finished a phone conversation I think you'd like to hear about."

Sally went tense. There was only one thing Rita could mean. She'd gotten a call about the show either from an affiliate or another local—but larger—station. Sally sat down, gripped the arms of the chair and looked at her boss. One side of her

Rita stared at her. "Have you ever heard that name before? Howard Atlas?"

Through the fog of her anxiety, Sally tried to concentrate. "It does sound kinda familiar."

"He owns two stations in Austin…"

"Ohmigod!"

"And one in San Antonio." Rita arched her perfectly plucked eyebrows. "He's got three more scattered across west Texas."

Sally fell against the back of her chair, her hand against her chest. "Are you kidding me?"

Rita ignored her question. "This is important, Sally. For the station and for you. KFFD is very interested and though they haven't made us an offer yet, it could be coming. I know you had some reservations about doing the show at first and I want to make sure you don't have those qualms anymore. If you have any concerns, now is the time to talk about them." Her steely gaze caught Sally's and wouldn't let it go. "*After* we start talking to KFFD is *not* the time. Do you understand what I'm saying?"

"I understand." Sally nodded slowly. Rita couldn't have spelled it out any clearer. Her reputation—and that of KHRD—was on the line, along with Sally's. "I—I do understand…"

"So tell me."

"Tell you what?"

"Tell me you don't have any more qualms. About the show, about the content, about anything. Tell me the only thing you'll ask is 'how high?' when KFFD says 'jump.'"

"How high?" Sally said tightly. "I got it... How high?"

JAKE HAD TRIED to lay low and stay out of sight, but he'd known it wouldn't last forever. He was in town, washing his truck, when Bob finally caught up with him.

The black-and-white slowed as it passed Jake then it did a U-turn in the middle of the street. Wheeling into the driveway of the three-stall car wash a second later, the cruiser stopped. Through the windshield, Jake could see Bob pick up his mike and call in to Dispatch. A moment after that, he opened the car door and sauntered over to where Jake stood, the pressurized wand in his hand spitting out the last of its soapy water.

"Hey, there, Jake. How's it going?"

Bob pretended to act casual, his hands in his pockets, his face neutral behind his mirrored sunglasses. Jake knew him too well, though.

"Go ahead on," Jake drawled. "You're here to pull my chain, so you might as well start yankin'. The quicker you start, the sooner you'll be finished."

"I swear I don't know what you're talking about, Jake." Bob's expression looked sincere. "You in some kind of trouble or something?"

"You know damn good and well what I'm talking about." Jake turned, the hose still in his hand. Bob did a quick step back to avoid the spray. "Your pup of a deputy is too good. I'm sure you have all the details, including a written report."

"That I do...that I do." Bob leaned against the wall of the car wash. "Including the name of the lady involved. You getting serious with Sally Anne, Jake?"

"Not as serious as I would have if Deputy Dog hadn't intervened."

"You'll have other opportunities...if she wants you to."

Jake flipped the switch on the wall and changed the soap to water. He began to hose down the truck, rinsing the white foam off. Bob stood by expectantly. Finally Jake turned to him. "What?" he demanded.

"Well—are you?"

"Am I what?"

"Serious about her."

"What are you—her father or something?"

"I'm *not* her father, but I am *your* friend." His attitude shifted. "So I just wanted to remind you of where you are."

Jake cut the water off, then faced Bob again, all without saying a word.

"If you're falling for Sally, I'll be your best man and break out the champagne. If you think you're going to have a fling, then I'm here to tell you it don't work that way. Not in Comfort."

Jake's stare was steady. "I know how to treat a woman, Bob."

"I know you do, and it's not my intention to tell you otherwise. All I'm saying is people are already talking. They've got the two of you behind a white picket fence with babies in the backyard. Sally Anne may think she wants out of Comfort, but you need to remember, she grew up here and she's lived here almost all her life. If other people are thinking that, you can bet it's crossed her mind, too." Bob took off his glasses and stared at Jake. "I think you should know her daddy came to see me yesterday. He asked me some questions—about you. What does that say?"

Stunned, Jake shook his head. "Damn! What'd he ask?"

"The usual—where you came from, what you're doing here. How long you plan on staying…that kind of stuff." Bob took off his hat and hit it once against his thigh before putting it back on his head. "Look, here, bud, I don't want to see you get in over your head so I dropped by to tell you what's going on. That's all. You're a grown man and you can make your own mistakes."

8

"I WANT TO KNOW more about M&M."

Sally glanced quizzically through the glass of the booth toward Linda. Linda shook her head in obvious confusion as well. Sally spoke into the mike. "M&Ms? You mean like the candy?"

"No, no. You know, like tying up people and whipping 'em and stuff. I saw this movie the other night and they talked about M&M all the time. What's that stand for, anyhow?"

Sally's forehead cleared, and Linda dissolved into giggles. Sally couldn't hear her, of course, but she could see her friend's face as it turned red and she started to shake. Sally managed to hold her own laughter back. She'd gotten really good at that.

"I think you're talking about S&M," Sally answered. "That stands for sadism and masochism. These are two sexual practices some people enjoy which involve the giving of pain—sadism—or the acceptance of pain—masochism. The partners may use a lot of different aids. As you mentioned, sometimes whips are involved and frequently bondage is employed as well." *Are you listening, Mom?* "Does that answer your question, caller?"

"Yeah, I guess. But one last thing...this dominatrix woman. What's she got to do with it all? Dish out pain?"

Sally grinned. "The job of a domimatrix is to administer whatever the client wants, but yes, that's what she basically does—dish out pain."

"Well, hell's bells, I think I've found a new profession for my wife! Thanks a bunch!"

Sally cued in the ending commercial. Who would think in little ol' Comfort, people would have questions like that? She leaned back in her chair and shook her head. You never knew what was going on behind all those closed doors.

She left the station an hour later, exhausted and wrung out. Doing the show took much more out of her than she'd ever expected, and the letters that had started to arrive every day, rain or shine, didn't help things. They were usually written with crayons but sometimes in lipstick, which Sally was pretty sure was Passionate Papaya by Merle Norman. The notes were hateful and ugly, but harmless. Sally had gotten to the point where she just sent them, unread, over to Bob. There had been no more rocks or slashed tires, so if the letter writing kept the unhappy listener busy, that was great. Today, though—for a switch—she'd gotten a box of

Godiva chocolates and a fan letter. The glowing compliments had made her feel great. Obviously, not everyone agreed the show was the sure way to hell. Sally had chosen the biggest, fattest chocolate in the box, one decorated carefully with pink sugared flowers and tiny green leaves. She'd left the rest of the candy on her desk, knowing that by the time she came back in the morning, the gold foil container would be long empty—temptation removed.

She paused by the front door before stepping outside and scanned the parking lot. There were no people, just cars, and she felt a tiny spark of disappointment. Jake had been waiting for her almost every day, and she'd come to expect it. He must have had something else to do, she told herself, something more important than sharing a hamburger with her at the Dairy Queen. After their dinner in Medina, they'd kept their evenings simple, but each one had ended the same way, with growing kisses and tight embraces.

It was only a matter of time, she thought, crossing the parking lot. Only a matter of time. Then she'd let him into her bed and what had been inevitable from the very beginning would take place. Jake would make love to her. She'd make love to him. Then they'd come to that awful crossroads a relationship always faced afterward. To keep going or stop. To take it to a different level, or forget about it.

She opened the door to her car, freeing a blast of furnace-like air. Standing there for a moment, she argued with herself. *It doesn't have to be that way! Remember what Jake said? Sometimes a kiss is just a kiss....*

If that was true, then couldn't sex be just sex?

She climbed inside the car and the hot leather seat sizzled against her nylons. Served her right, she thought. She ought to be paying attention, not thinking about sex with Jake. Hell, she'd just talked about S.E.X. for more than an hour with a bunch of total strangers. Wasn't that enough for her?

She answered yes, but was apparently lying to herself. Thoughts of Jake filled her mind as she drove home—Jake coming out of the lake, his long, bronzed legs sturdy and streaming with water. Jake without his shirt, sitting inside his pickup, steaming up the windows. And that first night, when he'd stepped into her house, a stranger, and she hadn't been able to take her eyes off him.

Suddenly, the lights of an approaching car focused her attention on the road. It was going fast, eighty, maybe ninety miles an hour, then all at once it swerved into her lane. She yelled and slammed on her brakes, jerking the wheel at the same time.

The rest was a blur. The other vehicle screamed

by, and Sally got one quick glance. A passing face—white and scared—but nothing more. A second later, Sally lost control and found herself blinded by towering stalks, bouncing through Ed Yasik's cornfield.

JAKE HEARD Bob's cruiser before he saw it. The siren was blaring like all hell had broken loose. He couldn't imagine what would necessitate the piercing wail, but it immediately made him uneasy. He was standing on the porch, waiting, when the car slid up in front of the house and rocked to an unsteady stop.

Bob opened his door and stepped outside the car. "C'mon. We got somewhere to go."

Jake didn't ask any questions. He sprinted to the car and barely made it inside before Bob was fishtailing out of the driveway and heading back down the lane.

"What the hell's going on?" Jake asked, gripping the door handle and looking over at his friend. "The local bank been robbed or something?"

"Or something," Bob answered grimly, throwing him a sideways glance. "Sally Anne just got run off the road. Some yahoo forced her car into Ed Yasik's cornfield."

At Bob's words, Jake's stomach took a bounce and fell to his feet. He'd never experienced this

particular sensation before so he wasn't quite sure
how to handle it. Throwing up seemed most likely.
"Is she—"

"She's fine, she's fine, but her car's banged up
and she's scared out of her wits."

Jake's stomach righted itself, but the sick feeling
didn't leave. A sweep of anger joined it. "Who in
the hell hit her? Was it an accident? Did they stop?
Are you—"

"They didn't actually hit her, but beyond that,
you know what I know, Jake. I was already home
when she called the station. Dispatch called me and
I headed straight out. Only stopped to get you first.
We'll be there in ten minutes and you can ask her
yourself."

They were there in five, Bob slamming on the
brakes in front of a white frame farmhouse, a cloud
of dust accompanying their stop. Jake jumped out
of the cruiser before Bob could even kill the engine.

The screen door squeaked open and a pudgy man
in a tan jumpsuit came out onto the porch. He had
on a John Deere cap and the right side of his face
looked as though he'd been in a prize fight, a knot
the size of a golf ball distorting his jaw. He spit off
the side of the railing, and Jake realized a wad of
tobacco was responsible for the man's appearance.

"Where is she?" Jake demanded.

"Where's who?" the man responded laconically.

"Sally Beaumont."

"Who're you?" was his answer.

Bob reached Jake's side and made the quick introductions. "Ed, this is Jake Nolte, a friend of mine—and of Sally's. Is she inside?"

The man's eyes shifted to Bob. "Yep. The gal's okay. Jes' shook up a little—"

Jake charged past the farmer and pushed through his front door. It took a moment for his eyes to adjust to the dimness. Then things came into focus. He was in a living room, made dark with blinds and drapes. Sally was sitting on the edge of a worn brown sofa while a woman in a faded housedress dabbed carefully at her face. Jake's heart thudded and suddenly he couldn't catch his breath; his chest was as tight as a lug bolt on a tire.

Sally jerked her head up and their gazes locked. Ignoring the protests of her erstwhile nurse, she leaped from the couch just as Jake took two steps toward her. They collided in the center of the tiny room and he wrapped his arms around her. Her body felt frail and shaky and something welled inside him. It was a mixture of anger and disbelief and horror. How could anyone in the world want to harm this incredible woman? He pulled back and looked down into her face.

"Are you all right?"

Her brown eyes warmed to a darker shade of

chocolate. "I am now," she whispered. "But don't turn loose, okay? I—I need you."

"Turning loose of you is not an option," he said roughly. "Don't worry about *that*."

With his arms around her, Jake led her outside onto the front porch, into the sunshine, and for the first time, he took a good look at her face. She had a small cut over one eye, which he wanted to lean down and kiss, but he held himself back because he knew once he started, he wouldn't want to stop, and Bob was coming up the steps.

Bob reached out to Sally, then dropped his hand when he saw that Jake was holding on to her. "Sally Anne—what the hell happened?"

She shook her head, then winced at the motion. "I'm not too sure. I—I was driving home, minding my own business, when this car just came out of nowhere. I thought it was going to hit me for sure. I was sailing over the ditch and into Ed's field before the damned thing even finished going by."

"The car was coming in the opposite direction?"

"Yes."

"What kind of vehicle was it?" Jake tried to keep his voice even, but it was a struggle with all the emotions fighting inside him. "Did you get the make? The model?"

She shook her head again. "I don't know. It was white—maybe tan. Some kind of pale color. And it was a car, not a truck. I saw the driver's face, but everything happened too quickly. All I saw was white skin, dark hair. I couldn't even tell if it was a man or a woman.''

"Where's your car now?" Bob pulled out a notebook. "Do we need to call for the wrecker?"

"It's still in my back forty," answered Ed Yasik, who had suddenly emerged from the house. He aimed a brown squirt over the porch railing and spoke from around the gob in his jaw. "I can pull it out with my tractor. She's scratched up a mite, but she'll start, I reckon."

Bob nodded. "Okay—we'll have you do just that, but I want to look at it before it's moved." He turned to Sally. "First, I'll take you over to the hospital."

"Oh, Bob, I don't need to see a doctor," she protested. "I'm fine, really. It's just a little cut." She looked up at Jake, dissolving him with her expression and her words. "Could you just take me home, Jake?"

He started to object—maybe she *did* need to see a doctor—but she spoke again.

"Please," she begged him softly, her eyes filling up. "I'm okay. I just want to go home. I want to go home and have you hold me."

WHEN THEY GOT BACK to Sally's place, Jake made a pot of coffee while Sally changed her clothes and cleaned herself up. She followed the tempting aroma of coffee outside to find that he'd already poured her a cup.

She sank to the swing where he sat and they drank their coffee in silence. Jake seemed to understand she didn't want to talk, didn't want to do anything but rest. Finally, he turned to her. It was almost dark on the porch; the sky behind them was streaked with purple and red. She could barely see his eyes, but she could see enough to know they were shining. His voice was gruff.

"It's not too late for me to take you to the hospital. Are you sure you're all right?"

"I'm okay, but I would feel better..." she said slowly, "if you'd put your arms around me and kiss me."

Taking the coffee mug from her hands, he set it down on a nearby table, then turned to face her once more. Very slowly, very tenderly, he put his hands on either side of her face, cradling her. "I can definitely do that," he said. He paused then slowly, he edged his thumb over her bottom lip.

The moment stretched on, then he leaned closer to her and replaced his thumb with his lips. He kissed her so gently that she could barely feel the caress. He pulled back. "Does anything hurt?"

She shook her head. "No."

He nodded once, then angled his head toward hers, kissing her again, still letting his lips barely touch hers. She realized she was going to have to reassure him in a more convincing manner, so Sally put her arms around his neck and pulled him toward her. He hesitated, but she deepened her kiss, edging her tongue into his mouth and moaning against his lips. He seemed to acquiesce and suddenly he was bringing her to him as well, pulling her into his lap as they'd sat in his truck before.

The T-shirt and shorts she'd changed into offered little protection from the heat of his chest and body. Curling against him, Sally could feel his warmth and his interest, as well. She slipped her hand under his shirt and threaded her fingers through the hair on his chest. It was coarse and thick and without thinking about it anymore, she leaned back and pulled his shirt over his head. She wanted to get as close to him as she could. She needed her skin against his. She needed to feel his heartbeat with more than just her hands.

She needed him.

He mimicked her actions, pulling her own shirt off, then leaning back and staring at her in the darkness. She hadn't bothered with a bra and his eyes went slowly down her body, his gaze as hot and compelling as if he were touching her with his hands instead. By the time his look came back to her face, her breath was nowhere to be found and her heart was pounding, fast and furious.

"You're beautiful," he said, his voice husky and deep. "Perfect."

Sally started to shake her head in denial, but she couldn't move. He'd reached out, and with one finger, he was tracing a line around her breasts, first one and then the other. Again his touch was so gentle, so fleeting, it barely registered, yet it left a trail of heated desire she couldn't have ignored if her life had depended on it.

She hadn't imagined the start of their lovemaking to be like this at all. Their previous encounters had been hot—to the flashing point—but now that they both knew the inevitable was about to occur, it seemed as if time had slowed down, almost stopped. Heart-racing desire was building up inside her—and him, too, she was sure—but both of them were overcome by the moment. Through the fog of her wanting, she realized why. She wanted to discover him, slowly and with appreciation. He didn't want to rush, either.

She reached for him, her hands tracing his chest, then pressing flat against the wall of his muscles. Beneath her touch, his skin felt fevered. She brought her face to the place where her fingers rested and began to kiss him, her mouth planting a crooked line up and down his chest to his shoulders and lower. He smelled clean and soapy and she wanted to get so close to him that she wouldn't be able to tell where he began and she stopped.

He groaned, his hands now on her breasts, spreading over their fullness. Could he tell how hard she was breathing? How fast her heart was pounding? She knew he could, but she didn't care. She didn't care about anything except getting closer to him.

He spoke against her mouth. "Do you want to go inside?"

"I—I have blinds," she managed to get out. "I put them up after you showed me the house from across the lake."

"Pull them," he said.

She tore herself from his embrace and reached over the swing to the wall behind them. Unwrapping a cord from around a bracket, she let the platted blind unravel. It fell down with a clatter, enveloping them in sudden privacy and even less light than before. She turned back to Jake and smiled.

He smiled back, but his expression changed quickly—a yearning intensity replacing everything else. Standing up beside her, he pulled her to him and began to kiss her, his tongue pressing into her mouth, his fingers going to the waistband of her shorts. She helped him. The rasp of her zipper was loud in the silence of the dusk, then the sound of his own echoed a few moments later. They squirmed out of their last pieces of the clothing, mouths still pressed against each other's. Sally's need grew to a level she'd never before experienced as they held on to each other, the length of their bodies touching in the darkness.

Her hands roamed over his back and buttocks. Everywhere they touched, her fingers found taut muscle and smooth skin...until she reached around, to the front of his thigh. His scar was slick and polished, a thick line against his skin. She ran her fingers over it.

"Does it bother you?" he asked, moving his lips from her mouth to her neck.

"Of course not," she whispered.

He pulled her even closer, sucking gently at her neck, biting a little bit and sending heated stabs of needy desire to her core.

She groaned in response, her hands moving over his erection to cradle him between her fingers. He sucked in his breath and seemed to hold it as she eased her hands up and down, slowly, provocatively.

"Don't plan on doing that too long." His voice was hoarse.

"I won't," she said, gasping slightly as his fingers eased down her leg to find the juncture of her thighs. "I—I promise."

"That's good," he said, slipping his hand between her legs. "That's really good."

She didn't know if he was referring to her touch or his, but she didn't care, either way. She gave herself up to the feel of his fingers, to the smooth rhythm of his hand against her body, his touch against her core. He seemed to know exactly what she wanted, exactly what she needed and with skillful delight, he brought her to an earth-shattering climax. She fell against him, breathing hard. He took her weight easily—as if it were nothing—and eased them down onto the swing. It moved gently, the ropes creaking, the night breeze easing in between the slats of the blinds, as he pulled her on top of him.

A second later, he was inside her, and once again Sally was lost. The world could have ended at that moment, and she would never have known. Beyond the feel of Jake's warmth inside her, the touch of his hands on her back, there was nothing. There was only Jake.

He gripped her shoulders and his head fell against the bench, the muscles and cords in his neck growing taut and thick as his rhythm built. He cried out her name and a moment later, she cried out his.

9

THEY WERE IN SALLY'S BED when the phone rang the next morning. For a fleeting second, Sally wondered what she'd say if her mother was on the other end, then she looked over into Jake's heavy-lidded eyes.

They'd made love three times in the past twelve hours and she didn't give a big fat flip who knew it. She and Jake could have rolled around on the lawn of the county courthouse and it wouldn't have mattered a bit. He was the most incredible man she'd ever met and a lover unlike any she'd ever had. In between their bouts of wild passion, they'd talked about everything imaginable, including his divorce and the reasons behind it and her near miss with Max.

On the fourth ring, she reached over to pick up the phone, breaking her stare and her thoughts.

Rita's husky voice answered Sally's hello. She spoke with no preliminaries. "You okay?"

Sally sat up slowly. Her body was sore and achy, but she suspected that had more to do with the man beside her than her car accident. "I'm fine," she said. "How'd you hear?"

"Bob told me. I had to call him when I got to the station this morning."

Her voice—and her words—tipped Sally off immediately. "What do you mean—you *had* to call him? What's wrong?"

"We had a problem."

"What kind of problem?"

"You know that box you got yesterday? The one with the candy in it?"

Sally glanced automatically toward her purse. She hadn't had a chance to eat the piece she'd brought with her. The wreck—and then Jake—had robbed her of all thoughts of beautifully decorated chocolates. Which said quite a bit, she thought belatedly. "The Godivas," she said. "I brought one home, but—"

"Oh, my God! You didn't eat it, did you?"

"No..." Sally let the word out slowly, her heart sinking. "Why?"

"Thank God... Ricky found Sonny and Frank in the bathroom this morning, sick as puppies. They came in early and apparently ate the whole box in lieu of their usual donut fest." She took a deep breath. "It wasn't pretty."

"Oh, damn... are they going to be all right?" Before Rita could answer, Jake was sitting up in the bed, his sleepy look gone, every ounce of him focused and leaning forward. The transformation was almost scary. When he motioned to her, Sally put her hand over the phone and quickly explained.

Rita spoke again. "Let's just put it this way… They'll survive, but it's going to be a long time before either of them want chocolate again. I'm not going to give you the details, but I'm so happy that Ricky found them instead of me, I may give him a raise."

Despite herself, Sally started to laugh, but the amusement died quickly. "Ricky found them?"

"That's right."

A buzz started behind her forehead and she blinked twice, her mind going dizzy. "He…he brought that box to my desk and said someone had dropped it off out front. He'd been in reception doing something for Loretta, he said."

The line went silent, then finally Rita spoke slowly. "I think you'd better get down here, Sally. And bring that last piece of chocolate, too. I'll call Bob and get him back up here."

THE SCENT OF Sally's light perfume filled the truck as Jake drove into town. He hadn't noticed it before, but her fragrance was branded into his brain now. He'd smelled it on her skin and in her hair and he'd never forget how it rose from her nape.

He wouldn't be forgetting a lot of things from the night before.

From their previous encounters, he'd thought he'd understood the level of her passion, but last night had proved him wrong. She'd wanted him just as much as he'd wanted her and she'd matched him move for move. There was a freshness in that, he realized now, and it made him feel great. Sandra had always acted as if she was doing him a favor when they'd made love.

He glanced across the seat, an inexplicable emotion hitting him hard. He was feeling things for Sally that he'd never felt for Sandra—and he'd *married* Sandra. What did that mean? He was halfway afraid to voice that question, even inside his mind, but sooner or later, he'd have to face it, wouldn't he? He'd have to face that and a helluva lot more, especially since Sally's one goal in life was to leave town. He'd come to Comfort to kick back, to recoup, not to fall in love....

Her voice broke his reverie. "It doesn't look too bad, does it?" She was gazing into the vanity mirror above her seat, lightly touching the cut above her eye. "I covered it up with makeup."

"You look gorgeous," he said gruffly. "You always look gorgeous."

She reached across the seat and patted his arm. "Right answer, sweetie."

He glanced over at her. "You're a beautiful woman, Sally. Inside and out."

She smiled one of those secret, satisfied smiles that women did sometimes.

"You're damned lucky, too," he continued, his hands tightening on the steering wheel. "Bob's got to get on the stick and figure out what's going on. We can't let this continue."

"Now, Jake—"

"Don't 'now, Jake' me. We need to stop whoever in the hell is behind this vendetta." He paused. "You could have been hurt last night, and who knows what was in that candy?"

"There's one way to fix the situation right now."

"What's that?"

He could feel her looking at him. He turned.

"KFFD in Austin may be making me an offer soon. They've requested tapes and they're interested in the show. This could be my break." She spoke softly. "If I leave, things would go back to normal."

Even though he'd just considered that very thing, Jake's reaction to her words was totally unexpected. When he'd been a kid—twelve or thirteen—he'd caught a helmet in his gut during a practice football game. He felt the same way now. Empty, winded, out of breath and unable to get any more. He covered up the best he could. "You could do that," he said evenly. "But whoever's behind this is breaking the law. They need to be stopped and dealt with, one way or the other."

"But if I'm gone—"

"It doesn't matter. There's a nut out there willing to hurt people." He shook his head, almost to himself. "You've never accepted the seriousness of this, Sally. You always say it's Comfort and things like this just don't happen here." He glanced toward her. "How bad does it have to get before you understand the situation?"

She didn't answer him and they spent the rest of the ride in an uneasy silence.

Bob met them outside. Sally said hello to him then went inside the station, her manner as remote to him as it had been to Jake. He tried to explain, but Bob just shook his head.

"C'mon, Jake, let's face it—the situation's not good, but I don't think Sally's in any serious danger."

Jake exploded. "What the hell do you mean? She's had a rock through her window, her tires slashed, she's been run off the road and now she's gotten poisoned candy. And you don't think it's serious?"

Bob looked at him with a puzzled eye. "Jake—that car was nowhere near hitting her. I looked at the skid marks myself. Sally panicked and that's why she went off the road. If the driver of that car had wanted to really hurt her, they would have waited till she went around the corner. She would have ended up in Dead Man's Creek—not Ed's cornfield. They were trying to scare her, that's all.'' He shook his head. ''And the candy wasn't poisoned.''

''What do you mean?''

Bob grinned. ''That wasn't Godiva in that box, Jake. Beneath that fancy decorating job, there was chocolate-covered Ex-Lax. I don't think anyone's ever died from that.''

Jake stared at his friend in disbelief. ''Ex-Lax?''

''That's right.''

The two men held back their laughter for as long as they could, but it erupted anyway. When they got themselves back under control, Bob spoke again, wiping one eye.

''Listen—I know you're concerned about Sally and I understand, but I'm taking care of things.''

''Not from where I stand.''

Bob stared at him patiently. ''I have Billy Ray drive by Sally's house three times a night, Jake. And once every hour or so, I call Rita while she's here at the station. I'm watching out for her, but this isn't Houston. Someone's just trying to make Sally's life tough. They aren't out to kill her.'' He patted his friend on the shoulder. "Let me do my job, Jake. You're retired now, remember?"

"Is IT TRUE you'll go blind if you...you know..."

The voice was young and squeaky, but filled with concern. Unfortunately, Sally was listening with only half an ear, her mind still on Jake and all they'd shared. She knew he thought she was mad because of what he'd said, but in fact, that had nothing to do with her quietness in the car. She was scared of what was happening between them. What was she going to do? Her feelings for Jake were almost overpowering, but it'd been her dream forever to leave Comfort.

Why now, her brain screamed. *Why now?*

At Sally's silence, the youngster's voice went up, desperation edging in. "You know what I'm talking about, don't you? If you stroke the puppy? Choke your chicken? Slap your monkey?"

Linda's frantic motions outside the booth finally caught Sally's attention. She jerked the mike toward her, horror finally coming over her. "You're abusing animals for sexual pleasure?"

"Arrhhhhhggh... Hellloooo? I'm talking about masturbating, okay?"

Sally's brain clicked. "Oh...oh, yes. I got it. I got it now."

"Well?" A pause filled the air time. "Will I go blind?"

"No. You will not go blind if you masturbate. That's a myth."

"Well, thank you. Finally!"

Sally punched in a tape and spoke over the music. "And now here's a message from our friends down at the feed store. Remember, Johnny carries food for all kinds of animals—puppies, chickens, monkeys..." The ad began and she leaned back, a prayer coming to her lips. "Oh, please, God. Don't let KFFD be listening today...please God?"

THE SUN WAS a huge ball of orange slipping behind the oaks across the street when Sally walked out of the station that evening and saw Jake. Her heart did a funny tumble, then began to race, and as she walked toward him, she could actually feel his stare. His eyes had an almost mesmerizing pull to them, and as she reached his side, she knew that before the night was out, they'd end up in bed again.

He had on his usual jeans and a starched white shirt, and now that she knew the body beneath the clothes, he looked even better than the first time she'd seen him. She pulled her eyes away and glanced into the back of his truck. Half a dozen grocery sacks filled it, one with a couple of steaks and a bag of salad greens sticking out from the top. Her gaze returned to his when he spoke.

"What do you say we go back to the cabin and get something cooking?"

At his sexy tone, she knew he'd forgotten her remoteness this morning. "I can't cook," she confessed. "You'd starve to death if you had to depend on me in the kitchen."

He grinned, those electric blue eyes sending a arc of desire straight into her heart. "That's not the kind of cooking I'm talking about..."

She took two steps and linked her arm in his, shamelessly batting her eyelashes and forgetting all the reasons she should just walk away. "In that case," she answered, "I'm all yours..."

They pulled into the driveway of Bob's cabin twenty minutes later. Jake carried in the groceries and set the sacks down on the kitchen counter, but that's as far as they got. He reached out for Sally, and she went into his arms, her heart thudding against her ribs as she breathed deeply and took in his now familiar scent.

He put his hand on the back of her head and tilted it gently, until their eyes met and held. "I've been thinking about this all day," he said. "From the minute I dropped you off this morning, until right now, this is all I've wanted. What have you done to me, Sally Beaumont?"

"I didn't mean to do anything—"

"But you have, haven't you?"

She nodded gently. "I think I have…and it's the same thing you've done to me. I—I didn't plan on this happening."

He lowered his head and began to kiss her, his lips pressing hard against hers. Sally lost herself in the feel of his mouth, his tongue insistent and demanding, the slick wetness echoing her own body's response to his touch. She couldn't say no to this man.

After a moment, he bent down and picked her up, then strode from the tiny kitchen toward the back of the house. Sally laid her head against his chest, wrapping her arms around his neck. If it could only be like this all the time, she thought.

He sat her gently at the edge of the bed and kneeled beside her, his hands going to the buttons of her suit. Slowly, one by one, he undid them until the jacket hung open and loose. He spread the jacket open, then undid the black bra she wore underneath.

All at once, she knew this time was going to be different. A thrill of anticipation coursed through her as she understood why. There was a urgency behind his features, a kind of controlled intensity that was almost frightening in its strength. She wondered what was going to happen when he let go.

She didn't have long to think about it. He pulled her to him, almost abruptly, and buried his face against her. He kissed her breasts greedily, then his lips went to her nipples, first on one side and then the other. A second after that, he was pulling on them, rolling the edges between his teeth with a gentle bite that only made her want more.

When she knew she couldn't stand it another minute, he pulled back abruptly, slipping her jacket off at the same time, and tossing it to the bed behind them. Her skirt quickly joined it and she was left, standing by the bed in her panties and heels.

Within seconds, he was naked, too. She pressed her body next to his, the hardness of his chest flattening her breasts as his hands roamed over her back with growing urgency. Cupping the weight of her buttocks, he lifted her off her feet, still in her heels. His hand went under her panties and then traced a line forward. Her pulse thundering, Sally cried out as he found her wetness and began to stroke her.

When she went limp, he released her and she eased down his body, her hands slipping from his shoulders, over his chest to the flatness of his stomach. By the time she was on her knees, she was holding him in her hands, the length of his hardness within her grasp. It was his turn to moan as she leaned closer to him and took him into her mouth.

The feel of him, hard and hot, filled her with satisfaction and when she moved her lips up and down, she knew he was feeling the same. A few seconds later, he pulled her away with a gasp.

They fell to the bed, and she reached out for him, to bring him closer, but instead he shook his head. With his hands pressing her into the bed, he kissed her breasts and then her stomach, making his way down her body, his lips leaving a pulsing path behind them. When he was between her legs, his tongue probing and hot against the very core of her desire, she cried out.

By the time she realized he had stopped, he'd lifted his head, pulled her to the edge of the mattress and was entering her.

She gasped and without even thinking she lifted her legs and wrapped them around his waist to bring him closer. She'd never felt this way before— wanting a man so badly, needing him so much. He thrust against her, his hips hitting hers, the rhythm building into something faster, hotter, deeper than she'd ever felt before.

Sally wanted it to go on forever, but as Jake's tempo increased, something seemed to break inside her, a liquid sensation, then suddenly she climaxed—a deep, shuddering climax that rocked her to her very core. Above her, Jake gave a final push, then he too, moaned in release, her name on his lips as he leaned over and buried his face against her damp, hot neck a second later.

They stayed that way, frozen against each other in a tableau of sated passion. Finally Jake pulled back and looked at her, his weight on his hands on the mattress beside her head. His eyes were heavy-lidded and glazed as he stared down at her.

He spoke slowly, almost reluctantly she thought later. At the time, her mind was still reeling from his touch, from the feel of him within her body, and she didn't hear the emotion in his words. She only heard the words.

"You're a helluva woman, Sally Beaumont."

She stared up at him, dazed, breathless, her chest rising and falling. "Wh-what? What did you say?"

He grinned, a slow, lazy expression that made her senses reel even more dramatically.

"I said you're incredible. I love the way you look right now—your eyes all smudgy, your lips all pouty, your hair messed up. I love the way you smell—like sex and damp sheets—and I even love those bright red high heels you've still got on your feet." He leaned down and kissed her gently, his blue, blue eyes drilling hers. "I think I'm falling in love with you," he said softly. "What in the hell are we going to do about that?"

10

JAKE HAD NEVER SEEN the inside of a radio station
before, so when Bob called him up and asked for
his help, he readily agreed to meet his friend there.
Monday morning, they strode into the reception
area together, their boots ringing out as they crossed
the lobby to the desk of the clerk. Bob had already
explained their mission. He wanted to ask Loretta
Smith about the package of candy and Ricky Carter's acceptance of it. Back in the days when they'd
been partners, Jake had always been the one who
could tell if someone was lying or not. Even though
he'd improved on his mind-reading ability, Bob
told Jake, he could always stand a second opinion.
Jake was more than happy to oblige, but he also
wondered if Bob had asked him just to pacify him.
Jake had made it more than clear he was getting
impatient for some results on Sally's investigation.

Loretta Smith glared at them from across the barrier of her curved desk. She had on a headset and
a dark blue dress whose white collar tightly circled

her neck. Above the pristine lace, several chins hung.

"I'm telling you the truth," she insisted at Bob's first question. "That candy was sitting right here on my desk when I came back from lunch. Me and Pearl went to the Dairy Queen for chicken salad sandwiches and when we walked in, that gold box was right there." She pointed a red-tipped finger to the edge of the desk.

"Was Ricky here then?"

"No sir, he wasn't. He came up here about five minutes later. I had called and asked him to look at my headset—it was on the fritz—and when he finished, he offered to take the box and the mail back to Sally Anne's desk. It saved me a trip, so I said okey-dokey." She crossed her arms and her chins quivered. "I didn't have nothing to do with that box. I didn't even touch it. No sir."

They asked her a few more questions, but it was obvious she knew nothing about the 'candy.' Stepping away from her desk, Bob looked at Jake. "I swear I don't know what to do about this. My only good suspect was Ricky and he's looking clean."

"Even for the car incident?"

"Especially for that. He drives a red pickup and he was here—still at work—when Sally drove off into that cornfield."

Before they could talk more, Sally's low, sexy

voice filled the reception area and Jake realized her show must have started. Loretta shot out her arm and cut off the sound with a sniff. She saw him looking at her and spoke defiantly. "I don't listen to smut," she sniffed.

Jake looked over at Bob, and the sheriff nodded once. He'd caught the word, too. "Let's go in the back," he said quietly. "I need to see Rita before we leave."

They made their way to the rear of the station, going down a long, narrow hallway. "Her office is this way." Bob spoke over his shoulder, pointing to a door. "You can come or you can wait out here."

Jake didn't hear him because he'd already stopped. The corridor had an interior window where visitors could watch the disc jockeys doing their show. Sally hadn't seen him, but he had a clear view of her.

Her cheeks were animated and flushed, the headphones on her ears looking big and awkward over the smooth cap of her hair. Her brown eyes sparkled with interest as she took her first call, and he couldn't stop the twist of emotion he felt as he watched her and listened to her voice over the speakers. It was obvious how much she loved her job.

"Go ahead, caller. What's your question this morning?"

"Well…it's not exactly about sex. Is that okay?"

"That's all right," Sally answered. "We're having an open forum today. Anything goes…"

"Well, in a way, it's kinda about sex, I guess. It's about my boyfriend. We've been dating for almost three months and we have a terrific sex life, but… Well, I think I love him, but I'm just not sure. How do you tell? How do you know when you're really in love and not just 'in lust?'"

Sally bit one corner of her bottom lip, then pulled the mike closer to her. "You've asked a tough question, caller. That's so personal, you almost have to decide on your own."

"Can't you give me a hint?" The woman's voice pleaded, an edge of despair coming into it. "He wants to move in with me, and I'm just not sure."

"Then that should tell you something, right there."

"Wh-what do you mean?"

"If you're not sure, you're not sure. Love hits you hard and if you have to think about it, then maybe it isn't love."

"But what if I'm wrong? I don't want to make a mistake. What if he's the one and I let him go?"

The words seemed to startle Sally, but she recouped fast and never missed a beat. If Jake hadn't been watching her, he would never have known.

"If he's the one, you know. Deep down inside." She closed her eyes. "You aren't able to concentrate on anything but him. When you aren't together, you want to be, and when you are, the rest of the world doesn't even exist. Your stomach stays in knots and nothing matters but his touch, his smile...his voice. You know, believe me. You know."

Then she opened her eyes. And that's when she saw him. There were two panes of glass and fifteen feet separating them, but Jake felt as if she'd reached out and grabbed him. He could suddenly smell her perfume, taste her skin, feel her hair.

And he knew she was talking about him.

Without thinking, he opened the door leading into the outer room. The blond woman inside sent him a startled glance, but he strode right past her and into Sally's soundproof booth. Just before he swept her into his arms, she hit a red button on the console and an ad began to play.

"Johnny's LP and Feed now has everything you need for your summertime pest control..."

But neither of them were listening. Crushing her into an embrace, Jake lowered his head and began to kiss her, the power of their emotions too strong to deny any longer.

JAKE WAITED in the hall while Sally wrapped up the show. She wasn't sure what she had said to anyone who called, including the one guy who wanted to know if you could overdose on Viagra. He was about to go on his honeymoon and wanted to be prepared.

All she knew was that she loved Jake and he felt the same way. They'd told each other so right after he'd kissed her and just as the Johnny's LP & Feed spot had ended. They'd told each other, and everyone else in Comfort. Their words had been broadcast, Linda jumping up and down frantically pointing to the 'On Air' sign. Sally hadn't really cared, though. What she'd told the caller was the truth. She did love Jake—now she just had to decide what to do about it.

Walking down to her office a minute later, she was still grinning. "Let me get my purse and then we'll leave," she said, smiling at him with what she knew was a goofy expression.

He smiled back. "I'll wait right here."

She dashed into her office and grabbed her purse, but just as she made it round her desk and to the door, her phone rang. It was Rita. "Come to my office."

There was nothing else she could do. Sally went into the hall where Jake still stood. "My boss wants to see me. There's probably some remote FTC law

I don't know about that says you can't declare love over the airwaves. Can you wait a little longer?''

He leaned down and gave her a look that weakened her knees, his blue eyes staring all the way into her soul. "I've got all the time in the world. I'll be right here."

With his hands gripping her arms, he kissed her deeply, his mouth covering hers for one, long pulse-pounding second. When he finally released her, she had to stand still for a moment and catch her equilibrium. She felt like she had the time she'd jumped off the Ferris wheel too soon at the county fair.

"I—I'll be right back."

He nodded and she tottered down the hallway, his eyes on her back. She knew because she stopped twice to look over her shoulder at him as she approached Rita's office.

The door opened just as she reached for the doorknob. Bob stood on the other side, and he grinned at her as she passed him. "Nice finish to the show," he teased. "I didn't realize you cared about your listeners that much."

"I love them all," she said airily. Turning around she blew Jake a kiss, then disappeared into Rita's office, the warmth of Jake's mouth still lingering on her own.

They loved each other, she thought with a dazed intensity. Nothing else *did* matter. The show probably wouldn't go anywhere, anyway, and if it did, well, they'd cross that bridge when they got there. Nothing mattered right now except loving Jake. That was the only important thing.

"KFFD just called." Rita's voice was excited as it rang out across the office. "They're buying the show!"

Sally's heart stopped. She could actually feel it cease to beat. "Are you kidding?"

"Hell, no! I'm not kidding and neither are they. They want you in Austin by the end of next week." Behind her glasses, Rita's eyes glowed. "It's part of the deal. You have to move there or they won't buy the rights." Grinning, she strode to Sally and held out her hand. "Congratulations, Sally. You've gotten exactly what you've worked for all these years."

JAKE KNEW SOMETHING was wrong the minute Sally walked out of Rita's office. Her face was pale and she wore an expression of shocked disbelief. He hurried down the hall to take her arm.

"What's up?"

She looked at him, her brown eyes two wells of confusion and disbelief. "The show…" she said in a stumbling voice. "It—it's been bought by KFFD in Austin."

"That's…terrific. Isn't it?"

"They want me to move," she answered. "To live there. In Austin."

"Well...great." His throat was so tight he could barely get the words out, but he made his voice strong and filled it with fake enthusiasm. "Isn't that just what you always wanted?"

She blinked at his hearty tone. "Y-yes. It's what I wanted."

"Let's go celebrate. I'll take you by the house and you can change, and we'll go to Medina. Have some steaks."

She nodded slowly. "That sounds wonderful."

He put his arm around her as they went outside. The sun was still beating down with fierce determination. Jake felt the heat, but it barely registered. Inside his chest a ball of frozen denial was building up and taking over. Sure, they'd had a good fling, and sure she'd been fun, but he'd known from the beginning it wouldn't be permanent and that's exactly what they both had wanted. He told himself her moving away would actually work out perfectly—it'd be a natural end to what they'd had and eliminate those messy breakups that always got so bitter.

They made their way to her car, and she handed him her keys without another word. The drive was equally quiet, the silence broken only once when the fire truck of the Comfort Volunteer Department passed them in a blaring hurry.

"Somebody's got trouble," Jake said quietly.

She stared at the red blur as it passed by. "Looks like it."

A moment later, they knew who.

11

SHE SAW THE FLAMES as they turned into her driveway. They were higher than the branches of the pecan tree and licking greedily at her roof. Sally's stomach flipped over in shock. "Oh, my God! It's my house! My house is on fire!"

"Stay calm, now, babe. Stay calm!" Jake wheeled his vehicle around the scattered trucks and cars. "I don't think it's as bad as it looks. It looks like it's just the tree—" Jake threw the truck into Park, but Sally was gone before he could reassure her any more.

She ran toward her driveway where a group of men stood. In the center was Earl Ellis, the president of the Chamber of Commerce and the chief of the tiny volunteer fire squad. He was directing the rest of the men as Sally pushed through.

"Earl, Earl! My God, what happened?"

"Someone driving by saw the flames and called us. It's all under control, Sally. We'll have it out in just a few minutes."

"How'd it start?"

"We don't know yet."

"My house…" she wailed.

He patted her on the arm and spoke soothingly. "It's not that bad, Sally. Really. I think it actually started out there under the tree. It only skipped to the roof because the branches were hanging over the shingles." Turning, he pointed to the edge of her house. "Look—it's already out…the flames are just in the tree. The roof's barely been touched."

Feeling sick, Sally walked closer and inspected the outside brick, her throat tight with anxiety. Earl was right—beyond a smudged window and a little black around the shingles, the place was hardly damaged. The pecan tree would need a serious pruning, though.

"I can't believe it," she said, shaking her head as Jake reached her side. "How could this have happened? I don't understand…"

Earl came toward where she and Jake stood. He held a container in his hand and was looking at it curiously. Smaller than a paint can, it was about eight inches tall and four or five inches in diameter. The label had been burned off. "Sally, is this yours?"

She stared at the container. "I don't know. What is it?"

Jake bent down to look at it better, then straightened, an equally curious expression on his own face. "You didn't throw anything out into the yard last night, did you?"

"Of course not."

Earl shook his head. "Whatever it was, this is where the fire started. Did you have anything outside that was flammable? Paint? Kerosene? Gasoline for the lawn mower maybe?"

Mystified, Sally tore her eyes from the can to scan Earl's face. "No, no. I can't imagine what in the world that could be. I don't store anything that can catch on fire. I'm real careful with stuff like that."

"Well, this can held an accelerant—some kind of fuel." His gaze went to Jake, then to Sally. He spoke gently. "And that tells us something else very important. This fire wasn't an accident, Sally. Someone set it deliberately."

SLEEP WOULDN'T COME, and finally Sally got out of bed at 4:00 a.m. and went outside to sit on the porch. The air still smelled smoky and dense even though the fire had been out for hours. Sipping her coffee, she let her brain wander. Who hated her show so much they'd want to set her house on fire? What was she going to do with the offer from Austin?

Could she really give up Jake and move?

Her thoughts were jumbled and confused and the

harder she tried to work it out, the more complicated they seemed to get. That's why she'd asked Jake to go home last night. She'd needed to be alone so she could think about everything.

From behind the house, the sun eased up, the reflection growing on the lake as Sally sat quietly and considered all her options. If she left, her stalker would be thrilled and that problem would be solved. If she left, she'd accomplish her goal and get out of Comfort. If she left, her career would finally take off.

But if she left, she'd never see Jake again.

She'd never had such a dilemma facing her before. Even when she'd come back to Comfort after college, she'd known what she needed to do and that had made it simple, even though she hadn't wanted to come back. Now half of her wanted to stay and half of her wanted to leave...no, no, that wasn't exactly right, she thought immediately. *All* of her wanted to stay and *all* of her wanted to leave. She wanted Jake and the new job and the peace of mind leaving would bring her.

She wanted it all.

The lake turned to fire as the sun rose higher in the sky. Somewhere behind her, on the roof or maybe in the blackened pecan tree, a mockingbird cried out, his call loud and strident in the early-morning stillness. Sally sat quietly and listened to her heart, but the answer never came. Standing up, she made her way into the house to get dressed and go to work.

JAKE WAS UP EARLY, his usual morning run stretching to eight miles instead of four, his feet pounding the shell driveway, then slapping against the asphalt of the road leading from Bob's cabin. He pressed his brain to turn to something besides Sally, and the first topic it came to was the fire. He and Bob had had a long telephone conversation about it last night and Bob had played the dispatcher's tape while they'd talked. Whoever had called the fire department had been upset and scared...obviously not just a passerby and most probably the one who'd actually set the fire, a not unusual circumstance. The flames had gotten out of hand, reaching for the roof, and they'd suddenly become afraid.

The caller had been a woman.

She'd tried to disguise her voice and to some extent had been successful. Bob had no idea who she could be, but again, both of them had agreed it wasn't Loretta Smith. The receptionist had a distinctive tone, high-pitched and whiny. The caller's voice had been slower, more Southern, even though she'd tried to cover up the accent.

A growing suspicion had been bothering Jake for some time, but he'd put it aside after talking to Bob a few weeks prior. His friend had assured him he was way, way off base, but just to make sure Bob had gone and talked to the person in question. She'd denied everything, of course, and Bob had believed her.

But Jake wasn't sure *he* did.

And that's why he'd asked Earl Ellis for a favor. Earl had looked at him with questions in his eyes, but after Jake had explained, Earl had been happy to oblige. He'd given Jake the can found in Sally's yard and in a few days, they'd all have some answers.

Wiping his brow, Jake forced himself down another turn. They'd have *some* answers, but not the one he really wanted. He'd have to wait on Sally for that one.

SALLY CALLED JAKE on Friday afternoon and asked him to come over for dinner. They'd seen each other only briefly since the fire and the announcement by Rita, and Sally missed him like crazy. If she would be leaving soon, it just didn't seem fair to keep seeing him. It was torture, though. Every night in bed, she would toss and turn and reach out for him only to wake and realize he wasn't there. Did she want to spend the rest of her life wishing for someone who was nowhere near?

She changed clothes three times before he pulled

his truck into the driveway. Wearing a haltered sundress and a pair of white sandals, she met him at the door that evening.

His eyes darkened as he got closer to the porch and saw her waiting. He didn't say anything at all. He simply reached out for her and she moved into his embrace, tucking her head underneath his chin. His arms went around her and held her tight. She laid her head on his chest and listened to his heart beat. It sounded steady and calm—unlike her own, which was pounding wildly.

She finally looked up at him and started to speak, but he shook his head and stopped her, leaning down instead to kiss her. His lips were as demanding and insistent as ever, and she gave in to the sensation, losing herself without thought. They broke apart a moment later.

"I missed you," he said quietly.

"I—I missed you, too."

He didn't beat around the bush. "Are you leaving?"

Her throat closed up. "C-can we talk about that later?"

He looked as though he wanted to say no, but he nodded and followed her inside the house. They stopped in the kitchen to grab two cold beers, then went outside to the back porch. She already had the coals going for the steaks and they sat down beside the pit, the smoky aroma rising from it reminding her of last week's disaster.

Bob had called and told her Jake was working on a theory regarding the fire. She turned to him now to ask him about it. It seemed easier to talk about that than what she needed to discuss with him.

"Have you found out anything about the fire?"

He leaned back, stretching his legs before him and sipping from his beer. "As a matter of fact, I do have some news," he said, surprising her.

She turned to him eagerly. "Tell me."

"I took the can to Austin and had the DPS boys analyze it. The label was gone, but there was enough residue left inside that they got a pretty good sample." His blue eyes gleamed even bluer in the evening light. "That can had shortening in it, Sally."

She looked at him blankly, not believing what she heard. "Shortening? You mean the stuff you cook with?"

"Exactly. Lard, it turns out, is an excellent way to start a mighty hot fire."

"Well, that's weird! Who on earth would start a fire with shortening? I could believe paint thinner or gasoline or something like that, but shortening?"

"How about someone who knows their way

around a kitchen? Someone well known for their cooking skills?''

Sally's mind twirled, then suddenly it stopped and she stared at him in amazement. ''Are you kidding me?''

He nodded once. ''Mary Margaret Henley. It's got to be.''

''No way...''

''Bob is checking out her fingerprints right now. He called her down to the office and took them, then shipped 'em off to Austin. They'll compare her prints to the ones on the notes.''

Stunned, Sally leaned back in her chair. ''God, first the candy, now the shortening...it makes sense, I guess, but why?''

''You can ask her yourself on Monday if the prints match.''

He leaned forward before she could speak again and enveloped her hands in his, his voice taking on a different tone. ''Listen, Sally, I've been thinking a lot about you leaving, and I want to tell you that I think the right thing is for you to leave. We don't have a real future between us, and when we started this, we both knew it. I came here to kick back and you're just starting your life. You'd be a fool not to go.''

The breath left her chest in a whoosh, and no air

came in to replace it. She stared at him and said nothing.

"You've always wanted to get out of Comfort and this is your big opportunity. Hell, if you didn't want to take it, I'd kick you in the butt and make you. Austin's just going to be a stepping stone for you, and you know it."

She took her hands from his and stood up, her chest actually hurting. Until this very moment, she hadn't been sure of what she was going to say. She'd played out all the scenarios—staying, leaving, commuting. In her mind, she'd worked out a dozen different solutions, but this had never been one—Jake telling her to leave.

He stood and came to her side. "This is your chance, Sally. You need to take it."

"But what about us?"

His expression took on a stony resolution. She wasn't too sure what that meant because she'd never seen it on his face before. "What we had was great, but we both knew it wasn't permanent, remember?"

"But I—"

He reached out and put his finger over her lips. The touch was warm and sensual, but he'd stopped her because he knew what she was about to say. That she loved him. That she didn't want to leave him. And he didn't want to hear the words. She wanted to get mad and yell and scream, but she couldn't because she understood exactly what he was doing. It was easier this way. More civilized.

"You have to follow your dream, Sally. If I told you I wanted you to stay here in Comfort and be with me, sooner or later you'd start to resent what you'd given up. The feelings between us would turn into something else, and all the good would go bad."

"I'm not sure I agree."

He took her chin in his hand and lifted her face. "You don't have a choice this time, sweetheart. You're going to go out there and be successful. That's all there is to it."

12

JAKE LEFT as soon as they finished talking, and Sally spent the rest of the night crying. She wasn't at all sure the right decision had been made, but there wasn't anything else she could do. Jake was adamant, and deep down, she knew he'd spoken the truth, at least partially. She would come to resent what she'd given up—but she couldn't help wonder if she wasn't giving up something even greater by leaving him.

She went into Rita's office Monday morning looking like hell.

"I'm taking the KFFD offer." Sally spoke quickly; she didn't want a chance to say anything different from what she'd decided upon. "Call 'em up and tell 'em I'll be there Friday. I want to do one more show here and then I'll go."

Rita's expression didn't hold the burst of excitement Sally had thought it would. In fact, she looked downright upset. "Are you sure, Sally?"

"Why does everyone keep asking me that?" she cried. "Of course, I'm sure. I wouldn't have said it if I wasn't sure. I think things out, remember? It's me, Sally, the analyzer.''

Rita stared at her without saying a word.

"I'm sure!" Sally insisted. "Leaving Comfort is what I've always wanted. It'll boost my career. It's the right thing to do.''

"And what about Jake?''

"What about him?''

"Have you discussed this with him?''

"I have his blessing.'' Sally's voice was bitter and the tone surprised her.

"You broke up?''

"There wasn't anything to 'break.' According to him, we didn't have a real relationship anyway.''

"Maybe he just wanted you to go and not feel guilty.''

Sally shook her head. "We talked about it, Rita. He told me to leave...and he's right. I—I need to go. I *want* to go. Comfort's not so comfortable anymore.''

"All right, then.'' Stepping briskly to her desk, Rita propped her glasses back on her nose and started jotting something down on a pad. "I'll call KFFD and give them the news. Then I'll call KPDC in San Antonio and tell them, too.''

Sally had already started toward the door, but she stopped abruptly. "KPDC in San Antonio? Why would you call them?''

Rita continued to write. "They made an offer, too." Finally she looked up. "Didn't I mention that?"

For some strange reason, Sally's pulse jumped. "N-no. You didn't say a word about it."

"Oh, I'm sorry." Rita pulled off her glasses and stared across the room. "KPDC heard your last broadcast and loved it. They called on Friday and made us an offer, too."

Sally waited, but Rita said nothing else. "Well? What was it?"

"Oh, you know…basically the same thing. They want to buy the broadcast and air it in their market. Promote you down there, expand the scope a little. Same thing, except for one minor detail."

"And that was?"

"They said you could record from here and just come into town to do promos. In fact, they insisted on you staying here in Comfort. They said the callers wouldn't be the same if they came from their market. Something about the questions being not as 'quaint.'"

Ten seconds ticked by, then ten more. Sally simply stared at the woman behind the desk. Finally she found her voice. "They said I could do the show…from here?"

Rita nodded. "Yes, but I told them you weren't

interested in that. I told them you wanted to leave—''

Her feet came unglued from the carpet where she'd been standing and Sally bounded across the office. She gripped the edge of Rita's desk for support. ''Call them back!'' she cried. ''Call them back right now. I don't want to leave Comfort. I want to stay here,'' she wailed. ''That's exactly what I want to do....''

Rita grinned and Sally suddenly realized what was going on. Dropping her glasses, Rita pressed a button on her phone and spoke. ''Tiffany, did you place that call I told you to?''

''They're on line three,'' the secretary said. ''I told them you said it was going to be a while, but the guy insisted on holding. Said it was important and he'd wait.''

Rita looked up at Sally and spoke. ''Put him through now,'' she said. ''I think we're ready to talk turkey.''

MARY MARGARET HENLEY glared across Bob's desk. Part of her evil eye was for Bob, but most of it was directed in Jake's general vicinity. Her bright blue eye shadow added a certain emphasis to the threat.

''She made me a promise,'' she said, her Southern drawl more pronounced than ever. ''Sally Anne *tole* me I'd be a radio star, but when that first filthy question came in, I wasn't about to sit thare and be humiliated."

Humiliated had more syllables in it than Jake could count.

"You didn't think you could work something out?" Bob asked mildly.

"Like what?" she said indignantly. "I don't answer to smut!"

Her lips quivered, and Jake recognized their piled-on color. It was the same shade of lipstick she'd used to write some of the notes.

"Well, Mary Margaret, I got to do something about this, now. I can't have you going around throwing rocks, and slicing up tires and setting people's trees on fire. Not to mention the candy and the car wreck."

"I wasn't even in her lane," she sniffed. "I pulled back way ahead of time. I wouldn't want to hurt my Cadillac! And I called the dad-blamed fire department as soon as I lit that can of shortening."

"And the candy?"

She smiled and patted her hair. "I did decorate that nicely, didn't I? If those two boys hadn't been so danged greedy they wouldn't have gotten sick. I wasn't trying to kill her, for goodness' sake! I just wanted to teach her a lesson, that's all."

"Well, what you did was against the law. I'm

going to have to charge you with malicious mischief at the very least.''

Her blue-rimmed eyes widened. "Am I going to jail?''

"That'll depend on the judge.''

"I cain't go to jail. I've got two weddings and a baby shower to cook for next week.''

Bob glanced in Jake's direction, barely holding back a grin. "Well, I guess we'll just have to see how things work out, then..."

Bob shook his head and laughed as the unhappy woman drove off a few minutes later in a dusty cloud, her white Caddy almost obscured. "Can you believe her?" he asked Jake. Rising from his chair, he pumped Jake's hand and grinned. "That was damn good detective work, Nolte! I have to say, she had me fooled. I'm glad you caught the cooking grease thing.''

"Yeah, yeah..." Jake conceded glumly. "I'm only glad I was able to help.''

Bob looked at him with an understanding gleam in his eye. "Too bad you can't resolve your love life as easily, huh?''

Jake looked up. "Is it that obvious?''

"'Fraid so, partner. You better do something fast, or you're going to bleed to death from that broken heart.''

"There's nothing I *can* do. Sally's leaving town

for a better job, and I'm not going to be the one to hold her back.''

"Why the hell not?''

Jake looked at his friend in disbelief. "I can't keep her from doing what she's always wanted! She'd hate me for it!''

Bob shook his head. "You may be a damn good detective, but you are one dumb son-of-a-bitch, Nolte. Go find Sally Anne right now and tell her you don't want her to leave. The two of you can work it out somehow.''

"How?''

"Well, damn, it beats me, but if you don't try, you'll always regret it, that much I *do* know.'' Picking up his cowboy hat from the rack by the door, he waved it in Jake's face. "Just leave and go on down to the station. You'll think of something when you get there.''

SALLY TRIED to call Jake five times, but no one answered out at the cabin. She wanted to hop in her car and track him down to give him the news, but with the show starting in five minutes, she couldn't. She barely had time to race into the booth, put on the headphones and take the first call.

"Good morning, Comfort,'' she said, somewhat breathlessly. "Today's topic is—'' She looked up from the sheet of paper in her hand with a chagrined expression. Linda shrugged her shoulders as if to say it was the best she could do. "—um, today's topic is 'Having Sex in Strange Places—Is It Okay?' Call us up and tell us about the most unusual place you've ever had sex." She reached out, her finger hovering over the red button. "First off, though, here's a word from our newest sponsor, Jitters Coffee Shop. Need a pickup before the big date? Trying to keep awake if you've hooked up with a bore? Stop by Jitters and they'll have you jumping in a minute..."

The jingle segued in and Sally hit her 'mute' button. "Who in the heck came up with this topic?"

Linda just grinned. "Hey, I'm doing the best I can, all right? You've been a little busy with poisoned chocolate and burning bushes..."

"It wasn't a bush, it was my pecan tree," Sally countered, "and for your information—"

"Back in three, two, one—" Linda pointed and the phones lit up. Sally picked up line one.

"You're on the air, caller. What's on your mind?"

"Sex in strange places." The man's Texas twang was so thick, Sally could barely understand him.

"Okay, caller." She rolled her eyes and pointed an accusatory finger at Linda. "Go ahead. Tell us the strangest place you've ever had sex."

"Well...uh...you sure these calls are anonymous? I don't want nobody knowing about this, ya unnerstand? You don't have that Caller ID shit, do ya?''

Sally reached for the kill button, but she was way too slow. The word made it to the air. She hoped KPDC wasn't listening just yet... ''Um, no, caller. We don't have any kind of way to identify you. Go ahead. Where's the strangest place you've ever had sex?''

The man paused long enough to make her think he'd hung up, then he spoke in a rush. ''The strangest place I've ever had sex was...'' He began to cackle wildly and then hung up, the sound rattling through her ear phones.

For one stunned moment, Sally let the dead air build then she managed to recover. Punching the next phone line, she said, ''You're on the air, caller. Do you have a comment?''

''I don't have a comment on today's topic, but I do have a question for you.'' His voice was sexy and deep, a growl that reached way down inside her.

''Yes...what's your question, caller?''

''I'm wondering what it would take to convince you that I love you and I want you to stay with me. Here in Comfort...''

Sally's mouth went dry as the words registered, then a movement caught her eye. She stared in amazement as Jake's tall form filled the window leading to the hallway. He held a cell phone to one ear and his eyes were trained on hers, pinning her with their intensity. She felt herself begin to melt under the heat.

"Wh—what you mean, caller?"

"I mean I love you, Sally Anne Beaumont, and I couldn't stand it if you left here. So…would you stay here and marry me? It's not a high-paying position, but it's the best counteroffer I can make to the one you've already received."

Her mouth fell open. "Marry you?"

"That's what I said," Jake grumbled. "I know this isn't sticking to the topic of the day, but if you like, I could call back later, after the honeymoon, and we could talk about strange places to have sex then."

"The ho—honeymoon?"

He grinned. "Hey, for a fast-thinking disc jockey, you need to work on your delivery a bit."

"I—I don't know what to s-say," she stuttered.

"Try yes."

She looked at him through the glass, her heart welling up with an emotion too big to contain. He didn't even know about the second offer—had no idea all their problems had been solved—but he was willing to take a chance and try to work it all out! Taking off the headphones, she walked out of the booth and straight into his arms.

He held her tightly, then she looked up into those bright blue eyes. Behind her, Linda was screaming, "Dead air! Dead air!"

Sally ignored her. "What's your question again?"

"Will you marry me?"

She kissed him long and deep, then pulled back and grinned. "Try and stop me," she said.

Coming in June 2000

Two single dads
(and their double dose of daughters)
seek the perfect wives (and moms!)
in this delightful duo:

Single
DAD
Seeks...

by

CHRISTINE RIMMER

JENNIFER GREENE

Two complete novels by two incredible talents!

Available June 2000 at your favorite retail outlet.

Silhouette®

Where love comes alive™

Three complete novels by bestselling author

DALLAS SCHULZE

Angel in your EYES

Half savior. Half sinner. *All hero!*

There's nothing like being safe in the arms
of the man you love.

Dallas Schulze turns up the heat
with these three stories of love and passion!

On sale June 2000 at your favorite retail outlet.

HARLEQUIN®
Makes any time special ™

Visit us at www.eHarlequin.com

PSBR3600